THE FORCE
OF WIND

ELIZABETH
HUNTER

The Force of Wind
Copyright © 2012
Elizabeth Hunter
ISBN: 978-1479153015

This is a work of fiction. Names, characters, places, and incidents are the products of the author's imagination, or are used fictitiously. Any resemblance to actual persons, living or dead, business establishments, events, or locales is entirely coincidental.

Cover Design: Damonza
Edited by: Amy Eye
Formatted by: Elizabeth Hunter

For more information about Elizabeth Hunter, please visit:
ElizabethHunterWrites.com

For my dear friends:
to those who inspire me
to those who challenge me
for all I have met along the way

ALSO BY ELIZABETH HUNTER

The Elemental Mysteries Series

A Hidden Fire
This Same Earth
The Force of Wind
A Fall of Water
Lost Letters and Christmas Lights
(novella, All the Stars Look Down*)*

The Elemental World Series

Building From Ashes
Waterlocked (novella)
Blood and Sand
The Bronze Blade (novella)
Shadows and Gold:
An Elemental Legacy novella
(December 2014)

The Cambio Springs Series

Long Ride Home (short story)
Shifting Dreams
Five Mornings (short story)
Desert Bound (October 2014)

The Irin Chronicles

The Scribe
The Singer
The Secret (Winter 2015)

Contemporary Romance

The Genius and the Muse

ACKNOWLEDGEMENTS

Many thanks, as always, to my amazing reading and editing team: Kristy, Lindsay, Sarah, Kelli, Sandra, and Molly. You girls are amazing. I couldn't do this without you.

Thanks to my editor, Amy Eye. Your work is as fantastic as your enthusiasm and dedication.

Thanks to my family: to my very patient husband and son, who often fend for themselves while I'm writing and who give me the love and encouragement to keep going. And to my parents, brothers and sisters, your pride and encouragement is an inspiration to me.

To the readers who buy my books, send me e-mails, review, and tell their friends; who offer encouragement, enthusiasm, and so much more, a thousand thanks. You've let me into your imaginations, and you've let these characters into your hearts.

I cannot thank you enough.

The little reed, bending to the force of the wind, soon stood upright when the storm had passed.

—AESOP

PROLOGUE

Wuyi Moutains
Fujian Province, China
September 2008

Fu-han watched the passing boats in the late afternoon sun, carrying their people and wares to the small town just a few miles away. The sun glinted off the surface of the Nine-Bend River and a breeze stirred, swirling the air and tickling the red and gold leaves from the trees. They whirled and twisted in the wind, fluttering down to lay along the edge of the water and drift downstream, carried away by the burbling river.

"Master, do we need more of the moss?"

The old man brushed a few leaves from his faded grey robes and glanced down to the young brother who was gathering moss from a rock along the bank. The young man had good eyes, stronger now than the eyes of the old man who taught him. Fu-han held his gnarled hand out and motioned to the young man, asking him to bring the basket closer to his eyes.

"No more."

"Is that all we need from this part of the forest? Are the mushrooms here the correct ones or do we need to go upstream?"

The old man gave a crooked smile. Elder Lu was wise to choose this young one to be his apprentice, despite his impatience. Impatience, Fu-han knew, could be mastered, but perception such as the boy's could not be taught. The young man already perceived even a slight difference in the hours of shade could impart a different character to an ingredient.

"We have enough for this remedy. These mushrooms are fine for healing. Do we have all the other ingredients?"

The young man glanced at the slip of paper in his hand. "Yes, Master."

"Then, let us begin our walk back," he said with a smile.

The young man held out his arm for his teacher, who grabbed it along with his walking stick. They started up the small dirt path to the monastery, which was tucked into one of the creeping river valleys of the Wuyi Mountains in Southern China. The humid air was soft in the early evening, and the old man was glad that one of the young brothers had already come down to light the lamps along the path.

"Is it true we will have visitors coming tonight?"

"Yes," the old man nodded, "Elders Zhang and Lu. They are bringing another immortal with them, a scholar. The scholar carries a book we will have the opportunity to study."

"What is the book?"

"It is an old manuscript. From the West. The Elders think we may be able to help the young immortal to interpret it."

"They honor us."

The old man chuckled. "They do. But then, I am only an apprentice to Elder Zhang."

"Why does he not study the book himself?"

"The Elders have many important things to do." *Like indulge in the new wine*, the old man thought with a private smile. "And I am Elder Zhang's oldest student. I accept the honor with happiness."

They walked for a few more minutes, slowly climbing the old stairs as twilight fell and the mist crept up the mountain.

"Master Fu-han?"

"Yes?"

"Why did you not join the Elders when they asked?"

The old man glanced at the setting sun and then up at the tall young man who helped him along the path. It was an important question, so he took his time in answering.

"You will choose your own path, but I am happy to know I have only a short time more in this body. It has been a good life, and I have learned much. I will be ready to move on when death comes for me."

"But the gift of immortality… is it not an opportunity for even more study? Think of the years you could teach others. Someday, you could be as wise as Elder Zhang."

He only offered the young man a knowing smile. "Ah, but the gift of mortality offers its own lessons, as well. And though I will never have the wisdom of Elder Zhang, he will never have the wisdom of Master Fu-han."

The young man's cheeks reddened at the old man's apparent arrogance. Fu-han was quick to continue.

"Do not mistake me, I do not compare myself to the Elders. Their wisdom is beyond our comprehension, but they have chosen to step off the path of enlightenment that mortality offers. Just as there is wisdom to be gained from a long life, there is wisdom to be gained from a short one, as well."

"I do not understand."

The old man gripped the young monk's arm as he avoided a thick tree root that had worked its way through the old stone staircase. "The immortals carry the wisdom of our ancestors, but their own enlightenment is slowed by their long life." As they climbed the stairs leading to the monastery, a small bird came and landed on one of the stone lanterns. Fu-han nodded toward it with a smile.

"Look at the thrush."

The young man glanced at the small speckled bird as it cocked its head to the side, observing the two men as they moved up the stairs.

"What of the thrush?"

"What lessons might be learned from living in such a small, weak body?" The old monk smiled at the bird, which flicked its tail before flying to perch on the branch of a low-hanging conifer.

"The thrush has a most beautiful song, Master. One could learn to appreciate that."

"You are correct. And is it a powerful bird?"

The young man smiled. "Of course not. It darts along the branches and eats only seeds and insects."

"And yet, it does not worry about its life. It is a humble bird, as many small creatures are humble, but it has a beautiful song." He paused to catch his breath on the stairs and looked up at the young man beside him. "We gain more enlightenment from weakness and loss than we do from strength and victory. That is the wisdom of mortality that our immortal elders cannot grasp. It is only the youngest of them that remember such humility."

"But that wisdom is lost when you die," the boy said with a frown.

"As it should be—to be discovered again by the young." He reached a gnarled hand up to pat the young man's cheek. "You will learn this. And when the time comes, and Elder Lu asks you if you would choose an immortal life, you will make your own choice, as all of those in your order do."

They continued to climb, and Fu-han felt every creak of his joints. Soon, he would not be able to join the young monks as they gathered the plants and roots in the forest. Soon, he would take refuge in the collected wisdom of all those who had come before him and stay in the library and workrooms of the monastery.

"Master?"

"Yes?"

"Which of the elements is most powerful?"

Fu-han smiled. It was a young question.

"There is no one element more powerful than the others."

"But surely—"

"It is *balance* that is most powerful. The elders know this; that is why there have always been eight, two from each earthly element."

But it was the fifth element, the space between, that Fu-han thought of as he climbed the stone stairs. It was the elusive energy he felt quicken his own senses as he looked to the top of the stairs to see his old teacher jump from the branch of a tree to land on his toes.

Fu-han smiled as his companion took a sharp breath.

"Elder Zhang Guo," the young monk said with a respectful bow.

The ancient wind vampire floated down the stairs, his white robes fluttering in the dark along with his long, black hair. Though he was called 'elder,' Zhang had been frozen in the prime of his human life. His broad face was open and jovial as he greeted Fu-han and reached out an arm to help him.

"How is my old student this evening?"

The old monk smiled and gave a deep nod. "I am well, my teacher. We were not expecting you until much later."

Zhang shrugged. "We took refuge in one of the caves today so we could be here early. Our guest was most eager to bring his book to the safety of the library."

The old man frowned. "Does this guest bring trouble?" He glanced at the young man beside him and thought of all the boys who trained at the monastery school.

The ancient wind immortal only smiled. "And who would dare harm the monks of Lu Dongbin? Your patron is far too powerful for anyone to challenge."

Fu-han bowed. "We are grateful for the protection of *all* the council, Elder Zhang."

Zhang laughed. "Some more than others, my old friend."

The three walked slowly up the stairs after Fu-han waved away the offer of a quick flight from his old teacher. The two friends spoke of the young monks and the school, about the visitor who would be staying with them and the curious book he was bringing.

"I am eager to hear your thoughts on it," Zhang mused. "You are familiar with its author, though I can promise you have not seen anything like this before."

"Oh?"

"I need your eyes, my friend."

"Have you asked your daughter to look at it?"

Zhang smiled a little. "My daughter has taken a vow of silence for many years. She has no time for me."

Fu-han chuckled. "I will always have time for you, Master."

"No," the vampire said as he looked at the bent, old man. "I'm afraid you won't."

"I suppose that is true enough," Fu-han said.

They reached the gates of the monastery to find a group of young monks scurrying about, preparing for their visitors. They were rushing in expectation of their patron and only a few stopped and stared at the three men as they made their way through the stone courtyard and the meeting room, winding their way back into the mountain and toward the library.

The dim hall was lined with books, scrolls, and manuscripts, a mix of modern and new writings, and small alcoves branched off into study rooms strewn with cushions. It was lit by some of the few electric lamps in the ancient building, the risk of fire outweighing the preferences of their immortal patrons.

The young man escorted Fu-han to his favorite corner of the room and left him to go put the herbs and other ingredients they had gathered in the workroom. He promised to return with tea.

Fu-han could feel the eyes of his old teacher on him as he arranged his aching body on the low cushions. Zhang stretched his legs out and relaxed against the cool, stone wall of the library.

"It's not too late to change your mind."

The old man laughed. "And spend eternity with an old and creaking body? I was tempted when I was thirty, considered it at forty, but at ninety-eight years?" The old monk shook his head. "I will welcome death when it seeks me out."

Zhang scowled. "You waste yourself."

"I move on to whatever is next." Fu-han shrugged. "That is all. Tell me about the young immortal."

"He has been hiding for many years, afraid of the knowledge he has."

"Why be afraid of knowledge?"

"This knowledge is power, and others seek it. His mortal life was taken because he found it."

"Ah," Fu-han nodded. That changed things. To be thrust into an immortal life without a choice was a harsh fate. "He is welcome here."

"I hear him approaching with Lu now."

"And his element?"

"He controls water, but is not very powerful. His sire was unwise and too prolific."

"And his mind?"

"Impressive," Zhang said with a slow nod. "Very impressive."

"I look forward to meeting him."

They paused when Fu-han felt the stirring of energy that signaled the presence of a powerful immortal. Zhang rose as Lu Dongbin, patron of the monastery and ancient water vampire, swept through the doors of the library, followed by a thin man in Western clothes. The proper greetings were offered along with quiet words of welcome as the three vampires situated themselves on low cushions in front of the old man, who examined the newcomer.

The young immortal was of moderate height, and his dark hair and dramatic features indicated Spanish or Mediterranean blood. He did not carry himself with the confidence typical of his kind, but his keen eyes darted around the room, taking in the massive library that Fu-han's order had tended for over a thousand years. He carried a wrapped bundle clutched to his chest that looked like a small book or box.

He was younger than Fu-han, in mortal years as well as immortal, and the old scholar could feel the vampire's nervous energy fill the small alcove, causing the lights to flicker.

This one, he thought, had not forgotten his own humility. This one was open to a greater wisdom.

When Fu-han's kind eyes finally met the brown gaze of his guest, the old man smiled.

"Stephen De Novo, you are welcome here. And you are safe."

CHAPTER ONE

En route to Beijing, China
August 2010

Giovanni Vecchio eyed the impassive water vampire from across the compartment, casually draping an arm around Beatrice's shoulders as she sat next to him on the plush couch.

"Remind me why he is here."

She rolled her eyes and refused to answer, so Baojia spoke for himself.

"I am here because Beatrice has a very concerned grandfather who offers her the finest protection of his clan."

"Are you sure you're not just homesick?"

The Asian vampire's face betrayed no emotion when he replied, "Unless we have changed course to San Francisco, I do not understand the question."

Beatrice snorted and laid her head on Giovanni's shoulder. "Leave him alone, Gio."

"I dislike having someone else on the plane." Particularly someone who looked at Beatrice the way her grandfather's enforcer did. Beatrice may not have noticed, but the quiet water vampire watched her every move with keen interest.

"You're overreacting," she murmured. "Besides, Ernesto wouldn't send anyone with us who wasn't on our side."

He saw an almost imperceptible smile flicker across Baojia's face, and there was a wry amusement in his eyes when he looked back at Giovanni.

"And it is always beneficial to have another interpreter," Baojia said in perfect Mandarin.

When Don Ernesto Alvarez, Beatrice's powerful ancestor whose clan controlled Southern California, had offered to send his child with them to visit the legendary Eight Immortals of Penglai Island, Giovanni could hardly refuse.

Baojia's prowess as a fighter was almost as well known as Giovanni's, despite his youth, and the offer was evidence of both how highly Ernesto viewed his granddaughter and how valuable he saw her connections in his world. Giovanni couldn't deny the offer without alienating a powerful ally and causing a rift in Beatrice's family.

Though she had initially been intimidated by the silent water vampire, Baojia made every effort to set Beatrice at ease in his presence. From casual observation, the vampire, who was only known by his given name, did not seem particularly intimidating, and his medium build and even features were unremarkable.

But the minute a canny opponent looked into his black eyes, Giovanni knew they would reevaluate. Baojia was one of the most lethal water vampires Giovanni had ever known, including his own sire. His mastery of his element, combined with a natural grace and training in various martial arts, had quickly become legendary. He was known for his ruthless and efficient combat and was also an exceptional swordsman.

The enforcer had monitored Beatrice for her grandfather in the years before Giovanni's return, and he could tell Baojia's interest in the young woman had been piqued.

"Gio?"

He looked down at Beatrice, whose eyes had begun to droop. "Yes, Tesoro?"

"I'm going to go lay down. When will we be in Beijing? Do I need to be awake?"

He shook his head. "We'll arrive mid-afternoon, but we'll remain in a secured hangar until nightfall. Sleep as long as you like."

She leaned over to place a kiss on his cheek, but he turned his head and captured her lips. Giovanni heard the small hum of satisfaction she made and the contented sigh when she pulled away. He let his eyes rake over her face, delighting in the slight blush that colored her cheeks.

"I'll join you soon," he said with a wink before she turned, gave Baojia a slight wave, and walked back to the secured bedchamber he'd installed in the belly of the cargo plane.

Giovanni watched her go, letting his eyes wander over her supple body and ignoring the instinct to follow her. Then he turned back to Baojia; he still had a few questions for the enigmatic man.

"Why are you really here?" he asked in Mandarin.

The water vampire offered a placid smile before responding in the same language. "As I said, I am here on orders from my father to guard Beatrice. As you have the same goal, I'm sure there will be no conflict. We will… cooperate, di Spada."

He flinched at the name he had used as a mercenary and assassin. Giovanni had chosen a different name for a reason.

"Please," he offered a stiff smile, "call me Giovanni."

Baojia nodded with respect before his eyes flicked to the room where Beatrice had gone to rest.

"So, you are here to guard my woman?"

He smiled again. "Does she like it when you call her that?"

Beatrice didn't like it in conversation, but he knew without a doubt she liked it in other, more intimate, moments. "She prefers it."

"That surprises me."

"Do you think you know her?"

"She's an interesting human," Baojia said, avoiding the question.

"She is." Giovanni paused. "And to what lengths will you go to protect my woman, Baojia? What did Ernesto ask of you?"

"That is between my father and me."

Giovanni cocked his head. "Is that so?" He looked between Baojia and the door Beatrice had walked through. "He told you to turn her if she is in danger, didn't he? Ernesto told you to sire her if her human life is at risk."

A shadow flickered in his black eyes, and Giovanni leaned forward. It was the truth, but Baojia was not pleased by the command from his sire.

"I was instructed to protect her by whatever means necessary."

Giovanni gave a rueful smile. "Not particularly pleased by that, are you?" He wasn't either, which was one of the reasons he was so eager to join Tenzin. The reassurance of Beatrice having the protection of another immortal—one he trusted implicitly—was vital to him.

"I have no desire for children," Baojia said.

Particularly not a human you are interested in.

Giovanni decided he was tired of parrying with the vampire, so he stood up and stretched his tall frame. "I'm going to retire for the day. I hope you're comfortable on the couch."

"I am perfectly comfortable, thank you."

Giovanni grunted and walked to the bedroom door, opening it, then locking it behind him with the multiple deadbolts, safety latches, and bars he used to secure the room. He turned to see Beatrice watching him with a sleepy smile.

"You're in a mood tonight."

He shrugged. "I don't trust him."

"I think he's fine." She yawned, reaching across the bed toward him. He stripped off his clothes and climbed in next to her. Tugging her arm, he pulled her on top of him and began kissing along her neck. Beatrice continued, "As interested in me as Ernesto is, I hardly think he'd send anyone to guard me that wasn't trustworthy."

He tugged at the small shorts and tank top she had put on to sleep. Her habit of dressing for bed annoyed him. Sleep clothing was an unnecessary layer, in his opinion, and highly uncomfortable against his skin.

"I'm going to donate all your night clothes to charity," he murmured against her neck as his hands slipped under her shorts, sliding them down her hips.

"And you know how much Ernesto is scared of you and Tenzin, so I hardly think—"

"Beatrice?"

"Hmm?"

He rolled them over and pressed his hips into hers, smiling when the sigh left her throat.

"I don't want to talk about your grandfather."

His gaze traveled from her dark eyes, across her pale skin, and down the slim column of her neck before his mouth followed.

"Okay," she breathed out.

"I don't want to talk." His mouth moved down her body, and he enjoyed the rush of energy that followed his lips and hands as he explored her skin. "At all."

"Okay." Her voice was higher pitched, and he smiled in satisfaction as he nipped at the inside of her thigh.

She may not have kept quiet, but he decided he didn't mind after all.

Giovanni woke the next evening to see her smiling at him.

"You think you're so sneaky."

"Hmm?" He rubbed at his eyes.

"I don't think you wanted me to be quiet at all, Mr. Possessive."

He grunted and blinked as she propped her head on his chest.

"I don't know what you're talking about."

She gave an adorable snort. "I should be pissed off, but—"

"We're going to a place with far thinner walls and far more vampires, so I suggest you get over any unnecessary modesty," he said as he ran a hand along her back.

She rolled her eyes at him, and he grinned at the gesture. The previous months had been the happiest in his memory. The move to Los Angeles had gone smoothly for the whole family, and he was satisfied with the security he had arranged for Ben, Caspar and Isadora while they were gone. Matt Kirby and Desiree Riley were aware of the situation, and Ernesto Alvarez had arranged his own security for Beatrice's grandmother, who had charmed him, to no one's surprise.

His family was as protected as it could be, and Beatrice was with him. Despite the danger and uncertainty he knew they were facing, Giovanni was content.

"I love you," he said quietly as he ran his fingers over her skin, causing her to shiver.

She sighed and laid her cheek on his chest. "I love you, too."

He knew the plane had landed, but he delayed leaving the safe cocoon of their cabin, knowing that an uncertain reality would face them as soon as they unlocked the door. They weren't meeting the boat to the island until midnight. Her fingers played along his chest, waking him and arousing his hunger. As if she could sense his fangs descending, she moved up his body, tilting her head to the side.

"You're hungry."

He growled low in his throat as her scent washed over him. Giovanni loved the fragrance of her skin when she first woke. His fangs descended, but he shook his head.

"I took too much yesterday. I'll drink a bag later."

Beatrice frowned. "I don't like it. You're not as strong from the bagged blood. I can tell."

She was right, but he shrugged anyway. "I'll be fine."

"I don't want you 'fine,' I want you as strong as you can be."

"Beatrice—"

"I know you don't like feeding from other humans, but we're going to have to figure something out eventually."

He rolled away from her, annoyed she had brought up the argument that had plagued them for months. "Can we not talk about this here?"

"You're not going to be able to feed from me forever. Not if you want me to—"

"I don't want to talk about this when we are about to go into a very unknown situation!"

She glared at him and sat up in bed. "And I don't want you going into an unknown situation at anything less than your strongest. It's not smart."

He snarled, pacing the small cabin, but she didn't back down. Instead, she rose to her knees, brushed her dark hair to the side, and took a fingernail to her neck, scoring it so deeply she bled.

Giovanni hesitated only a second before he rushed her, licking at the thin line of blood that marred her skin for a second before he latched on. He could feel the quick bite of her nails on his shoulders when he pierced her neck, but the flash of pain was quickly overwhelmed by pleasure as his amnis spread across their skin, and the rich, warm blood flowed down his throat.

She held his head to her neck and arched her body against him, but he took only a few deep swallows before he stopped and sealed the wounds by piercing his tongue. He closed his eyes and looked away from her, angered by her actions.

"Gio?"

He shook his head and walked to the small washroom attached to the cabin.

"Don't do that again," he said before he shut the door.

The boat from the mainland left at midnight, ferried by a young water vampire who greeted them with a nod and a polite smile. They climbed aboard the small junk and walked toward the seats the pilot indicated near the bow of the vessel. Giovanni's senses were on alert, but he could only feel faint traces of old energy signatures and the expected hum of their escort.

"Just us," Baojia murmured in English, his eyes scanning the water around them. "Nothing in the sea, either."

He nodded and placed a hand on Beatrice's back to lead her forward. They had come to an uneasy truce since their argument earlier in the evening, and he caught her eye, giving her a slight smile as they took their seats. As soon as they were seated, the young water vampire held out his hands at the stern, propelling them forward in the dark water and toward the hidden island in the Bohai Sea.

"How does he know how to get there?" Beatrice whispered, looking around the boat, which was devoid of any modern navigation equipment.

She had dressed in her typical uniform of slim black jeans and a black T-shirt before they left, but had failed to bring a coat in the warm summer air of the city. The wind on the water was brisk, so he put an arm around her and drew her closer as he answered.

"Penglai Island has a particularly strong energy signature because of the high immortal population. Even I can feel it, and it is not my home."

"And you're sure they're expecting us?"

"We wouldn't be going if they weren't."

"Tell me what to expect again," she said. "I feel like I'm going to forget."

"There will most likely be some sort of reception when we arrive, since we are expected and friends of Tenzin's."

"Why is Tenzin so important?"

Baojia chuckled quietly. Even Giovanni had to smile.

"Tenzin's sire is one of the Eight Immortals, Beatrice. The one I think your father sought out, Elder Zhang Guo."

He heard Baojia mutter something under his breath, clearly displeased by their destination.

"So, what? Tenzin's really important, then?"

"Tenzin could be one of the Elders if she wanted," Baojia said. "Unfortunately for them, she's too smart and has too low a tolerance for bullshit."

"She's older than most of them, Beatrice. And far more powerful."

"And her father's one of the main guys? Is he a good guy?"

Giovanni glanced back to their pilot. Though he was smiling and looking straight ahead into the night sea, he knew the vampire was memorizing their every word.

"Elder Zhang Guo is a great and powerful immortal. We are fortunate that he chooses to see us. He is deserving of great respect." He nudged her shoulder when she frowned at his rote answer, and she looked up at him. Giovanni made sure she caught the long look he gave the unknown vampire out of the corner of his eye, and he saw her mouth part as she nodded in understanding.

"I'm looking forward to meeting him, then," she said in a cheerful voice. "And to seeing Tenzin. It's been weeks since I've talked to her."

Giovanni smiled. Beatrice had proven to be a natural at the more political side of his life, and there was no way their pilot had missed the implied intimacy between the legendary wind vampire and the young human woman.

The sky had become strangely overcast, and a swirling fog covered the surface of the sea the farther they sailed away from the mainland. He glanced to the side to see Baojia curl his lip. The water vampire lifted a hand to reach out in front of him and, with a broad sweep of his arm, brushed the fog away. The dark blanket parted to reveal a great, glowing mountain, rising out of the water. Its stone walls were lit with golden lamps, and a wide avenue curled around, leading to a large palace that spread across the summit. The whole island shone like a jewel in the moonless night, and Giovanni could feel the energy rolling out from it in waves.

"The Elders do like their fancy castles," Baojia said as he stared at Penglai.

Giovanni turned to him. "You really didn't want to come here, did you?"

Baojia shook his head.

"I thought you were Chinese," Beatrice said.

"I've been an American far longer than you have, Beatrice De Novo." He curled his lip again as he stared ahead. "There's a reason I was willing to enslave myself to the Pacific Railroad in order to leave this place."

Giovanni glanced back at the silent water vampire who piloted them. Baojia caught his look, but only shrugged, seemingly unconcerned to make his opinions public.

They entered a small bay and approached the dock that reached into the ocean. A crew of humans met the junk and tied it up before helping them off with quick movements and near-constant smiles.

The sounds of Mandarin filled the air, though the humans looked to be a mix of ethnicities from all over China. Giovanni pushed the humans back to help Beatrice off the boat and up the walkway, only to be met at the road by two hand-drawn carriages that were pulled by even more human servants. He tossed their small bags into one, which Baojia boarded with a quick nod, then Giovanni helped Beatrice into the second, and they started up the cobbled road toward the castle at the top of the hill.

Taking advantage of the weak human ears, Giovanni whispered to Beatrice in English.

"Remember what we talked about. Be very cautious what you say or what you commit to when talking with anyone. You are taken at your word here and must always follow through or you will lose face."

"Got it. I'll be careful."

"And remember, everyone will smile. Even if they want to kill you, they'll do it with a smile to your face and a knife to your back."

He felt her begin to tremble and he pulled her closer.

"I won't ever leave you unless I absolutely must. Trust me and Tenzin. No one else."

"And now I'm scared."

Giovanni was too, and he hated bringing her into such an unknown situation, but he knew that the possibility of open conflict on the sacred mountain in the middle of the sea was also very low.

"Don't be scared. Be smart. You'll do fine. Just remember, everyone has an agenda."

He tucked her head under his chin and stroked her hair. A part of him wanted to force the carriage around and take her back to the safety of the plane, but he knew that running was no longer an option. Lorenzo had forced their hands with Ioan's death and Beatrice's abduction. Giovanni was convinced they had to find her father and the book he carried if they were ever going to end this.

Their carriage approached the grand gate to the Temple of the Eight Immortals. Two giant stone lions guarded the steps leading to the entrance and Baojia waited nearby. He held a hand out for Beatrice and helped her down when the carriage came to a stop. Two human servants in dull brown robes rushed off with their bags, and the carriages sped away, leaving the two vampires and the human woman standing at the gate of the palace.

He heard Baojia sigh. "Let's get the circus over with. I'm hungry."

The two vampires flanked Beatrice, Giovanni walking slightly forward and to her right, while Baojia stepped behind her and took up her left side. Their eyes scanned the long staircase and the surrounding forest as they began climbing.

When they reached the top, two human servants met them and swung open massive doors painted gold and decorated with semiprecious stones set in elaborate patterns. The entrance to the palace was designed to impress, and by the look on Beatrice's awestruck face, it was working.

A hum seemed to come from beyond the antechamber when they walked in and two smaller, but more richly decorated, doors swung open. They walked into a massive stone courtyard lit with more golden lamps and decorated with ancient stone statues. Fountains and pools cut through the space and a huge open lawn ran through the center.

The flaming lanterns and flowing water, the open earth and empty sky all combined to provide a perfect balance of the four elements mastered by the immortal Elders that dwelled in the palace. Giovanni, Beatrice, and Baojia crossed the lawn dotted with tall, twisting rocks and walked up another set of steps leading to the main hall of the complex.

Through it all, Giovanni kept an eye on Beatrice, watching her as she took in the grandeur of the palace and the wealth on display. She was subdued and looked around with curiosity, but no great outward reaction. She was handling herself perfectly, he thought as he reached back and gave her hand a quick squeeze.

They climbed the steps and waited for an even more elaborate set of carved doors, overlaid in pure gold, to be pulled open by saffron-robed monks. Finally, they entered the Hall of the Elders and Giovanni paused, taking a deep breath to sense the air.

The few times he had come to this place in his five hundred years, the sheer spectacle of it was enough to start his heart. The hall was lined by enormous malachite pillars, and the walls were coated in silver. The oil lamps were gold, and the floor was a pure, white marble. Deep red rosewood benches lined the walls, but his eye was drawn to the end of the hall, where eight ancient thrones were placed, each from the era and province of the immortal who sat upon it.

His eyes moved from left to right as he faced them.

Elder Zhang Guo, the oldest of the eight, was Tenzin's sire and a warlord of some kind from the ancient steppes of the North.

Royal Uncle Cao, the youngest of the eight, was still over twelve hundred years old. An earth vampire of unknown origin, he usually wore a pleasant smile.

The Immortal Woman, He Xiangu, sat next to Cao. Giovanni met the eyes of his fellow fire vampire, who nodded at him with respect.

Lu Dongbin, the ancient water-master, scholar, and reluctant leader of the eight, sat near the center next to Zhongli Quan, a wind vampire who met him in an uneasy truce. The two had been embroiled in a somewhat-polite tug-of-war for power for almost two millennia.

The earth-master and legendary healer, Iron Crutch Li sat next to Zhongli, and next to him was possibly the most enigmatic immortal Giovanni had ever met.

Lan Caihe was a fire vampire who had been turned at a very young age, but that was all anyone knew about him... or her. No one even knew that much, and Lan wasn't sharing.

The last of the eight was the philosopher and water vampire, Han Xiang, a watchful immortal with a smile that never reached his eyes.

Giovanni estimated that at least sixty other vampires and numerous humans milled around the room, positioned in relation to their allies and associates. All of them paused and turned when Giovanni, Beatrice, and Baojia entered the room.

As one, the Eight Immortals, wearing identical white robes, rose to greet them, and the rush of energy that rolled through the room was enough to make Beatrice stumble back.

"Welcome, Giovanni Vecchio," Zhang greeted him in Mandarin. "And welcome, Baojia. Your presence is unexpected, but not unwelcome."

Baojia nodded, but refrained from bowing toward Zhang.

He Xiangu, the Immortal Woman, smiled as she surveyed the group. "It is pleasant to have such respected vampires in our midst, particularly a famed one of my own element." She nodded toward Giovanni. "But who is this young human you have with you? Who is this girl who warrants protection from both the lion and the dragon?"

Giovanni stepped forward. "Elder He, may I introduce the granddaughter of Don Ernesto Alvarez of Los Angeles, a friend of Tenzin, and my companion, Beatrice De Novo." He motioned Beatrice forward, and she nodded respectfully toward the Eight, as Giovanni had instructed her. When she spoke, it was in English, which Giovanni knew all the Elders spoke.

"I am honored to be introduced to the hall. Thank you for your invitation, Elder Zhang Guo."

"You are welcome here, Miss De Novo," Zhang answered with a smile. "It is my pleasure to meet my daughter's dear friend." He looked to Giovanni as if searching for a reaction when he continued. "I believe there is another present in the hall who is even more pleased to see you than the Elders."

Zhang looked at Lu, who lifted an open hand and motioned to the side of the enormous room. The crowd parted to reveal a slim vampire dressed in the blue-grey robes common among scholars of the court. Giovanni recognized him immediately and turned to Beatrice to hold her hand as she gasped in recognition.

"Dad?"

CHAPTER TWO

Mount Penglai, China
August 2010

He looked exactly the same.

Beatrice's mind flashed to the last time she had seen her father the summer she was twelve. She'd been angry with him because he was leaving for Italy and worried because he wouldn't be there for her first day of junior high school.

"You're always leaving. You love books more than me."

"Don't be ridiculous. I'll be back on Friday afternoon. You and Grandma can pick me up at the airport and we'll meet Grandpa for dinner to celebrate your first week of school."

"I can't believe you're leaving again! You just got back from Boston."

"And I was only there for the weekend. I can't turn down this invitation, Beatrice. Try to understand."

She hadn't understood. Beatrice hadn't understood anything except the last words she had ever spoken to her father had been in anger. Five weeks later, her grandparents sat down with tears in their eyes and told her she would never see him again.

And fifteen years later, Stephen De Novo looked exactly as he had when he'd stepped out the door that summer morning.

"Daddy?"

Beatrice could feel Giovanni's hand on her arm, and she knew he wanted her to stay still. He worried so much. He shouldn't have. Her feet were as frozen as her gaze while she stood, staring at the man she thought she would never see again.

His thick, black hair was shorter, and he was paler, but no wrinkles touched the corners of his eyes. No grey sprinkled his hair. His dark brown eyes, the exact color of her own, stared at her as he stood in utter, immortal stillness. Her father was thirty-five years old for eternity.

Her hand slid down to Giovanni's, gripping it in her own as she heard him start to speak.

"Elder Zhang, you can imagine that you have… surprised us, though I am pleased to see Mister De Novo in good health. I'm sure his daughter is eager to meet with him, and—"

He broke off when the doors to the hall swung open and an irritated stream of Mandarin rung out. Beatrice tore her eyes from her father and turned to see the disturbance. For some reason, the sight of Tenzin's tiny figure stalking into the hall brought tears to her eyes and an overwhelming wave of relief.

Giovanni pulled her closer, slipping an arm around her waist and sighing. "*Grazie a Dio*," he whispered.

Beatrice leaned into him, her eyes darting between Tenzin and Stephen, who had stepped forward with a smile.

"Why are they doing the bowing thing again?" Tenzin barked in English. "Did you get new humans? Don't you tell them I hate the bowing thing?"

Elder Zhang stepped forward. Beatrice could have sworn he rolled his eyes when he saw his daughter. He issued a very polite-sounding stream of Mandarin that Beatrice didn't understand a word of until Tenzin interrupted him.

"Don't be rude in front of B. You know she doesn't speak Chinese, and your English is perfect. And why is Stephen in the hall? I told you I wanted to be here when he was introduced."

She could feel Giovanni start next to her, and she looked up at him in confusion. Tenzin had known her father was here? How long? She could tell the same questions were running through Giovanni's mind at lightning speed. The minute she saw his face, she realized he was furious, and she could feel his skin heating as she held his hand.

"I knew you were coming tonight," Zhang said with a shrug.

"Why would I delay their reunion for your whims, my daughter?"

"Because I asked you to." Tenzin let loose a string of incomprehensible words that Beatrice couldn't even begin to translate. It didn't sound like Mandarin. It didn't sound like any language she'd ever heard before. She looked around, but no one looked as if they understood a word.

Zhang was arguing with his daughter in the same guttural tongue. Beatrice looked up at Giovanni, whose eyes were darting between Tenzin, Zhang, and Stephen with steadily mounting anger.

She slipped her hand along the small of his back, trying to soothe him. Beatrice was starting to feel overwhelmed. The last thing she needed was to worry about Giovanni bursting into flames while she was in a completely foreign environment, her father had suddenly appeared, and her friend seemed way more familiar with him that she ever would have expected.

"What, um… what language is that?" she whispered, trying to distract Giovanni, as Tenzin and Zhang continued their argument, seemingly oblivious to the audience in the hall.

"What?"

"What language are they speaking? No one looks like they understand what they're saying."

"They don't." Beatrice saw him take a deep breath and a calm mask fell over his face. "It's their own language. I suspect anyone who speaks it died long ago… or Tenzin and her father killed them so they could converse without eavesdroppers."

Somehow, that didn't seem implausible.

Most of the vampires were riveted by the loud argument. The humans skittered to the edges of the room, but the vampires were still and utterly silent. The Elders in the front of the room looked bored, except for Elder Lan. The childlike immortal's mouth was covered by his or her hands as the vampire looked on with laughing eyes.

"Enough. I'm taking them to my rooms," Tenzin cut her father off. "You can meet with them there if you want. Tomorrow night."

"Of course, dearest daughter," Zhang said with an indulgent smile. "There has been enough excitement for tonight. We have disrupted the business of the court long enough." He looked over to Beatrice and Giovanni with a smile. "Giovanni Vecchio, Beatrice De Novo, Baojia, you are welcome here. My daughter will see to your needs."

She felt her arm being pulled toward the back door, but she was still frozen in confusion. "What? Where are we going now?" She looked back toward where her father had just been standing, but he was gone. Beatrice started to panic. "Gio, where's—"

"Shh, Tesoro, he'll meet us there. Follow Tenzin. Follow her now."

"But—"

"Beatrice, do not linger. We have been dismissed."

His arm was like iron around her waist, but she craned her neck, trying to see where her father had gone. Over her shoulder, she spotted Baojia, who shook his head slightly before catching her eye and giving her a nod toward the door and a quick wink.

Beatrice swallowed the feeling of panic and leaned into Giovanni as he led her from the room, following behind Tenzin, who swept the doors open with a flick of her wrist and a gust of wind. She strode into the dark night, growling at the humans who bowed before her.

He still looked exactly the same.

They were sitting in one of the windowless rooms in Tenzin's wing of the palace. Beatrice and Stephen sat on low couches across from each other in awkward silence as Giovanni and Tenzin carried on a vicious argument in yet another unknown language. Baojia lounged on another couch across the room, glancing up from his book occasionally with a smile.

Beatrice stared at her father for a few more minutes until the silence became overwhelming. "What language are they speaking?"

Stephen blinked, apparently shocked that she'd spoken to him.

"I—I think it's Mongolian. Or some variation of it. There are several dialects that Tenzin speaks."

His voice sounded different. Deeper, somehow, but then she wondered if she had only forgotten what he sounded like in the fifteen years they'd been apart. He stared at her and a pink sheen came to his eyes. He smiled.

"You're so beautiful."

Blinking back her own tears, she crossed her arms and took a deep breath, wishing that Giovanni would finish his argument and take her away so she could collapse. "Thanks."

"You look like Mom… but different, too."

She stared at him, completely confused by the churning emotions in her gut.

"You look exactly the same."

He gave her a wry smile. "Part of the package, you know?"

"Yeah, I know."

He had no response, only nodding as he continued to stare at her. "Grandma's doing okay?"

"Yeah. You know about Grandpa, right?"

"Yes. I… uh." Stephen cleared his throat the same way he always had when he was nervous. "I heard a few months after he passed away. But Tenzin said Mom got remarried earlier this year?"

"Yeah." She gestured toward Giovanni. "Gio's friend… well, kind of his son. But not a vampire son. But he raised Caspar, so he's like his son. But he's not a vampire. I mean, that would be weird, because he's old. Like Grandma. Well, a little younger. They're good. Great, really. Really in love and… happy. They're really happy." Beatrice couldn't seem to stop rambling, and her father was looking at her the same way he had when she would tell him a story as a child.

"I'm happy for her." Stephen nodded. "Tenzin has nice things to say about Caspar. And Giovanni, too."

She wanted to hug him. She wanted to hit him. Beatrice wanted to break down in tears and beg his forgiveness for her childish anger when he left. Then, she wanted to scream at him for putting her life in danger so many times.

"I don't know what to say to you," she choked out.

His eyebrows furrowed, and she saw a pink tear slip out of the corner of his eye as he shrugged his shoulders.

"That's okay. You don't have to say anything. I'm kind of enjoying just sitting across from you right now."

She fought back tears and twisted her hands together. "There's just… so much. There's so much that's happened. I'm really different than I was when I was little. And you're…"

"What?"

"You're just the same! But you're not. I just—I don't know who you are anymore."

Stephen nodded and took a deep breath before he spoke in a hoarse voice. "I know it's confusing, Beatrice. And I know we have a lot —a *lot* to talk about, but… I'm still me, Mariposa. I'm still me. And I love you so much. That has *never* changed."

Tears rolled down her face, and her father held out a tentative hand.

"Dad—" she cried before she stood up and met his arms as he embraced her.

His hands were cool when they brushed the hair out of her eyes and tucked her head under his chin as he had when she'd had nightmares as a child. She felt the rush of energy as Giovanni sped toward her side. He didn't pull her away, but Beatrice felt his quiet presence at her back as her father rocked her silently.

"I missed you so much," she whispered.

"I missed you, too. More than I could ever say."

Beatrice let him hold her as she soaked the front of his grey robes with her tears. After a few minutes, she heard him softly singing a lullaby she remembered from childhood.

"*A los ninos que duermen, Dios los bendice...*" His low voice took her back to the small bedroom where she'd grown up. *The children who sleep, God bless them...*

"*A los padres que velan, Dios los asiste,*" she whispered along, remembering the old words as if he'd sung them to her the night before. *The fathers who watch them, God helps them...*

"I missed you every day, Beatrice. Forgive me for putting you in danger. Forgive me—"

"Don't," she said, pulling back and wiping her eyes. "Don't start apologizing for that. This has all been..." She shook her head. "I know it's not your fault, Dad."

She saw her father glancing over her shoulder and knew he was looking at Giovanni. She could feel his heat radiating on her back and knew her lover was showing enormous self-control to be standing still instead of whisking her away. Giovanni hated to see her cry. It seemed to disturb him on a very deep level, and he often reacted in anger toward the perceived cause. Feeling for his hand, she grasped it and pulled him closer.

"I think Beatrice needs some answers, Tenzin." She heard Giovanni speak in a low voice as he pulled her away from her father and into his arms. She kept hold of Stephen's hand for a moment, squeezing it before she retreated into Giovanni's embrace.

"What were you two arguing about?" She sniffed. "It better not have been about me."

"Of course it was." Tenzin snorted. "You know how he is."

Tenzin walked over and motioned toward a grouping of plush cushions on the far side of the room. A small fountain trickled in the corner, and Giovanni sat next to it, pulling Beatrice into his lap as Tenzin and Stephen sat across from them.

"Tell her how long."

Beatrice's eyes narrowed at her friend. Tenzin sat, perfectly relaxed and looking like the queen of her own personal castle. Which, in a way, she was. The palace complex was two-tiered, and Tenzin's rooms took up a full half of her father's buildings. Giovanni had explained it as they walked out of the Great Hall, trying to distract her from her whirling emotions.

The two earth Elders and their clans stayed below ground in a complex series of caverns that had been dug thousands of years before. The four wind and water Elders each took a wing of the outer palace walls with their retinues; and Mistress He and Elder Lan, the two fire vampires, lived in smaller homes within the palace walls, since they preferred to keep less company.

"Tell her how long you've known where her father was."

"Don't be rude. I don't have to explain myself to you. You're in my home."

"Tenzin," Giovanni growled.

"And, I'm here in this crazy house as a favor to you. You know how much I dislike being around my father and all the bowing people."

A bevy of servants scurried about, most of them overseen by a quiet, sweet-faced woman named Nima, who was a personal assistant of some sort. She was older than Caspar, easily in her eighties or nineties, and issued quiet orders as each human servant hung on her words.

"Tenzin," Beatrice finally said after a silent woman brought a tray of tea. It was hot and sweet-smelling, suffusing the air with the scents of honey and cardamom. "Please tell me how long you've known my father was here. You know we've been looking for him."

"You even asked me to call you when we got back from Brasilia, Tenzin. You knew then how upset she was, and you still said nothing," Giovanni bit out, obviously still angry with his old friend.

"You found my house in Brasilia?" Stephen asked, looking at her with delight. "You did remember the game!"

"Yes, it might have been a bit easier to just leave a note, De Novo," Giovanni replied. "Or show up to expected appointments. Either one would have worked so your daughter didn't have to worry that you were dead."

Stephen's eyes flashed. "And how was I supposed to know *you* were trustworthy, di Spada? How was I supposed to know you wouldn't take advantage of her?"

"Dad..." Beatrice squirmed.

"Maybe because I protected her. Which is more than what you did. Maybe because—"

"Stop it, both of you," Tenzin broke in. "This is ridiculous. Save your posturing for another time, or leave B and I alone so we can talk."

"Don't get mad," Beatrice said as she grabbed Giovanni's hand. "Just... let's talk for a bit, then I want to go to bed. I'm exhausted." In the back of her mind, she felt as if she should be slightly embarrassed to talk about going to bed with Giovanni when her father was right across from her, but she was too tired to be mortified. "Tenzin, tell me what's been going on."

Tenzin looked at Stephen and something passed between them that caused Beatrice to sit up slightly straighter. It wasn't exactly—

"If you found the house in Brasilia, then I'm assuming you found my journals," Stephen said. "So you know I came here in August of 2008."

"And what have you been doing since?" Giovanni asked. "You've been here for two years."

"Working, mostly. I was in a monastery in the Wuyi Mountains for over a year, studying with one of the Bön scholars trained by Elder Zhang. Then I came back here when I was called."

"And Tenzin? When did you meet her?"

Tenzin curled her lip and reached her foot across to kick Giovanni's shin.

"Shut up. It's none of your business, and you don't ask him. Ask me."

"Fine." Beatrice saw the collar of Giovanni's shirt start to smoke and she put a hand on his shoulder, willing him to calm down. "Tenzin," he said through gritted teeth, "when did you meet Stephen and why didn't you tell me you'd found him?"

"I met him about a year and a half ago, and I didn't tell you because it wasn't time to tell you yet." She gave a slight shrug and reached for her tea again.

"Okay!" Beatrice jumped in, knowing Giovanni was about to lose his temper with his oldest friend. "I'm exhausted, and I want to go to bed before I collapse. Gio, where are we sleeping?"

Giovanni pulled back from the argument he was about to jump into and rested his chin on her shoulder. He and Tenzin appeared to be in some kind of staring contest for a few moments until she heard him take a steadying breath. He brushed a kiss across her temple and helped her up before standing himself. She put an arm around his waist and almost pushed him away from her father and Tenzin.

On their way out the door, she paused by Baojia. Giovanni waited next to her with a blank expression, his mind obviously elsewhere.

"Are you calling Ernesto tonight?" she asked.

Baojia cocked an eyebrow at her. "Perceptive as always. Did you have a message for him?"

"Yeah, tell him he has a new family member around."

"Already on the agenda," he said before giving her a wink.

"Goodnight, then."

"Gio," Tenzin called across the room, still drinking tea with Stephen. "Nima put your bags in the same room as last time."

"Please, tell me it has more than chamber pots now."

"Yes," she sounded bored. "I made Father put a full bathroom in all my rooms here."

"How very modern of you, Tenzin," he muttered as they walked out the door.

"Can we pretend all that stuff out there didn't just happen?" Beatrice asked when they were finally alone. "I just need to be normal with you tonight. That was... too much. There's a million things to talk about, but I don't want to talk about any of them right now."

Giovanni nodded and gave her hand a quick squeeze before he started looking around the room. Even though they were in his friend's home, he did his typical precautionary search, zipping around the room, pulling back any draperies and generally searching every corner for any unknown threat.

While he did that, Beatrice fastened the series of locks on the heavy wooden door and slipped off her shoes. She sighed when she turned around to survey the room where they would be living for... she had no idea anymore. "Wow, this is so beautiful."

"It's different. It's all red."

Giovanni was looking around their room with some confusion, but she could do nothing but admire the space. The ceilings were vaulted, and she could see what she guessed were the original dark wood beams crossing the center. The rest of the room was a stunning mix of modern simplicity and Chinese elegance. There were no windows, but carved wooden screens lined the walls and an intricately worked arch lined with silk curtains separated the bedroom from the sitting area.

Giovanni was still frowning. "She definitely redecorated since the last time I was here."

"When was that?"

"About… a hundred years ago? I don't remember exactly."

She took a deep breath. "I forget how old you are most of the time."

"*I* forget how old I am most of the time."

Beatrice walked over to a low chaise, covered in red shantung. The whole room was decorated in rich crimson and black fabrics. "Somehow, I never pictured Tenzin having a flair for interior design."

He chuckled. "I can almost promise you this is Nima. As rough as Tenzin can be, Nima is as cultured. They've been companions for many years."

Thinking of the odd mood she'd picked up between her father and Tenzin, she asked, "Is Tenzin… well, were she and Nima *together*? Or… I don't know anything about that part of her life, to be honest."

He shrugged. "Neither do I."

"Really?"

He cocked an eyebrow at her and walked over, placing his hands at her waist. "It's not something she talks about. You have to remember, Tenzin has been alive for over five *thousand* years. I expect she sees those kind of relationships in a very different way than you or I do."

She sighed and embraced him, wrapping her arms around his waist and putting her ear to his chest. His heart gave a single, quiet thump.

"Are you very angry with her?" She cursed herself for asking, but she had to know.

"You were crying."

"That's not her fault."

"No, it's your father's fault."

"No…" She looked up at him and traced around his lips with her finger. "It's not anyone's fault. You can't blame anyone this time."

He frowned as if her explanation was unsatisfactory, so she asked another question.

"Who are the lion and the dragon?"

He pulled back. "What?"

"Elder He, the other fire vampire?"

"Yes?"

"She said, 'Who is this human who's protected by the lion and the dragon?' Was she talking about you and Baojia?"

Giovanni chuckled. "Yes, she's quite dramatic, isn't she? She always has been."

"So, are you the dragon?" Beatrice teased, pulling at the back of his shirt as she walked backward toward the silk-covered bed beyond the arched doorway. "The dragon that breathes fire?"

He bent down and hitched up her legs around his waist, carrying her toward the bed and laying her on the red pillows. "We're in China; the dragon is a water symbol here."

"Oh?" she asked as his warm hands stroked along her waist. "So you're the lion? Why are you the lion?"

"I'm from the West, and the lion is a symbol of the sun," he said as he laid gentle kisses along her collar. "The sun is the mother of fire."

"But…" She sighed as she felt the quick lick of amnis wherever his lips touched. Her heart began to race. "That seems kind of cruel. You can't go out in the sun."

He only smiled, and she could see the length of his fangs gleaming in the low light of the candles that lit the room.

"*Tesoro mio,* the lion may be a symbol of the sun…" He bent down, lifted her body toward his, and gave one long, slow lick from her collarbone to her ear. "But he hunts at night."

CHAPTER THREE

Mount Penglai, China
August 2010

Giovanni left Beatrice sleeping a few hours before dawn, after exhausting her body and quieting her mind. She wouldn't talk about her feelings toward her father yet. He knew it was too soon. As she did with all new developments, she would take her time observing and thinking before she came to a decision.

But Giovanni could still be angry.

He was angry with Tenzin, who had kept the secret of Stephen's location for her own cryptic reasons. He was angry with Stephen for running and questioning his motives with Beatrice. He was angry that he had to be in this place that tried his patience and set every instinct on edge. He knew exactly why Tenzin avoided her father's court. It reminded him of the strictly choreographed social scenes of his human childhood, where even the color of a hat could have some hidden meaning.

Giovanni walked out of Tenzin's rooms and into the central courtyard, spending a few quiet moments breathing the night air and wandering among the large limestone rocks placed around the garden. The scholar's stones had been shaped by wind and water and were a popular symbol among the Eight Immortals, as they combined three of the four natural elements in harmony.

He stepped over a small footbridge and spied Beatrice's father reading a book near the edge of a stream. The vampire must have sensed the changing energy because he immediately looked up and narrowed his eyes. Giovanni walked over, sitting on a stone bench opposite Stephen. He looked around the garden, but picked up no indications they were being observed.

"How's my daughter?" Stephen asked.

Giovanni debated for a moment, but decided he would answer him. "She'll be fine."

Stephen nodded and closed his book. He set it on the bench next to him and folded his hands, the picture of practiced serenity.

"Have you had any word of Lorenzo?"

"I suspect he knows you are here. Or at least has some suspicion. The last time we had information about him, it indicated he was heading to Eastern Asia."

Stephen took a deep breath. "I've been in this place long enough that I knew it would trickle back to him."

"Then why did you stay?"

"I was tired of running." He sighed. "And I hoped that Beatrice would find me somehow."

Giovanni felt a spurt of anger. "You knew that I was looking for you. You must know my reputation. Why did you not seek me out? I was protecting your daughter; I could have protected you, too. And then you wouldn't have worried her."

"And how did I know you were trustworthy?" Stephen cocked an eyebrow at him. "Do you know the stories your son tells about you? The picture Lorenzo painted of you would make a thousand-year-old vampire run screaming, much less someone as young as me."

"Good."

"Do you know what it did to me to think that Beatrice was under your aegis? I had the most horrifying thoughts and conflicting reports. I had no way of knowing what the truth was."

Giovanni snorted. "Your daughter is more than safe with me, De Novo."

"I realized that when I met Tenzin."

"Tenzin…" Giovanni curled his lip. "I'm quite angry with both of you."

"She said you would be, but that we were doing the right thing and that things had to happen in a certain order."

He shook his head. "Damned mystic. Who does she think she is?"

"Your friend," Stephen said as he leaned forward, "and a friend to my daughter."

Giovanni remained silent, sitting with a stoic expression as he examined Beatrice's father. Stephen had the thin countenance common among those who spent their lives immersed in books, but he also looked as if he had been feeding regularly, and he no longer wore the gaunt look Beatrice had described from her childhood. There was something about his energy signature that bothered Giovanni. If he had no idea who the vampire was, he would have guessed he was much, much older.

Perhaps even older than him.

"Is Beatrice very angry with me?"

Giovanni shrugged. "You'll have to ask her."

Stephen sighed. "You explained to her what he's like, didn't you? Lorenzo?"

"She didn't need me to describe Lorenzo's madness for her. Unfortunately, she's quite well-acquainted with it on her own."

Stephen's face fell, crumbling with guilt as he remembered why Beatrice was familiar with Lorenzo's cruelty. "I know she may not forgive me. I understand that." He looked up. "Do you understand?"

"Why you ran? Of course I do. I could even feel some guilt for it, since I created him, but ultimately, Lorenzo is a creature of his own making. And frankly, Stephen De Novo, you are only as important to me as you are to your daughter. If she did not want to find you, you would be nothing to me. A mere annoyance in my otherwise very long life."

Stephen looked at him silently, taking a deep breath and closing his eyes for a moment. "You really do love her, don't you?"

"That is between Beatrice and me. I do not know you well enough to confide in you; however, Tenzin may decide to trust you. And if I think that your presence is a danger to Beatrice, I will not hesitate to be rid of you, manuscript or no manuscript."

"You killed to get her back. You've spent vast sums to protect her. Does she even know?"

Giovanni shifted slightly. "It is irrelevant."

Stephen only nodded. "I'm glad you found her. She could have come to a far worse end."

"Yes," he murmured, "she could have." The rage Giovanni had suppressed for over five years bubbled to the surface, and he felt his skin begin to heat. "Do you have any idea what you did? How you endangered her? What it did when you abandoned her?"

"What? Abandoned—"

"How could you be so careless? With your own daughter? Do you realize what could have happened to her?"

Stephen scowled. "I didn't plan on being murdered by your son, di Spada. If he hadn't killed me, my daughter never would have been in danger."

Giovanni rose to his feet. "And if you hadn't left her unprotected, she wouldn't have been, either."

Stephen shook his head. "What do you even know about—"

"You are not a man without skills, Stephen De Novo. You could have sought protection for yourself and your family through someone more powerful of your choosing. Then she and your mother—"

"I thought I was doing the right thing!" Stephen rose to his feet. "I thought—"

"You thought like a petulant child!" Giovanni glared at him, clenching his hands and trying to restrain himself. "You gave no thought to your daughter. Do you realize that every man in her life has abandoned her at some point?"

Stephen blinked, cocking his head at Giovanni before he sank back to his seat. "But I thought you—"

"I left her, too. Like a fool. After I came back, it took me months to realize what I had done, how I had hurt her." He took a deep breath and calmed the rush of his heart, taking a seat on the bench once again. "I was arrogant, probably even more than you. I thought I knew what was best for her, what she could 'handle.'"

Stephen sat with his arms resting by his side and his shoulders slumped. He took a hand and waved it in a scooping motion toward the stream. A ball of water floated toward him, and he tossed it in the air between his upturned palms like a baseball.

"I never thought about it that way. I really didn't think she'd remember me."

"Don't get me started on your clumsy mental manipulations. You're lucky that I'm feeling generous and she has such a strong mind."

Stephen winced and let the ball of water splatter on the neatly trimmed grass. "My father, Hector—"

"Your father was a good man, De Novo, but he died. He didn't want to leave her, but he did anyway. You left her. Your father left her. I

34

left her. Don't even get me started on the woman who calls herself her mother. Frankly, some days I think it's a miracle she'll talk to either of us."

Stephen looked at the ground, nodding. "I understand what you're saying."

"She's far stronger than either of us gave her credit for. Just remember that."

"Will she…" Stephen looked at him with pleading eyes. "I mean, does she want this life? Have you talked about it?"

Giovanni looked away. "You'll have to ask her. It is not my business to speak for her."

"I understand," Stephen said, nodding again.

"Do you?" Giovanni leaned forward, capturing Stephen in his vivid green gaze. "Make sure that you do."

Stephen did not flinch under his stare. "She's lucky she found you."

Giovanni shook his head and muttered, "I am the lucky one." Just then, his eyes darted to the right as he registered an ancient immortal coming toward them. Giovanni held up a hand to silence Stephen and took a deep breath, waiting for their host in a pose of meditation.

"Giovanni Vecchio. Stephen." Elder Zhang spoke as he approached them. "You are enjoying the hours before dawn in my favorite place."

Giovanni smirked. "I thought your favorite place was the banquet hall."

Zhang chuckled. "You know me too well. I have to thank you both for giving my daughter a reason to come visit me. It has been too long since I have seen her."

"You know Tenzin only does what she wishes, Zhang." Giovanni had always liked Tenzin's sire, enjoying his jovial personality that often reminded him of Carwyn. But he knew Zhang and Tenzin's history was complicated, so he didn't often express his feelings to his old friend.

"My daughter has always done what she wishes," the ancient wind vampire said. "I suppose I should be grateful she visits at all."

Giovanni fell silent, wary of saying the wrong thing. Zhang looked Stephen up and down. "Stephen, have you fed tonight?"

"I have, Elder Zhang. Thank you for asking."

"And how are you finding the palace after the austerity of the monastery?"

"I am grateful for my time in both, Elder Zhang. I am grateful for your hospitality, as well as the hospitality of Elder Lu Dongbin's monks."

So, Beatrice came by her political side naturally.

Stephen answered graciously, with none of the hesitation that would typically mark a vampire speaking to one so much older than himself. In fact, Stephen had carried himself with a surprising amount of confidence in the main hall earlier in the evening, as well.

Interesting.

"And your book has remained safely at the monastery, has it not?" Zhang said, looking at Giovanni out of the corner of his eye. Giovanni cut his eyes toward Stephen, curious what the young immortal would reveal with his expression, but Stephen had mastered the art of the impassive face. His expression revealed nothing but contentment.

Giovanni spoke up. "It is quite safe, from what Tenzin tells me. No one knows the location of the monastery except the Elders, is that not true, Zhang? Even Stephen was prevented from knowing where he was going on his journey."

"Very true." Zhang quirked a smile and shrugged his shoulders in an unusually dramatic fashion. Tenzin's sire was from the ancient steppes of Northern Asia and had always been more expressive than his younger Chinese peers. His mannerisms reflected it. "I feel the pull of the dawn coming. I believe I will retire."

Zhang nodded at them both before taking his leave, lifting off the ground in front of them and skipping across the top of the stones as he flew toward his rooms.

Giovanni looked at Stephen. "A good suggestion for all of us, I think."

Stephen and Giovanni rose and walked across the lawn.

"We'll talk about the book tomorrow, Stephen. At first dark, when Beatrice and I are awake."

Beatrice's father nodded quickly. "Fine, I'll be expecting it." Then he smiled as he watched Zhang's retreating figure. "You realize he doesn't really sleep, right? Neither he nor Tenzin have to sleep more than an hour or two a day."

"I know." *But I find it curious that you do, Stephen.*

He couldn't help but notice, as they walked toward the windowless rooms of Tenzin's palace and the morning sky began to lighten, that Stephen hadn't slowed at all, as a younger vampire normally would as he felt the pull of day.

Very interesting.

"Tesoro," Giovanni whispered into Beatrice's ear the following evening, trailing a hand from her knee, over the curve of her hip, and slipping it around her waist as he pulled her back to his chest. He had woken before her, which was unusual. She must have been overwhelmed from the night before.

"Beatrice," he whispered again.

"Hmm?"

"Time to wake up."

"Okay." He felt her shift into his chest as she stretched. "Can you rub my legs?"

"Of course." He sat up and pulled back the sheet. "Were you practi —what the hell?" His mouth dropped open as saw the bruises on her legs. There was one particularly large one near her hip. He let loose with a string of old curses she probably didn't understand.

"I was sparring with Tenzin today," she said in a sleepy voice. "You know, Gemma has nothing on Tenzin. Tenzin's mean." Beatrice chuckled a little. "And did you know she doesn't have to sleep hardly at all? She never mentioned that when she visited me in L.A."

He was still speechless as he examined her. There were fat bruises along her torso and arms, though none so severe that they could cause internal injuries. He continued muttering in Italian and he felt his skin heat up.

She must have sensed his anger, because she turned and narrowed her eyes. "Don't do the thing again. And calm down, you're getting hot."

"Beatrice, if you—"

"If I what?" She sat up, glaring at him. "I'm the one that asked her to practice with me. And it's not the first time we've sparred, Gio. Remember? You were gone for a few years. We always practice when we're together, and I usually get pretty bruised. It's nothing to worry about."

"Does she always treats you as her own personal punching bag?" He was angry. All he could see were the startling bruises that marred his lover's fair skin.

"You know what? Forget it. I'll take a bath and find some aspirin." Beatrice sat up and swung her legs over the edge of the bed. "I'm sure one of the bowing people—"

"Don't," he said as he pulled her back. He wrapped his arms around her, gently heating his body to soothe her aching muscles when she winced. She began to relax, but he kept her on his lap, pulling her legs around to straddle his waist as he heated his hands and placed them on the worst of her abdominal bruises. He buried his face in the crook of her neck.

"Warn me next time," he said. "I was surprised. You know my reaction to seeing you hurt."

"Okay, consider yourself warned." She played with the hair at his neck, twisting the curls in her fingers as she slowly relaxed her muscles. "When Tenzin and I hang out, I end up bruised from practice. But she's a great teacher, and she never does more than I can handle."

He made no reply, but moved his hands down her legs and began to massage them.

"Gio?"

"Mmmhmm?"

"Maybe... maybe we need to think about doing it sooner."

His breath caught and his hands halted. "I thought we were going to wait until Benjamin was older, so at least one of us—"

"I think we could work around it." Her fingers twisted in his dark hair. He took a deep breath and continued her massage.

"And I think it's not something I want you to do because you're fearful for your life. That's not a good reason to—"

"It's not the reason. You know that."

"Then why—"

"Because it's still a factor, love." She tilted his head back so they were eye to eye. "Gio, my safety is still a huge liability."

He took a deep breath and stared into the eyes of the woman he loved. "I think..."

"What?"

Giovanni frowned as he met her worried brown eyes. "I feel like we're rushing this. You're still young. You should have time—"

"Ugh." She rolled her eyes and looked away. "Not this again."

"It's not a small thing, Beatrice."

"I'm not saying it is. But it's not a big thing—not for me."

"I just think we should wait. Don't you trust Tenzin and me to guard you?"

She took a deep breath. "Of course I do. That's not the issue."

"Then—"

"We should get out of bed." She climbed off his lap. "I want to ask my dad a few questions tonight. I think I deserve some answers from him."

He sighed when she made the obvious subject change, but smiled at the determined expression she wore as he rose to join her.

"Are you feeling better?"

"I am, thanks." She squeaked as he scooped her into his arms and walked to the bathroom.

"Good. I think a nice, warm bath is in order, Miss De Novo. Just to be safe, I'll join you."

"Well," she laughed. "If it's for my own safety…"

"Oh yes," he said with a pinch to her knee, which was thankfully not bruised. "Safety first."

Giovanni was far more relaxed an hour later when they met with Tenzin and Stephen in the main room. Baojia was out hunting, no doubt informed that they had planned a private meeting. Stephen and Tenzin were already sitting at a table, sipping tea, when they walked in.

"Good, Nima had dinner prepared for you," Tenzin said, nodding to one of the servants standing near the door. "Did I bruise you too much?"

"I'm fine," Beatrice said with a wave.

Tenzin cocked an eyebrow at Giovanni, as if challenging his cool demeanor, but he didn't rise to the bait. "She's very good, you know. When she changes, she'll be formidable. We should have Baojia give her weapons training while she is here. I have a full practice room with many options."

"Oh?" Beatrice perked up. "What kind of weapons?"

He sat down and waited for Tenzin to stop teasing him. Though, really, it wasn't a bad idea. Because he had such a ready weapon in his fire and rarely needed to behead an enemy, Giovanni wasn't as well trained in swordsmanship as most vampires were. He was proficient in fencing and the older Greek and Roman forms of hand-to-hand combat, but he suspected that Beatrice would take to the Asian styles better, considering her background in martial arts. Baojia, despite Giovanni's personal reservations, would be an excellent teacher.

"We'll talk later; I'm sure she'll consider it," he said. "In the meantime, try not to bruise any internal organs on my woman,

Tenzin."

"Hey!" Beatrice scowled and smacked his arm. "Enough with the 'my woman' stuff already."

"Really?" He cocked an eyebrow at her. She blushed and looked at the bowl of noodle soup the servant had just placed in front of her.

"Well," Stephen said when the servant finally closed the door. "Speaking of awkward silences, let's talk about what's been keeping me running around the globe for the past thirteen years, shall we?"

Giovanni leaned forward. "First, do you know where Andros's library is?"

Stephen shrugged. "When I escaped, it was in Lorenzo's villa in Perugia, but who knows where it is now! I'm sure he moved it; it could be any number of places."

Giovanni sat back, stunned into silence by the simple confirmation of the mystery he'd followed for so long. He felt Beatrice's hand grasp his own, and he looked over at her. She had tears in her eyes as she stared at him, but he gave her a small smile and squeezed her hand.

He heard Stephen still speaking. "You knew about the library, right?"

Giovanni looked up, his voice a little hoarse when he finally spoke.

"No, Stephen. I have suspected for some time, but when Lorenzo and I parted many years ago, I thought my father's and uncle's collections had been lost or burned in Savonarola's bonfires."

Stephen's mouth dropped in horror. "No wonder you were looking for me. Andros's library was... magnificent! It would take a thousand years to detail it. The tablets. The scrolls." Stephen turned to his daughter. "Beatrice, Andros had scrolls from Alexandria. Things from Baghdad that he'd rescued from the Mongols. Books humanity thought had been lost for—"

"Dad," Beatrice interrupted. "Trust me when I say, we could talk about that library for years—and probably someday, we will. But right now, I think there's one book we really need to know about."

"Of course." Stephen nodded, taking a deep breath and leaning back in his seat, though Giovanni could still see the energy snapping off him. "Of course. I just... I had no idea you had no confirmation of its existence, Giovanni. I'd be happy—"

"Another time, Stephen." Tenzin rolled her eyes. "Tell them about the manuscript. Tell them about Geber's work."

"Geber?" Giovanni's ears perked up. "I wondered. So it was alchemy, or early chemistry? A lost manuscript? An experiment?"

"An incomplete work, but his greatest achievement. Of that, I have no doubt."

"Okay," Beatrice broke in. "Geber. I know I've heard the name, but remind me."

Giovanni turned to her. "Jabir ibn Hayyan. He was called Geber during my time, Tesoro, but he was an eighth century Persian alchemist."

"One of the first to apply modern scientific methods to his work," Stephen said. "He was hugely influential in the Middle East and later in Europe."

Tenzin piped up. "His work mostly related to the artificial creation of life. Not achievable, that we know of, but his formulas held promise and were better tested than others of the time. He wrote in deliberately cryptic ways, so many of his original formulas are still a mystery."

"But what is so special about this book? The book you stole, Dad? Why is it worth killing for?"

"'Knowledge is power,'" Giovanni murmured, still haunted by the words of his father. He shook his head and squeezed Beatrice's hand. "Humanity steals it. Trades it. Covets it. Many have killed for it. What is the knowledge that Lorenzo seeks from this, De Novo?"

Stephen sighed and spread his hands on the table.

"Life. The secret mankind has sought for centuries. Geber found the elixir of life. He discovered its source."

Beatrice shook her head. "That's not possible, that's—"

"And it's not just for humans."

CHAPTER FOUR

Mount Penglai, China
August 2010

"The elixir of… life?"

Beatrice could hear the skepticism dripping in Giovanni's voice.

Stephen only nodded. "Yes, the elixir of life."

"Let's pretend I believe that this is possible," he said. Tenzin barked something in Mandarin, but he just waved a hand in her direction and continued looking at Stephen. "I'll pretend this is possible, and you tell me why on earth an immortal vampire like Lorenzo wants this elixir enough to start a war with me."

"I told you, it's not just for humans."

Beatrice's eyes were darting around the table. She was as skeptical as Giovanni, but she knew her father had never been easily fooled, and he looked dead serious.

"I'd like to know why you think this is plausible, Dad." She spoke quietly, but every head at the table swung toward her. She had forgotten about her food almost as soon as it was set in front of her, but she played with her chopsticks nervously. "I mean, from all accounts, alchemists have tried for thousands of years to create a magic formula to prolong life, but none of them ever accomplished it."

Tenzin finally spoke. "But, none of them—as far as we know— had the advantage that Geber had."

"And what was that?" Giovanni leaned back in his chair as he spoke.

Stephen said, "Four vampires willing to work with him."

All attention was on her father again.

"What?" Giovanni narrowed his eyes, glaring at Stephen.

"Geber had four vampires, one of each element, that he was working with. I finally figured it out by reading one of his journals in Andros's library. It's one of the other books I took. I took the manuscript with the formula, along with three of Geber's journals and a few books I knew I would be able to sell for quick cash."

"Some of *my* collection."

He offered Giovanni an embarrassed frown. "I'm sorry. I'm sure some of them were yours, but I had nothing."

"I'll get them back. Continue."

"The key to the elixir is the blood. No one knows why we have an affinity toward the elements, but all vampires do. And it's our blood that seems to hold the key. Geber was smart and probably knew that his contemporaries would doubt his use of blood that wasn't even supposed to exist—except in myth—so he never names the ingredients in the formula, but from reading his journals, I was finally able to figure it out."

"But why would that even—"

Stephen turned to Beatrice. "You have bruises all over, why can't Giovanni heal them?"

She frowned. Surely her father knew that much. "Because I'm human. Gio says my digestive system would break down his blood before it could have any positive effect. That's why it only works on open cuts or scrapes."

"Exactly, your human system doesn't know what to do with it. Whatever magic animates our blood—"

"It's not magic," Giovanni spit out. "We just haven't figured out what it is yet."

"Damn it!" Tenzin said. "You're so damn arrogant, Gio. Do you think your science can explain everything? There are things in this world—"

"That haven't been explained yet. And once upon a time, humans didn't know what the stars were, either. But that time has passed. The mysteries of the natural world—"

"Are not going to be revealed at this table," Beatrice interrupted. "But the super-secret mystery of the elixir of life might be if you all quit arguing and let my dad talk."

Stephen chuckled, but Giovanni and Tenzin looked annoyed to have been interrupted. Still, they fell silent and Giovanni gestured to Stephen. "Continue."

Her father turned to Tenzin. "If you were injured, would you go to another wind vampire for blood?"

"You know I wouldn't." She seemed content to play along with the rhetorical question. "I would go to a vampire of another element that I trusted if I needed strength. The blood of your own element—"

"Does very little to heal, unless it is your own sire," Giovanni said, a sudden light of interest coming to his eyes. "It is the combination of elements that seems to heal. Tell me about the four types of blood."

Stephen took a deep breath. "Geber must have researched extensively, and his subjects must have been very open with him. What he discovered was that, combined, the four elemental bloods would create an elixir that would heal and prolong human life. Possibly indefinitely."

"Oh, wow," Beatrice whispered. "So—"

"How?" Giovanni asked. "How would a human even be able to ingest it?"

Tenzin spoke softly. "That's where his alchemy came in, my boy. It seems that somehow, Geber was able to stabilize it. That's what the formula is for. It's the formula to stabilize the four combined immortal bloods in a way that will allow the human body to reap the benefits in the same way that a vampire body does."

"But…"

She could tell from looking at him that Giovanni had been rocked. She was feeling a little overwhelmed herself. He looked at her and traced a hand along her cheek, letting his thumb rest at the pulse in her neck.

"Beatrice," he whispered. "This could be…"

"Gio, we don't know enough about this."

Tenzin spoke up again. "No, we most definitely do *not*. And I'm highly suspicious of the next part of the findings."

"What findings?" Beatrice asked.

"Geber tested it for almost a year," Stephen said, "and the results seemed very promising. He gave it to a human that was diseased—he only described it as a 'wasting disease'—but the recovery was almost instant. The human was observed for another few months before Geber sent him home, apparently totally healed. Another subject was very elderly. While the elixir didn't reverse the aging process, it seemed to halt when he took the blood, and his quality of life improved. He was healthier and exhibited a 'younger' level of health.

"But you said this was not just for humans," Giovanni said, leaning forward over the table. "What did you mean?"

"I mean that one of the vampires that drank from a human who had taken the elixir only had to drink once."

Beatrice frowned. "Drink once for what?"

Stephen looked at her, spreading his hands across the table. "I mean, he only had to drink once, Mariposa. He drank once in the year of testing."

She still didn't understand what he was trying to say. "And then what?"

"And then he didn't have to drink again," Tenzin said. "At all."

She turned to Giovanni in shock. His face was completely frozen.

Beatrice said, "What? At all? As in, he drank once from a human that had taken this elixir, and he didn't have to drink any more blood in the entire year of testing?"

"That's exactly what I mean," Stephen said. "He drank once, ate the amount of food he normally would have, and never had to take another drop of blood."

"There's something we're not seeing," Tenzin said. "Gio, I can see the look on your face, and I know what you're thinking, but this is not a cure for bloodlust. It's not. There's something—"

"But what if it is, bird girl?"

Beatrice didn't think she had ever heard him sound more vulnerable.

Despite his pragmatic views on vampire life, she knew it still bothered Giovanni every time he had to feed from a human, even a criminal. It made him feel barbaric, like a parasite. When they were together and she received pleasure from him, it was one thing; but he couldn't drink from her all the time, it simply wasn't healthy. That was why he bought donated blood, even though it affected his health.

"It is not the answer. There's something we're not seeing here."

"But what if it's true? What if—"

"Then why would your son want it?" Tenzin shouted. "Why would he kill for this? He has no need of eternal life, and he has no compunction about drinking, or even draining, humans. He's no kind of humanitarian, so why does he want it so badly? I'm telling you, there's something here we are not seeing!"

They broke into a heated argument in Mandarin that Beatrice couldn't follow, while Stephen watched, occasionally glancing at her as if she might know what to do. Tenzin and Giovanni had both risen to their feet and showed no signs of stopping.

"Enough!" Beatrice finally said, standing to join them. "This isn't something we can solve tonight. Even I can tell this book needs more investigating before we all run out and drink the Kool-Aid, so to speak."

"That's why it's still at the monastery," Stephen added. "Zhang wanted his oldest student and Lu's monks to take a look at it. Their knowledge of alchemy, particularly plant alchemy, which is what the formula required, is far better than my own."

"Or even mine, to be honest." Tenzin stepped away from the table. "Now, I'm going to find Baojia. I want to talk to him about training Beatrice. B, take him away and calm him down, will you?"

She could hear Giovanni growl next to her, but he didn't feel hot, so she wasn't overly concerned. She glanced at her father.

"Um… Dad—"

"I'm going to the library; then I'll be in the Great Hall," Stephen said. "I'll talk to you both later."

He slipped out of the room, and she and Giovanni were alone. He stared at her with the most tender expression she had ever seen.

"Tesoro, if this means—"

"We don't know what it means yet, Gio. And we don't know if we can trust this information. There are too many unknowns."

He put a warm hand over her heart. "But, if you didn't have to give up the sun, if you didn't have to be a slave to your own hunger to be with me forever…"

She drew him down for a gentle kiss. "There's still a lot to think about, love."

He nodded, but pulled her into his arms, wrapping her up in his warm embrace as she tried to think past the feeling of dread that still churned in her gut when she remembered Tenzin's warning.

Beatrice had to agree. There was something they weren't seeing.

"I don't trust that damn formula," Tenzin muttered as they

practiced late that afternoon. Beatrice was still astonished by how comfortable she was in the middle of the day. Though she couldn't go out in the sun, the ancient vampire showed not a hint of reduced strength, although Tenzin claimed that flying wasn't a very good idea.

They were taking some time off from heavier sparring to concentrate on tai chi forms.

"I don't really want to talk about the formula any more right now, if that's okay. I think there are too many questions."

"Thank you for being skeptical. It's a relief. I was worried that you were going to go crazy at the possibilities, and I'd have to restrain you both. I don't trust it."

Beatrice moved deliberately, focusing on the slow movement of her limbs and the steady rhythm of her breathing. "I'm skeptical of anything that seems too good to be true, and this formula falls into that category. Why are we doing basic forms again? And why are we doing them even slower than normal?"

"Because, when you turn, my friend…" Tenzin moved in front of her and started to mirror her in the "push hands" technique she employed when she wanted Beatrice to slow her movements. The technique always made Beatrice feel as if she was moving through heavy water.

Languorous. Flowing. Forceful, but still fluid in her body and mind.

"You must remember how your body feels right now. How you control every muscle, every bone, every joint and tendon. Deliberate. Everything must be deliberate. That is what will enable you to control yourself when your senses have been heightened, so you will not become overwhelmed. If I had known this discipline when I had first turned, my younger years would have been much more pleasant."

They moved as mirrors of each other, an achingly slow ballet of combat forms, pared to their most essential movements. This was not about speed or strength; it was about the total focus of the mind and body. The meditation of the mind was as central as the physical control.

"What were you like when you were younger?"

Tenzin paused, and Beatrice wondered if the secretive vampire would answer her.

"I was very angry and very violent. Why doesn't Giovanni want you to turn?"

She sighed and closed her eyes, moving through the familiar movements.

Bend. Sweep. Push. Yield.

"He's sentimental, for one. He uses the idea of one of us being available during the day for Ben as an excuse, but it's not really what's bothering him."

"What is it, then? Your human life is a liability at this point."

"I agree, but he's pretty stubborn."

"Why?"

"I think he's worried about the motherhood thing, to be honest. He thinks I'm going to turn and then regret not having children."

Tenzin snorted. "So you'll adopt."

"That's what I told him. We already have Ben, for heaven's sake. If we want more children someday, we can adopt, but he thinks I'll regret not giving birth or something. It's not something I take *lightly*, but being pregnant, especially when it wouldn't be his, isn't something that I consider vital to happiness."

"It's not. And pregnancy doesn't make you a mother. I gave birth to three children, but I was only mother to one."

Beatrice stumbled back, stunned by Tenzin's admission. The vampire just looked at her, clearly annoyed she had fumbled their practice. She stepped closer, pushing Beatrice to mirror her graceful movements.

Bend. Stretch. Push. Yield.

"How old were you?"

"When I birthed my children?" Tenzin shrugged, moving into a more complex routine. "*Focus.* I have no idea. We didn't celebrate birthdays back then. I'd been bleeding for one winter when I became pregnant with my first child."

"What—"

"She was small. She didn't survive the winter. Neither did her father."

Bend. Sweep. Push. Yield.

"Your husband died, too?"

She frowned, folding at the waist as they swept down into a new form. "I suppose you could call him my husband. His older brother took me after that. He already had a wife, but she hadn't given him any children, so he took me. I was luckier with him. My babies were born in the spring the following year, and both survived."

48

"What happened to them?" Beatrice concentrated on keeping her tone easy as they moved. She was shocked Tenzin was sharing as much as she was.

"The oldest one, the stronger one, was given to my husband's first wife. I was allowed to keep the second child. He was small, but strong."

Her mind was still reeling at the casual tone in which Tenzin was relating her story. She almost sounded like she was talking about an acquaintance. They continued to move with each other, as Beatrice focused on her breath and the stretch of her muscles.

Bend. Stretch. Push. Yield.

"Where did you live?"

"It was on the Northern steppes. I have no idea where exactly. I lived in a village that was raided a lot. That's how I was turned."

"What happened?" She held her breath, half expecting Tenzin to clam up. She didn't.

"We were raided one day, and the first wife sent me out to check the goats. They never took everything—how else would we have more goats for them the next time they came? But she wanted to know how many we had left and if any kids had dropped, so she sent me out after dark. I was happy to go. My son had been crying and he always liked it better when I walked, so I tied him to my back and went out to check the pens. There were three men there."

"The raiders?"

Tenzin cocked an eyebrow and moved into a new routine. "No, definitely not. These 'men' didn't need horses to get around."

"They were vampires," Beatrice whispered.

"Yes, they were vampires."

She fell silent for a few moments, and Beatrice saw her close her eyes as she moved through the forms.

Bend. Push. Sweep. Yield.

Even though her heart ached, and part of her didn't want to hear the rest of the story, Beatrice still asked.

"What happened?"

"They were feeding on the goats, but stopped when they heard me. My son started crying, and I tried to hush him so I could run away, but they were already coming toward me. I thought they were demons of some kind; they moved so fast. They swept me up and took me away."

"And your son?" she whispered.

Tenzin paused for only a second in her silent exercise.

"He fell to the ground. He was crying when they took to the air. It's possible someone from the village found him. Probably not."

Tears fell down Beatrice's cheeks, but Tenzin's eyes were still closed, silently practicing the meditative forms of the tai chi routine. Her face was serene, and her hair flowed around her, brushing her shoulders as they moved together.

Bend. Stretch. Push. Yield.

"And Zhang?"

"The men who took me were Zhang's sons. His own band of raiders. There were four of them then. He turned more as the years passed. His sons sired sons. Eventually, my father had over fifty wind vampires to do his bidding."

"Why did he turn you?"

"For his men. They usually killed the human women they took, so Zhang turned me. He thought I would be more... resilient."

Beatrice's stomach twisted in horror, but she took care not to halt her steady movements. She could not comprehend the cruelty of Elder Zhang turning a young girl, just so she could be a plaything for his other children. No wonder the vampire disliked her sire.

Tenzin was still moving with her eyes closed, her face a picture of placid meditation as she practiced.

Bend. Sweep. Push. Yield.

"How long were you with him?"

"Two or three hundred years. Just long enough to kill off all of his children."

Beatrice was speechless, but Tenzin never stopped moving through the complex combat forms. Eventually, she continued without prompting.

"They would take turns with me. At first, I was frightened. After all, I was a child. And I had no idea how to use my new body. But I slowly gathered more skill. I was probably twenty years immortal when I killed the first of his sons."

Bend. Stretch. Push. Yield.

"Eventually, they avoided me. But I didn't stop until I had killed them all."

"What did Zhang do when they were all dead?"

"He laughed. Then he told me I was his finest creation, his fiercest warrior, and sent me out into the world with half of his wealth. He came to Penglai soon after that, and I was on my own. I never had another companion until I met Giovanni."

Finally, she slowed her movements, finishing the routine before she bowed to Beatrice, who mirrored the movement. Tenzin opened her storm-grey eyes.

"Do not pity me, Beatrice De Novo. My life has been as fate dictated, and now I am master of it. Do not waste your regret on the past."

Beatrice nodded as they moved to the benches that lined the room and drank from the pitcher of water that had been set out. "Why didn't you kill Gio when you met him? He told me that he'd been sent to kill you. Why did you have mercy on him?"

She smiled. "I saw him. I saw his eyes in a dream. They were the same color as my son's. I knew our fates were intertwined."

Beatrice gulped down the water as Tenzin looked over her shoulder. She smiled just a few seconds before Beatrice heard the door open.

"Nightfall," Tenzin said. "You boys will have to wait to play with her," she shouted at the door. "She's still mine for another hour."

Beatrice turned to see Giovanni and Baojia leaning against the wall of the practice room. Her heart skipped a beat when she saw the two handsome men outlined against the pale walls. Baojia wore a look of amusement. Giovanni's eyes were narrowed at her; he looked hungry.

"Give me back my woman, Tenzin. You've borrowed her for too long."

Tenzin rolled her eyes and turned back to Beatrice. "How do you put up with him? That's so annoying."

She laughed. "He just hates it when I'm not there when he wakes up."

The small vampire lifted up and flew toward the two men, swiping at them and smacking both on the back of the head before she flitted back to Beatrice's side.

"Well, they'll have to learn how to be patient. You have more important things to be doing than entertaining his libido." She looked up at Beatrice and gestured toward the mat. "We're running out of time."

CHAPTER FIVE

Penglai Island, China
September 2010

The longer he watched her, the faster his heart beat.

She was astonishing.

A vision of her transformed assaulted him. Lithe grace turned into preternatural strength and speed. Fangs gleaming in her mouth as she pierced his skin. Her smooth, pale skin crackling with energy when she touched him.

Imagining Beatrice as an immortal was undeniably alluring. Yet, it still filled him with guilt.

"She'll be stunning when she turns," Baojia said as he sat next to him.

Giovanni glared at him, irritated that his thoughts had been so closely mirrored by the other vampire.

"She's stunning now."

Baojia just cocked an amused eyebrow at him.

"She plans on it. Why else would she practice as she does?" He folded his legs and hands in a meditative pose. "I think it was in the back of her mind even before you came back."

"Oh?"

"I remember the first martial arts class she took. Introductory tai chi. Ernesto was very pleased. Beatrice says Tenzin suggested it. Very forward thinking of your old partner; it will help immeasurably with physical control."

Giovanni wanted the water vampire to shut up. He disliked being reminded of the years where Baojia had watched over Beatrice, and he had not. He decided to change the subject.

"What weapons do you plan on introducing?"

"I'll start her with the *jian* and *dao*. She doesn't have any experience with weapons yet, and those will be a good start for her."

Giovanni nodded. The double-edged straight sword, or *jian*, and the curved single-edge saber, or *dao*, would be light enough for a human and versatile enough for Beatrice to carry regularly. Moreover, both were weapons he had some experience with and would be able to practice with her.

"Eventually, she will wield the *shuang gou*."

"What?" Giovanni looked up, frowning. "The hook sword?"

"Two," he said, watching Beatrice move in the faster *wushu* that Giovanni remembered practicing so many years before with Tenzin. Baojia leaned forward, tracking Beatrice with his eyes. "She'll carry two. Watch her move, di Spada. She's quick as a human; imagine her after. And she doesn't favor either side. She's adaptable and smart enough to wield them effectively." Baojia smiled. "Yes, we will start with the *dao*, but the *shuang gou* will be her weapon."

Giovanni frowned. The wicked curves of the traditional hook swords used in the northern part of China may have been brutally effective, even Zhang favored them, but they were also dangerous.

"Any sword is dangerous," Baojia murmured, as if reading Giovanni's thoughts, "but the *shuang gou* has many advantages to the one who can wield it effectively."

In the end, Giovanni had to admit that the water vampire's knowledge of weapons was far more extensive than his own. "I will accede to your expertise, Baojia, as long as it is what Beatrice wishes."

"I will make sure to demonstrate a variety of weapons with Tenzin. That way she will be able to observe them all."

"But keeping the *jian* and *dao* for her weapons at first?"

Baojia chuckled. "I never would have taken you for such a cautious immortal."

Just then, Beatrice's laugh rang through the practice room. Tenzin had picked her up, flown her to the corner of the room, and was hanging her by her feet.

"You crazy vampire," she called out, laughing. "Put me down,

Tenzin! No fair."

Giovanni smiled as his old friend flipped her upright and floated them both toward the ground. Beatrice looked toward him with laughing eyes and a brilliant smile, her face flushed and happy. She winked and blew him a kiss before walking over to the bench to drink a glass of water.

He glanced at Baojia. "And what fool would risk that?"

Baojia opened his mouth, as if to speak, but suddenly, Tenzin barked at him in Mandarin.

"Get over here. Do you want my help demonstrating or not?"

Baojia tossed a few insults back at her before he stood and walked to the thin mat that spread across the center of the room. Tenzin's practice room was exactly as Giovanni remembered it. He doubted it had changed in five hundred years. The ceiling was retractable, the walls were bare except for the impressive collection of weapons that covered two of them, and a small channel of water cut through the room, diverted from the gardens outside.

Giovanni caught the look of obvious interest that Baojia directed toward Beatrice as she crossed the room and headed toward him. She was covered in sweat, and her skin was flushed. She was still breathing heavily when she plopped down next to him.

"Hey," she said, kissing his cheek. "Sorry I smell."

He shrugged and pulled her into his lap. "You forget that I lived long before people bathed regularly, Tesoro. A little sweat won't scare me off." In fact, as he kissed her neck, he realized that her natural scent was only heightened. She smelled of salt, soap, and the unique honeysuckle and lemon scent that had drawn him from the beginning.

"I love practicing with Tenzin."

"No bruises today?"

She shook her head. "We were mostly doing tai chi earlier." A shadow fell across her face, but her gaze was quickly drawn toward the center of the room as Tenzin and Baojia parted and went to opposite walls to choose weapons.

Tenzin selected the long Chinese *jian* and skipped the ancient curved scimitar she usually fought with. She was ruthless when she carried it, but it would not be a good choice for Beatrice since she could not fly.

Baojia chose the *dao* he had spoken of, a single-edged weapon with good reach and a subtle curve. It had greater slashing power and, since beheading was the intention, Giovanni thought the choice was a good one.

"I'm really excited to start learning this," she whispered, wiggling on his lap.

"Of course you are."

"Relax. I doubt I'm in any danger from my grandfather's favorite son."

"I'm not worried about him hurting you."

"Then why the surly vampire act, old man?"

He bared his fangs playfully, pulling her head to the side as if going for a bite. She only laughed and reached up, pulling his head closer until his lips met her skin in a kiss. He was suddenly distracted by the steady beat of the pulse in her neck and the warm fingers entwined in his hair.

If she didn't have to give up the sun...

"Hey, why so quiet?"

"I'm thinking about the elixir."

"Gio—"

"I know there is more to investigate, but I am allowed to have some hope that you might not have to become a vampire to be with me."

She paused a moment, a slight frown creasing her forehead.

"What?" he asked.

"I've chosen *you*, Gio. I've chosen this life. I knew what it meant. I haven't changed my mind about turning."

"But, Beatrice, if you didn't have to—"

"If I could drink this elixir and remain human forever, then I would always be your physical inferior."

"That's not important to me; you know that."

"Who said it was up to you?" she asked. "This is something *I* decided." She turned in his arms, placing her cheek against his and whispering so they couldn't be overheard.

"I know you have to hold back with... so much. I don't want that forever. I want to be your partner. Your equal. I don't want to live a life separate from you, even in the hard things."

She pulled away and stroked his cheek as he looked at her.

In five hundred years of life, he had rarely met a human more stubborn or independent than Beatrice. It wasn't a foolish kind of disregard; she simply took her time to make up her mind, and when she did, she was determined. And he loved her for it.

"We'll talk about it more later."

That didn't mean he wasn't just as stubborn.

He felt her small elbow in his ribs, but she turned back to the mat, watching Tenzin and Baojia as they practiced with their chosen weapons. Eventually, they bowed toward each other in the way common among older immortals, bending from the waist while never breaking eye contact, arms outstretched so that all weapons were visible.

They began circling from their bow, both eyeing the other as Baojia murmured instructions to Tenzin about the techniques he wanted to demonstrate. Tenzin held the *jian* high in a pointed stance while Baojia's arm came out and his elbow pulled the *dao* back as if preparing to strike. They began moving in concert, demonstrating the most common strikes for each weapon as Baojia narrated to Beatrice what they were doing with each thrust or parry.

Giovanni glanced at her as she sat on his lap. She was completely enthralled. Her eyes lit up and she leaned forward, her complete focus on the two masters in front of her.

"This is so cool."

He saw them relax into the combat, and they began moving in more natural fight patterns for immortals. Baojia would use the water as a second weapon, sweeping his arm out to spear it in Tenzin's direction as she leapt into the air, dodging out of reach. At one point, Baojia sent a thin stream of water toward her as she flew above his head. The silver ribbon curled around her ankle, almost too thin to see, until Baojia reached a hand out and touched the stream, sending a shock of amnis through it, which brought Tenzin to the ground.

"Oh!" Giovanni cried, leaning forward and forgetting Beatrice on his lap. He had never seen a water vampire with that kind of control. "That was brilliant! Clever dragon."

Tenzin didn't seem to agree; as she rose up, she snarled at Baojia before launching herself into the air again. Baojia smirked, but Giovanni knew the vampire would only be able to use that trick once.

Not long after, they began to vary their routine, tossing weapons back and forth, calling out to Beatrice as they did, explaining each one as they demonstrated the proper way to use it.

Swords, pikes, axes, chains, daggers, spears, poles. Beatrice was transfixed.

"Oh," she drew out a breath as her eyes followed Baojia, who was drawing two ancient swords from the wall. "What are *those*?"

Giovanni growled when he saw the two wickedly curved swords that Baojia wielded. They were the length of the *jian*, but each had a long hook on the end. The hilts were sharpened into daggers, and the hand guard on each was a sharp crescent moon, suitable for either blocking or slashing an opponent.

Damn, prescient vampire.

"Those are *shuang gou*, Beatrice. Hook swords."

As Giovanni spoke, Baojia leapt toward Tenzin, whirling in dizzying circles toward her, as she parried with the *jian* and a chain, which she threw toward his neck. Baojia hooked the chain with the end of one sword, pulling it away as he slashed at the blade in her other hand. Giovanni could barely follow their movements, and Beatrice held her breath as they continued to fight for several minutes. They were a blur of movement as they spun around the room.

In one final flurry, Tenzin came to a halt, *jian* held out as Boajia pressed the *shuang gou* to her neck, the hooks curved toward her bared throat, and the blades crossed in a scissor formation.

"No way," Beatrice whispered.

Giovanni narrowed his eyes. "It's debatable whether she let him win, but that was still very impressive."

"I want to learn how to use those."

He shook his head as Baojia looked toward him and laughed. His eyes only said one thing.

Told you.

"You let him win, didn't you?"

Tenzin shrugged as they walked through the garden. They had left Beatrice with Baojia in the training studio. His woman scarcely gave him a second glance before she rushed toward the weaponry, peppering Baojia with question after question. Tenzin pulled him out of the palace and forced him to walk through the grounds so he didn't hover.

"Maybe. He's very good, and he'll be a much better instructor than I would."

"Why is that?"

"I revert too quickly to flying, and she won't be a flyer."

Giovanni halted, leaning against a wall of carved stonework.

"Oh, she won't?"

Tenzin turned and smiled, her face a picture of innocence.

In the back of his mind, Tenzin had always been Giovanni's first choice to sire Beatrice, though he knew Beatrice and Carwyn had discussed it, and the choice was Beatrice's in the end. Still, there was no one he trusted more than the small woman in front of him. Tenzin was his oldest friend, and she had one other advantage that Giovanni greatly desired.

Tenzin was immeasurably powerful.

She had lived for over five thousand years, and as far as he knew, she had never sired a child. Her blood would be unspeakably potent, and any vampire child she sired would be a force to be reckoned with. If Giovanni guessed correctly, Beatrice turning from Tenzin would put her almost immediately on par with his own physical strength. She would quickly outstrip him, but she would be able to defend herself from almost any other immortal, and that was all he cared about.

He narrowed his eyes. "Are you so averse to siring your own friend, bird-girl?"

"Did I say that?" She shrugged in her irritatingly vague way. "Even if she is sired from wind, the flying always takes time to develop."

"Not for your child, it wouldn't."

They continued walking. He knew Tenzin wouldn't tell him anything more, even if he pestered her, so he switched to a topic he knew would irritate her.

"I'm very curious to learn more about the elixir."

Her string of Mongolian curses was impressive. Most of them had something to do with horses and obscene acts. Giovanni just smirked.

"You have such a foul mouth for a little girl."

Tenzin punched his side. Then she threw him several meters away purely out of irritation.

"I knew you were going to be excited about that. If I could have destroyed that book when I learned about it, I would have been far happier, but Stephen was too attached to it."

"Not to mention that it rightfully belongs to me. Why destroy it? Maybe it really would allow us to stop feeding off humanity like parasites."

She shook her head. "It's so ridiculous, this guilt you feel. And don't pretend that it has anything to do with being a humanitarian, Giovanni."

58

"What?"

"You don't have a problem feeding from Beatrice, do you? You don't have a problem buying blood from banks when you need to. No, you just don't like being dependent on anyone, even a human, for your own survival. That's why you would prefer to conquer the bloodlust."

He frowned, unwilling to admit that part of her judgment was correct.

"It would be better for Beatrice if—"

"You didn't try to dictate her actions again?" She cocked an eyebrow at him. "If you allowed her to make her own decisions? I agree. The choice has always been hers."

"Damn you, woman."

"Stubborn old man."

"That's highly amusing, coming from you."

She laughed the tinkling, wind-chime laugh as the breeze picked up. "Why do you fight your own fate, my boy? She is your balance in this life."

"In every life. I know."

"Do you?" She stopped and placed a hand on his cheek, looking up at him with the loving, almost maternal, gaze she allowed herself at times. Giovanni didn't know much about her human life, but he knew that at one point Tenzin had mortal children of her own. He had a feeling their fate had not been pleasant.

"I know you sent me to her, Tenzin," he whispered, sensing the approach of a servant. "I know you saw her."

A slow smile grew on her face. "I thought you didn't believe in that stuff?" She winked and flew up, perching on one of the scholar's stones as she looked across the garden at the servant hurrying toward them in brown robes. She closed her eyes and turned her face into the breeze.

"Trouble is coming," she murmured into the wind. "No…" She shook her head and looked down at him with stormy eyes. "Trouble is here."

"Mistress Tenzin," the servant said as he bowed low, "your father requests your presence in the great hall with Dr. Vecchio." The man did not look up, and Giovanni had the impression he was purposely avoiding Tenzin's gaze. She floated down from the top of the tall limestone pillar.

"Stop bowing. Has Stephen been called to the Elders?" Her eyes darted across the dark garden toward the glowing lanterns in the center of the complex.

"He is already there, Mistress."

"I said stop bowing. Go to my chambers and inform Nima."

"Yes, Mistress." He started to scurry off. "Wait!" she called before she turned to Giovanni. "Have you fed tonight?"

He frowned. "No, I fed last night. I don't need—"

"Feed." She pulled the servant in front of him. The man immediately held up a wrist, bowing his head so as not to meet Giovanni's eyes.

"Tenzin, I told you, I don't need it."

"Giovanni…" She glanced toward the glowing lanterns again. "*Feed.*"

Narrowing his eyes, he took the servant's wrist and bit, numbing the man's skin so it wouldn't be painful. Despite his initial irritation, he couldn't help but enjoy the rich flow of blood from the servant, who obviously kept to an older diet free from processed foods. The surge of strength was immediate, and he felt his amnis pulse within him as he opened his senses and sent them across the palace grounds. A faint energy signature caught him off guard, and he pulled away from the man's wrist, quickly sealing the wounds he had made.

"What is this?" he hissed before taking off at a run. He felt Tenzin's amnis at his back and forced himself to hold back and wait for her. He paused before entering the hall, pulling back his fury and calming the rush of fire beneath his skin. Tenzin put a hand on his arm, pulling him back so she could enter the Great Hall ahead of him.

"My boy, I cannot emphasize how important it is for you to let me speak. Whatever you hear, remain silent."

She strode forward, the jeweled doors swinging open with a flick of her hands that made the human servants scurry. The silk curtains blew back as Giovanni followed her into the glowing hall. It was filled to capacity with curious humans and wary immortals, and he could feel the tension roiling when Tenzin spoke.

"Lorenzo!" she called out as the press of immortals parted in front of her. "Get your hands off my mate."

CHAPTER SIX

Penglai Island, China
September 2010

Step, thrust, sweep, turn.

"Again."

Baojia mirrored her movements, guiding her in the steps of the drill as she worked the *jian*. It already felt natural; the light balance of the old sword allowed her to move through the complicated routine with ease. It was as if some long ago muscle memory had been awakened.

Step, thrust, sweep, turn.

"Again."

She realized about halfway through the lesson that Baojia had switched to giving commands in Chinese, but by then, his instructions were so predictable that she hadn't even noticed. They moved in concert, both wearing the loose black pants and shirts that Tenzin had provided for them. Beatrice may not have liked most of the bland food that the palace provided, but she really liked the feeling of going through the day in what felt a lot like pajamas.

"Stop after this series and watch."

She finished the last turn and moved to the benches to watch him. Baojia was not an ordinarily eye-catching figure. His even features were handsome, but not striking. He spoke even less than Giovanni did, but she had discovered that when he did, he had a dry humor that put her at ease.

It wasn't until he moved that her eyes were drawn to him. If she hadn't been studying martial arts for years, he might have made it look easy. But Beatrice could detect the iron control and carefully restrained ferocity of the vampire. No matter what move he made, he looked smooth, effortless, as if the complicated sequences he performed came as naturally to him as breathing did to her.

He had picked up the shorter curved saber Tenzin used earlier and was going through the basic movements when his eyes darted to the door. A few moments later, she heard Nima quietly enter the room, and the two had a quick exchange before Baojia returned the sword to its place on the wall and walked to her, his face unreadable and his gaze distant.

"What's going on?"

"Come with me."

"What's going on?" she asked again, standing when he held out a hand. He pulled her up and stepped close. Beatrice suddenly realized that he was not much taller than she was, and she only had to glance up to meet his dark stare. She could see the barely concealed tension in his face, and for a second, she felt as if she could not breathe.

"Baojia… what's going on?"

"There is"—he hesitated—"a new guest in the Great Hall. Tenzin has requested our presence."

"Who—"

"No more questions." He hooked her arm with his own and shuffled her toward the doors, grabbing a red robe hanging by the door.

"Maybe you don't know this about me, but I really don't like being kept in the dark," she said as she pulled on the silk robe.

He snorted. "Maybe you don't know this about me, but I don't really care."

"Would Ernesto care?"

Baojia chuckled bitterly. "I am very clear on what my father wants from me, Beatrice De Novo. Why don't you spend a little time worrying about your own father?"

"My own…" She fell silent as a sick feeling began to churn in her gut. "Where's Gio?"

"With Tenzin in the hall."

They left Tenzin's wing of the palace and strode across the grounds, Baojia almost dragging her behind him. As they climbed the steps, she could already hear Tenzin's stream of angry words pouring out of the hall, though she had no idea what her friend was yelling.

Beatrice knew not to open her mouth. She simply followed along, her fists clenched at her sides as Baojia ushered her into the opulent room with a hand at her back, his quick eyes sweeping the room.

Beatrice spotted Giovanni's tall figure immediately. He stood at attention at the foot of Zhang's throne, his gaze flickering over the crowd that had gathered toward the center of the room. She saw him glance at her, nod, then he locked his gaze with Baojia and tilted his head toward the left side of the hall, where Beatrice noticed some of the humans and vampires in Zhang's retinue had gathered. She couldn't see Tenzin, but she could hear the woman arguing in Mandarin from the center of the mass of vampires.

They picked their way through the crowd, and Beatrice was glad that her dark hair and short stature allowed her to blend in far better than Giovanni's striking figure. They stopped about ten feet away, their backs to a large green column, and Baojia seemed to relax slightly at her side.

"Where's my dad?" she whispered.

Baojia leaned over to murmur in her ear. "He's in the crowd with Tenzin. I can hear him."

"Can you translate for me? What's going on?"

He sighed, and she could tell he didn't want to do it, but he continued leaning over, translating as the argument progressed.

"Tenzin says, 'You've always been needlessly worried about me. I have no interest in your throne…' and she calls him a foul name."

"Who?"

"Zhongli Quan."

"The other head guy? The one below Lu?"

"Some may say so. He is a wind vampire, like Tenzin. Do you understand?"

"No."

"There are only two of each element on the council."

'No interest in your throne…' "Oh, he thinks Tenzin wants to take his place or something?"

He only cocked an eyebrow at her and tilted his head back toward the crowd.

"Zhongli responds that Zhang may invite his guests without fear of them coming to harm, and he may do so, as well."

"What? Guests? Who—"

She broke off when an eerily familiar voice rang out. Beatrice may not have recognized the language, but she would never forget the dulcet tones of her former captor.

"Lorenzo," she gasped as her heart began to race. Her eyes searched for Giovanni's; he was looking at her, his lips pursed in a hushing motion, and she began to move toward him. He gave a tiny shake of his head at the same time that Baojia gripped her forearm.

"Let go!"

"No. You need to calm down and look at me." She couldn't look away from the front of the room; her eyes darted between Giovanni, who stood in a position by Zhang, and the clutch of people who surrounded the arguing voices. She could feel the vampires pressing around her begin to react to her agitation, and it only made her more nervous.

"Beatrice," Baojia said, "you need to look at me. Now. Take a deep breath and look at me."

She finally tore her eyes away from the crowd and looked at Baojia. She let herself rest in his calm, dark gaze as he continued to speak in a soothing voice.

"Giovanni needs to stay by Zhang. He is publicly allying himself with the Elder right now, so he must stay there. You are here under his aegis, and under the protection of Tenzin, Zhang, and all their allies, who are more numerous than you can imagine. He will not touch you here."

"But—"

"Beatrice," Baojia continued, "he will not touch you. I will not allow it."

Something in his eyes pulled her in. Some flare of emotion touched his normally placid face, and she pulled away in surprise, only to have him move with her. She leaned back against the pillar and made a conscious effort to calm her breathing. Baojia stared at her, his hand still holding her forearm, and she could feel his finger brush against her wrist. A calm began to steal over her, and her breathing smoothed out, so she was able to look back at the group at the front of the hall.

The crowd had thinned, but all eyes were on the ongoing argument between Tenzin and Elder Zhongli. She could see her father through the crowd and relaxed more when she saw his calm expression. She looked at Giovanni, whose eyes continued to scan the room, glancing from her and Baojia, to the back doors, across the crowd, over the arguing immortals, and back again.

For a moment, his eyes met hers and he gave her a quick wink. She tried to smile, but she was worried it came out more pained than optimistic.

"What did you study at university?"

Beatrice turned at the sound of the unexpected voice to her left. The odd Elder Lan Caihe had sidled up to her in the crowd and was staring at her with a curious expression. He… or she glanced at Baojia, and the two exchanged a friendly nod. Lan was no longer wearing the brilliant white robes of the Elders, but a dull grey set that blended with the crowd.

She frowned. "What? What did I study?"

"Yes, what was your course of study at the university? Your father says you are very bright for a human. What did you study? Medicine? Theology?"

"Um… library science."

Lan laughed. "You did experiments with books?"

"No." Beatrice had to smile. "Information Technology. I studied… well, how to be a good librarian. The best ways to preserve books and manuscripts and how to get that information to the people who need it. It's called 'library science,' but—"

"Oh!" Lan smiled, his or her round face creasing into a delighted smile. "You are a scribe."

She smiled, happy to be distracted by the strange vampire, even if she was confused why exactly Lan was talking to her. Lan's dark hair was pulled into a topknot, and while she had heard the immortal was mysterious, his or her face seemed open and friendly. Beatrice, like everyone else, was at a loss to guess whether 'he' or 'she' was the correct pronoun.

"Um… I guess that's accurate. I don't write the books, though. I just take care of them."

"But that is a heavy responsibility, as well. A scribe was a very honorable position when I was a human. Only the wisest could write and were given care of the scrolls."

Beatrice smiled, a little embarrassed by Lan's eager face.

"I don't think people take librarians quite that seriously anymore."

"That's because humanity is foolish," Lan said with a shrug. "And what do you do with my brother fire-vampire?"

She smiled when she heard the casual acceptance in Lan's voice. Most vampires, even those who knew and seemed to like Giovanni, spoke about him with a kind of reservation, almost as if they expected him to erupt at any minute. Lan's gentle voice held no judgment, and even though she didn't know the vampire, she was immediately set at ease by Lan's manner.

"I had to quit my job a while back. So I'm traveling with him and currently hoping I can stay away from Lorenzo. We don't get along very well."

Lan squinted at the mess of arguing vampires. "I do not think you should be concerned for your safety. You have many protectors."

"But my dad doesn't."

Lan's eyes twinkled. "I do not think your father looks worried, Mistress Scribe. And you should not, either."

She cocked her head at Lan before glancing at her father, who she was surprised to realize really didn't look concerned. He seemed completely relaxed and... taller, if that was even possible. She frowned and glanced back to her left, expecting to see Lan there, but the elder had disappeared into the crowd and the only one to her left was one of Zhang's guards, who began a quiet conversation with Baojia that she couldn't understand.

She really needed to learn Chinese.

By that time, the arguments had died down, and more vampires had dispersed, allowing her to see Tenzin and Zhongli speaking more quietly. Tenzin held an open hand toward Stephen, who reached out to grasp it in his own.

"Well," she heard Baojia murmur, "that is... interesting."

"What? What's interesting?"

Zhongli looked irritated, but resigned. Elder Lu Dongbin, who she remembered Giovanni telling her was a close ally of Tenzin's father, looked quietly pleased, and the Immortal Woman looked as if she wanted to laugh.

Elder Zhongli turned to Lorenzo, who was still arguing quietly. Suddenly, Zhang Guo stood from his throne and walked toward the center of the room with a scowl on his face. The crowd parted as he approached. When he reached his daughter, he grabbed her hand and bit. Tenzin curled her lip and pulled her hand away, but lifted Stephen's hand toward her sire, as well. Zhang bit Stephen's hand, licked at the blood, then dropped it before he spoke to the hall.

"My daughter is telling the truth. I want no more of this arguing," he said in English, glancing at Beatrice before he looked back at Lorenzo with a pointed glare. "You cannot have him. He is my daughter's mate, under her aegis and my own."

Everyone in the hall seemed to disperse after Zhang issued his proclamation, but Beatrice was frozen stiff.

"What just happened?" she asked.

"Well, it seems—"

"Shhh." She held up a hand to Baojia's mouth, cutting him off before he could finish his sentence. She felt him smile beneath her fingertips. "Just... hush. I need to think. I need everyone to be quiet so I can think for a minute."

Beatrice heard Baojia chuckle, but she couldn't tear her eyes from her father, who stood next to Tenzin, tall and confident in the face of his sire, the vampire he had run from for fifteen years. She felt warm fingers grasp her own, and she looked over her shoulder to see Giovanni standing behind her. He looked down at her with an expression that told her he was carefully concealing his feelings from the rest of the room.

"Tesoro," he murmured, bringing her hand to his lips and brushing her knuckles with a kiss.

She dropped her hand from Baojia's mouth and the vampire took a careful step back.

"What just happened there?"

"Tenzin has claimed your father as her mate," he said quietly, "and Zhang just confirmed that they have exchanged blood. Therefore, Lorenzo's claim on your father, and his request to take him, has been overruled."

"That's a lot of stuff happening."

"Yes, it was an eventful meeting."

"That's kind of an understatement."

"Beatrice—"

"Can we kill Lorenzo now?"

"Unfortunately, he is here as a guest of Elder Zhongli Quan. Unless we want to risk the wrath of—"

He was cut off by Lorenzo's voice ringing through the hall in clear English.

"I have another request for the great court of the Eight

Immortals."

All eyes swung back to the center of the room, and Beatrice could finally see Lorenzo clearly as he stood on the steps in front of Zhongli's throne. He looked the same as he had when he had taken her five months before. His curling blond hair came to his shoulders, and he still had faint smudges of scaring along the edges of his Botticelli face. He stared right at her with a smile before he spoke again.

"There is a book that my son stole from me. A very valuable manuscript that I petition the court to return to me. I understand that it has been taken for study by the scholars of Elder Lu Dongbin, and I would like it returned. My child did not have permission to take it."

She glanced at Giovanni, whose eyes had narrowed. He dropped her hand and stepped forward toward the center of the room.

"The book in question is mine, wise Elders of Penglai." Giovanni was the picture of calm respect as he stood before the hall. "My son took it from me without permission, and his son took it from him. I have no objections to Elder Lu's wise scholars keeping it for study."

No one spoke after that. It was almost as if the whole room waited for… something. There was so much tension in the air, Beatrice almost felt as if she would choke on it.

Finally, it was the Immortal Woman, Elder He Xiangu, who spoke. It was in Mandarin, and Baojia leaned over to translate.

"Honored Elder Zhongli, it appears that there is some disagreement regarding the owner of this valued book."

Royal Uncle Cao, the earth vampire who sat between the Immortal Woman and Tenzin's sire, leaned forward, finally showing some interest in the proceedings. "Perhaps this is a disagreement we could help to resolve, for your guest, Elder Lu. And yours, Elder Zhang."

There seemed to be a murmur of agreement around the hall. Baojia chuckled.

"Clever imp," Beatrice heard him whisper.

"What?" she asked, leaning toward him. "Is there going to be some kind of trial or something? What are they going to do?"

"Oh," Baojia nodded, "there will be a trial, but not now."

"Why not? Why—"

"Alas," Zhang stood, once again speaking in English and glancing at Beatrice. "It appears that Honored Elder Lan has departed the hall. If only I had known, I would have asked our fellow Elder to stay. Lan was departing on a journey of some kind. Of course, I did not question the Elder's plans."

"What?" Lorenzo hissed before glancing at Zhongli and falling silent again. There was a murmur of dissatisfaction from the right side of the hall where Zhongli's allies had congregated, and many vampires seemed to be searching the hall for Lan's small, white form.

But Beatrice knew the elder would not be found; Lan's earlier appearance in the inconspicuous grey robes suddenly made more sense. For whatever reason, Lan had delayed Zhongli and Lorenzo. To what end, she had no idea, but as she looked around the room, she realized that Tenzin, Giovanni and her father looked pleased, and Lorenzo and all the vampires on the other side of the room looked annoyed.

That was probably a good thing.

"We cannot decide this matter without Elder Lan," Zhongli conceded in English. "Lorenzo, you may remain at the palace as my guest until his return. All here"—he glared at the six elders surrounding him—"will guarantee your safety upon this sacred island. And to Elder Zhang's guests." He turned to Tenzin. "And to yours, Mistress Tenzin, we will guarantee safety as well."

Giovanni stood casually in the center of the room. He nodded toward Elder Lu and Elder Zhongli in the center thrones. "No one under my aegis would doubt the honor of the Eight Immortals. We stay here at your leisure."

After that, the hall turned back to the business of the night and hummed with energy again. Lorenzo was whisked away by Zhongli's entourage, and Tenzin walked over to speak to her father, leaving Stephen and Giovanni in the center of the room, both wearing completely blank expressions. Finally, her father nodded to Giovanni and brushed past him, walking toward Tenzin, who reached her hand back to grasp his.

Beatrice wondered whether she was just noticing, or whether they were now being more open, but the intimacy between the two was apparent. They almost seemed to circle each other, reacting instinctively to the other's movements as they passed through the room and out one of the side doors, leaving her alone with Baojia.

Giovanni was speaking with one of Zhang's people in a low voice, and the room began to swirl around her. She turned to Baojia, who was watching her. His steady, silent presence remained at her elbow as she felt her exhaustion begin to creep up. She gave one last look at Giovanni, who was still deep in conversation, before she raised her eyes to her silent guard.

"Can we go now?" she asked.

Nodding, he took her arm and led her toward the back doors, where other vampires and human servants were exiting the hall and dispersing through the palace grounds.

"I will wait outside your room until Giovanni can join you. You should get some sleep."

"Will Lorenzo—"

"Do not worry about Lorenzo."

"You know," she said, shaking her head, "I'm pretty tired of people telling me that when he's kidnapped me twice."

Baojia pulled her to a halt near the base of a large white limestone rock dotted with tiny shells. He stared at her for a few minutes, and she was beginning to squirm under his steady gaze.

"Giovanni is embroiled in this," he finally said. "He has many roles to play in this game. I respect that."

Beatrice frowned. "What are you trying to say?"

"I have one role to play here, Beatrice De Novo. I have one objective and one purpose. I was entrusted with your safety by your grandfather, my sire. I have one job, and it is you. So I tell you, do not worry about Lorenzo."

He stepped closer, and the same flare of emotion she had seen earlier in his eyes leapt out again. Her heart began to beat more quickly, and a faint heat rose to her cheeks. Baojia's eyes never wavered from hers, and she forced herself to tear her gaze away before she continued walking toward her room, his ever-present footsteps trailing behind her.

CHAPTER SEVEN

Mount Penglai, China
September 2010

Giovanni gritted his teeth as she left. The fact that Baojia had been the one to comfort her in her distress had not escaped his notice, even as he stood watch over the hall. His need to claim her had been overruled by caution, but he wasn't pleased.

"Doctor Vecchio? Did you have any other questions?"

He turned back to Zhang's administrator. "None. As long as Zhang can spare the extra security to make sure Miss De Novo is fully protected through the daylight hours, I am comfortable remaining on the island."

The old wind vampire gave a respectful nod. "You honor us with your presence. And your support of Zhang's interests will be remembered."

"Thank you, Quan. Your master's offer of protection will be remembered, as well."

"Is there anything else?"

"I will return to Tenzin's quarters at this time. I have some phone calls to make. I understand there is a phone connection on the island now?"

"Yes, a custom satellite system was installed last year. There are insulated phones that connect in each wing of the palace. I believe Tenzin does have one." He leaned in a little closer. "The connections, of

71

course, are shared. One must always keep that in mind."

In short, don't say anything on the phone that you don't want spread around the palace. Giovanni received the veiled message with a quick nod before he took his leave from Elder Zhang's efficient administrator.

He walked across the grounds, glancing toward the opposite side of the compound where Lorenzo was carefully sheltered within Zhongli's entourage. He gritted his teeth and kept walking.

What was the wind immortal's purpose? Why would he invite the water vampire to Penglai? Had his jealousy and paranoia of Tenzin finally reached its limit?

Elder Zhongli Quan may have been the second-ranking political leader of the Eight Immortals, but the old wind vampire had long been insecure of his position and suspicious of Tenzin. Zhang's daughter dwarfed him in age and power, and it was only her disinterest in politics and her desire to avoid her sire, which kept her from attaining a position of leadership in the hall of the Elders. She could have had Zhongli's throne with a flick of her small wrist, but had always been quite vocal that she had no desire for it.

Had her recent activities on Giovanni's behalf caused suspicion that Tenzin had taken an interest in political life? If it had, he regretted it. He'd had no quarrel with Zhongli in the past, but now, the wind vampire was an enemy.

He was mentally running through the web of alliances within the council as he entered Tenzin's quarters. He immediately turned down the hall to check on Beatrice. As he passed their room, he saw Baojia sitting on a bench, reading, nearby.

He looked up briefly. "She's sleeping. She was exhausted."

Giovanni came to a halt. He had nothing to criticize, even though an instinctive protest at the vampire's presence wanted to leap to his mouth. The water vampire was doing the job his sire had assigned him, and as much as Giovanni may not have liked the interest Baojia showed his woman, he knew that Beatrice was safe under his care.

He finally nodded. "I have some calls to make to Southern California. Do you know where the phone is located?"

"It's in the front library. You have to put it on speaker phone to use it, even with the insulation for the wiring, so be careful what you say."

"Has Ernesto been informed?"

"I told her I wouldn't leave the door until you returned, so no."

"I'll make my calls and be back shortly."

Baojia shrugged. "It's morning there anyway, so I can only talk to his secretary. Take your time."

Giovanni frowned. "I'll be back shortly." He turned and walked toward the small library just off the main sitting room. The walls in Tenzin's rooms were all decorated simply, with pale paint, sparse wall hangings, and a few wood screens. It suited her while still being formal enough for her father's tastes.

He passed Nima in the hall, and the old woman nodded in his direction. Her face, as always, was set in a pleasant expression that concealed the calculating mind he knew she possessed. Nima had been in Tenzin's company for so long, she was almost like another half of his friend, though Tenzin took care to not place the old woman in any position she feared could be dangerous.

No, Nima had always been carefully protected. As the old woman continued down the hall, he turned to watch her slow gait. Giovanni had always assumed that Tenzin and Nima had been more than merely companions at one point, and he wondered what Nima thought of her mistress's involvement with Stephen. Giovanni had to wonder himself.

He walked into the library; there was a small man working; a servant of Zhang's was dusting the books.

Giovanni spoke quietly. "You may leave now. Shut the door." The man bowed silently and left.

He spotted the phone and walked over. It was a speaker unit, as Baojia had said, in some sort of bulky, protective case with a stylus sitting next to it for dialing.

The fact that there was any phone on the island was a huge advance. For thousands of years, Mount Penglai had been cut off from the modern world, with electricity only coming in select locations fifteen years before, and most correspondence was still sent by courier. The human population of the island was just as isolated, though all stayed by their own desire, as far as he knew.

He quickly dialed Matt Kirby's number in Pasadena.

"Hello?" The connection was slightly delayed.

"Kirby, it's me."

"Gio?" His tone was cautious. "How's everything?"

"Going well." *In a manner of speaking.* "How are Caspar and Isadora?"

"Enjoying the gardens here, which look amazing. They're both enjoying the house and the weather. Dez and Isadora are thick as thieves and are spending a frightening amount of time shopping lately. They miss your girl, though. Give her our love."

"I will. And how is the puppy?"

Though Lorenzo knew of Ben's existence, the knowledge that Giovanni had adopted a human child was not widespread, so he and Matt had agreed that, if lines were not secure, Ben would only be referred to as Giovanni's "puppy."

"Active as always. His obedience classes are going well, but he still has discipline problems occasionally." They had enrolled Ben at an exclusive school used by many of the human families under Ernesto's aegis and others involved in the immortal world. Some of the students boarded there, though Ben lived at home. Most importantly, it was private, and the security met Matt's stringent requirements.

"Any accidents in the house?" *Any fights with Caspar or Isadora?*

"Nothing serious."

"Well, give him a scratch behind the ears from me."

"Will do," Matt said. "Anything new there? Was everyone there that you expected?" *Was Stephen there?*

"All the expected players. Beatrice was pleased. And then we had some unexpected company tonight."

"Oh?"

"Yes."

"The one I thought?" Matt had been convinced that Lorenzo would make an appearance while they were in the East; Giovanni hadn't been as sure. Luckily, "I told you so" wasn't Matt Kirby's style.

"You may have mentioned him."

"Do we need to make adjustments?" *Did Giovanni need Matt to fly out?*

"It's not anything I'm not equipped to handle. Things seem secure on our end. I just wanted to let you know."

"Thanks. I'll take appropriate precautions." Realistically, if Lorenzo was in China, it was unlikely that he or his associates would target Giovanni's family in Southern California. Still, it never hurt to be cautious.

"Thank you, Kirby. Please give my regards to everyone."

Giovanni wanted to talk to both Ben and Caspar, but it wasn't smart to advertise his human attachments. They were simply too vulnerable. Sending greetings through Matt was the best he could do.

"I will," Matt said. "Take care, and say hi to B for me."

"I will."

He hung up and immediately called Carwyn in Ireland. The priest was staying with Deirdre and helping the widow cope with losing her mate. He was also looking through Ioan's library in the hopes that it would reveal some sort of clue why he was targeted.

Lorenzo's child had confessed that his master had tortured Ioan while questioning him about vampire blood types, and Giovanni wondered whether Ioan had somehow stumbled into the mystery of the elixir, or whether there was some other reason Lorenzo had wanted the information from the doctor.

"Carwyn?"

The tricky delay caused him to talk over the priest when he answered, "Hello?"

"Carwyn, it's me."

"Gio, are you there?"

He frowned. "Yes, it's me."

"Are you calling from Penglai?"

"Yes."

There was a crackling pause. "When did they get a phone? Also, the connection is horrid."

Giovanni chuckled. "I'll let them know. It's fairly recent."

"Have the finally put bathrooms in that crazy palace?"

"Yes, even showers."

"Will wonders never cease?" He heard Carwyn laugh. "And how's the ancient and drafty one? Has she killed anyone yet?"

"Not yet, but we haven't been here that long."

"She's got time, then. Excellent. Is the food still awful?"

"Even you would have trouble eating it."

Carwyn laughed again. "And has her dad been there?"

"Stephen *is* here, Father."

There was a long silence on the line. Carwyn was one of the few people that knew how much finding her father had meant to Beatrice. His voice was slightly hoarse when he spoke again. Or, it might have just been the connection.

"How is she?"

"Well. She was shocked, of course, but they're catching up. It's... good."

"And he's safe?"

If Stephen had been exchanging blood with Tenzin for some time, it would explain the strange level of energy from the young vampire. Simply ingesting a little of Tenzin's ancient blood would strengthen Stephen immeasurably. If the point of the blood exchange had been to make him stronger than Lorenzo, it was most likely already accomplished. The young vampire was no longer holding back, and the strength of his amnis had been evident from across the room that night.

Giovanni had to laugh. "Oh, yes. I think Stephen is very safe."

"What do you mean 'very?'"

"He and Tenzin are mated."

There was nothing but silence on the other line.

"Um…" Carwyn finally sputtered. "Well, that's… what? Tenzin and…"

"Stephen, yes. They're mated." It was probably common knowledge on the island within minutes of the revelation, so Giovanni had no qualms revealing it over the phone.

"Has she… I mean, has Tenzin ever taken a mate?"

"Not that I know of."

"That is very… interesting."

"I thought so, too." Giovanni heard shouting in the background. What was his old friend up to?

"Well, on that very interesting note, I should probably go. It's nightfall here, and I have much to do tonight. Lots of news, but it can wait."

"Anything vital?"

"No, it can wait. If you need to contact me, I might be in Scotland visiting the boys for a bit. So try there if I'm not here."

"Are you sure everything's fine?" Giovanni heard a crash.

"Oh, nothing I can't handle. Give my best to B."

"I will. And hello to Deirdre and the boys, too."

"Goodbye, my friend."

Giovanni ended the call and hung his head. He took a deep breath. Something odd was going on with Carwyn. Stephen and Tenzin were essentially married by ancient tradition. His son had arrived with an unexpected and very powerful ally. It was too much. He thought he had escaped this life three hundred years before. He did not relish returning to the wily manipulations of politics or the constant danger and tension he found himself embroiled in.

He just wanted Beatrice.

So, he left the library and sped down the hall, waving at Baojia as he unlocked their room and entered. He heard the vampire slip away, and Giovanni locked the reinforced door behind him, leaning against it for a moment as he listened to her soft breathing while she slept.

He smiled and crept silently into the room, gazing at her as her chest rose and fell. The tension had left her face, except for her eyebrows, which were slightly furrowed. He undressed and slid behind her, grateful that she hadn't worn nightclothes so he could feel the warmth of her skin against his own. He wrapped his arms around her waist, cradling her against his body and taking comfort in her scent and the soft beat of her heart.

"Beatrice," he whispered against her shoulder. Giovanni knew he should let her sleep, but he needed her. He needed the comfort of her touch, and he needed to see himself in her eyes.

"Tesoro," he murmured, as his lips trailed down her back. His hands brushed along her sides, tracing over her hip under the red silk sheets. She shifted onto her back, and he was able to see her small form. Her pale skin was luminous in the soft lamplight. Her breasts peeked above the sheet, and her hand was thrown over her head in a plaintive gesture. He drew the sheet down and kissed along the ripples of her ribs as her brown eyes flickered open.

"Gio?"

"Hmm," he hummed when she tangled her hands in his hair. He had cut it again, so she wasn't able to grab the length of it as she liked, but her fingers played along his neck as he tasted the skin on her belly.

"I missed you," she said, her heart already racing. "Come here."

She tried to pull him up, but he slipped under the sheet, determined to continue his leisurely exploration. Her soft cries filled the silent room as he slowly brought her to climax, piercing her thigh with his fangs as she arched her back and whispered his name. He drank her sweet blood before he slid up her body and into her, finally meeting her mouth as they moved together. Beatrice's hands gripped his shoulders, and she met his gaze, staring at him as he moved over her.

She was worth it. Worth every worry, every pain. Her safety and security was everything to him. After five hundred years of existence, she had become the singular desire that animated his immortal life.

He drove her harder when he felt her peaking again, and he chased her pleasure, burying his face in the crook of her neck as she stroked his back and he shuddered. They lay together in silent communion, his body and mind refreshed from her love.

Giovanni finally rolled onto his side and pulled her under his arm, cradling her head on his chest as he played with the ends of her hair and ran gentle fingers up and down her back. He smiled to see the way the small hairs on her body reached for him.

"I'd say I was sorry to wake you up, but I'm not."

He felt her shoulders shake. "You can wake me up that way anytime."

Giovanni laughed quietly and hummed a tune he knew she liked.

"I love it when you hum."

"I know."

They lay in peace for a few more minutes.

"Have you called Matt? Did you let him know? How's Ben?"

"Yes, I called Matt. Benjamin is fine. It sounds like school is going well. Caspar and your grandmother still love the house."

"Carwyn?"

"Still in Ireland."

"How's Deirdre?"

Giovanni shrugged. "He didn't say much." He paused. "I'm sorry I couldn't be with you in the hall."

"Shh," she whispered, reaching a hand up to stroke along his cheek. "It's fine. I was fine. After the initial surprise, I was fine."

"I should have expected it. Matt said he would make an appearance."

"But we had no way of knowing. Just like we had no way of knowing…"

She trailed off, and he knew she was thinking of her father and Tenzin.

"Beatrice? Do you want to talk about it?"

"Did you have any idea?"

"No. I sensed there was something we weren't seeing, but with Tenzin, you never know."

"Why? Why would she—"

"Your guess is as good as mine. It's possible they simply have a connection. I'm not going to lie and say it's not odd to me, but she certainly doesn't have to ask my permission to have a relationship."

"With my dad."

"Is it that strange?"

She screwed her face into an adorable frown. "You have to understand, he never dated when I was young. Not that I ever knew of. So to see him again, after so many years. And he looks exactly the same as when I was thirteen. We look like we're almost the same age. And then Tenzin, who I know is way older than you or even Carwyn, but she looks like she's a teenager…"

"It's strange to you."

"Yes!" She shook her head. "And I know it's my own problem. But she's my friend, and he's my dad. And it just feels…"

"What?"

"Weird." He began shaking in quiet laughter, and she hit his shoulder. "Shut up. I know I'm being ridiculous, but it's weird. There's no other word for it."

"What if they have found love together? As we have? Would you begrudge them that?"

"No." She propped herself up and lay a gentle kiss on his mouth. "No, everyone should be as lucky as we are."

"Lucky?" he smirked. "Kidnapped. Blackmailed. Chased around the globe. Targeted because of who we are and what we know. We're lucky?"

She smiled and laid her head on his chest, looking at him and trailing a finger along his lips. He opened his mouth and let a fang peek out. She flicked it with her fingertip, and he growled in pleasure.

"Born five hundred years apart? Finding our way to each other through pain and loss. All that so we can have hundreds, maybe thousands, of years together? Lucky."

This time, it was Beatrice that moved, stroking his face and kissing his lips as they lost themselves in each other again. After another hour, he had exhausted her, and she was sleeping again. He dressed and slipped from the room to walk through the gardens, calling one of Tenzin's guards to watch Beatrice's room. Baojia showed up anyway.

Giovanni strolled through the palace grounds, working his way across the gardens until he was wandering through the stones in front of Elder Zhongli's wing.

"Well, *you* smell like you've had a good night."

He turned to his son, who was sprawled on a bench, pleased to have found him so quickly.

"I've had an excellent night, thank you."

"Your human is very alluring, but I'm surprised you haven't killed her yet. I tend to break human women. That's why I gave up on them years ago. Too fragile."

"Not all of us are barbarians."

"Oh"—Lorenzo threw out a laugh—"yes we are. Just because we fool ourselves with the trappings of courtly life does not mean we're not monsters."

"Becoming a philosopher in your old age, Lorenzo?"

"Oh no." His blue eyes gleamed in the darkness. "I quite enjoy being the thing that goes bump in the night. In fact, I revel in it."

Giovanni stepped closer to his only child. At one point, he and Lorenzo had been almost like brothers, lashed together, trying to survive the whims of a madman. That they had gone such drastically different directions still bothered him.

"Why do you want this elixir?"

Lorenzo's eyebrows lifted. "Ah! So Stephen did figure it out, did he? I thought he would, especially when I discovered he was here. I wonder how he put the pieces together to come here. It's very curious."

Giovanni had wondered that himself, but he did not voice his suspicions to Lorenzo. "How did you know he was here?"

"Oh, what's the saying?" Lorenzo glanced over his shoulder toward the Zhongli's guards that shadowed him on the palace grounds. He smiled. "'A little bird told me?'"

"Of course." So Zhongli Quan did have some ulterior motive inviting Lorenzo to the island. Otherwise, why would he have tempted him with Stephen's whereabouts?

"You never answered my question. Why do you want this elixir?"

Lorenzo grinned. "I'm a humanitarian."

"You're a monster."

He shrugged. "I'm a monstrous humanitarian?"

"Why?"

Lorenzo only rolled his eyes. "As if I would tell you, *Papà*! What do you think? I'm going to reveal all in some strange, enlightening monologue? What makes you think I even have a reason? Maybe I just want it so others can't have it?"

"You're too calculating for that."

Lorenzo stood in the blink of an eye. "Yes, I am."

His son stepped closer, and Giovanni could feel the heat running along his skin. It would be so easy… But he saw Lorenzo's guards step closer, so he smiled and turned to go.

"I'll see you around, Lorenzo. We'll have to have some father-son bonding time when your guards aren't around."

"So sentimental, Giovanni. I do love a good family reunion. If only Niccolo was here."

Giovanni turned, cutting his eyes toward the guards before he looked at Lorenzo. "If Andros was here," he whispered, "you wouldn't be."

"Oh, I know." Lorenzo's mouth curved into a wicked smile. "I remember. Everything."

CHAPTER EIGHT

Mount Penglai, China
September 2010

"Stupid, irritating, obscure, dead, Persian guy." Beatrice muttered as she scanned a copy of a sixteenth century manuscript, searching for the exact ingredients of a curative concoction that her father thought might be similar to one of Geber's ingredients. "Why couldn't he just write in clear language instead of putting everything in code?"

Stephen glanced up. "Trust me, I understand. Having his journals was the only thing that let me decipher the manuscript at all. Otherwise, it would have been complete gibberish."

They were buried in Zhang's personal library, which Stephen said rivaled the monastery library where the manuscript was being kept. Zhang Guo's selection of manuscripts and scrolls was… intimidating.

Beatrice stretched her neck and looked around. "Is this library bigger than Lorenzo's collection? Well, it's rightfully Gio's, I suppose."

"It's comparable." Stephen nodded and looked around. "The subject matter is just wildly different. I really could go on for ages about Andros's collection from the ancient world. He seemed to have a particular fascination with the near East and Minoan culture." Stephen chuckled. "If *you* got your hands on it, you could spend an eternity cataloguing its contents. It wasn't exactly organized in any fashion. And, of course, Lorenzo moved it periodically, so I'm sure some things have been lost or damaged."

She shook her head. "So, in addition to kidnapping and murder, the bastard's guilty of putting ancient documents at risk. I really have to kill him now."

Stephen shook with laughter. "Oh, Mariposa…" He reached across the table and brushed her cheek. "I'm so lucky to see you again." Stephen sighed a little, and she could see his eyes line slightly with pink tears. "I never really thought I would, you know? I hoped, but I never thought it would be safe for us to be in contact. If you hadn't come under Giovanni's aegis—"

"My life would be…" She laughed. "I can't even imagine."

"You'd probably be safer."

"Yeah, but I'd be bored silly. I'd get myself into trouble."

"I doubt that. Though you do seem very suited to all this. It's rather amazing, if you think about it."

She shrugged and continued scanning the pages. There were numerous mentions of mercury, but she had yet to find the original formula for "mercury of life" that Tenzin had recommended she look for.

"Dad, why didn't you just memorize the damn formula with your super-duper vampire brain? I'm trying not to be judgmental here, but —"

Stephen barked out a laugh. "It wasn't exactly a cookie recipe. There were so many steps, and I didn't know half of what the terms were, much less how to concoct them or process them. I mean, I was an assistant professor of medieval literature, for heaven's sake. It probably would have made more sense to a chemist or a holistic doctor, though so many of the ingredients were obscure, even a trained alchemist might have had problems."

"But Lu's monks seemed to understand them?"

"I spent most of my time at the monastery learning Mandarin first, then translating the book from Arabic into Mandarin so Fu-han could read it. Then, I had to explain what a lot of Geber's codes were, and all of his journals were written in Persian." Stephen shook his head. "I had a feeling things were becoming clearer to him, but then I was called here. I'm still sending letters back and forth to him, explaining this or that word or phrase. And he and Zhang are the Spagyric experts, not me."

"And that's the plant alchemy, right?"

"Yes, which is a specialty even within normal alchemy. If Geber

83

hadn't written his findings in his journals, I'd have had no idea what the book was or what the formula was supposed to do."

"But Lorenzo knows?"

"He doesn't know what the formula is, clearly, but I believe he knows what it's supposed to do. I saw him examining the journals and smiling that creepy, satisfied grin he has."

Beatrice shivered involuntarily when her father mentioned his name. "Did he really torture you?"

Stephen's eyes clouded in pain. "Beatrice, I don't want to talk to you about that. It's not… it's just not something…"

She shook her head and looked back to the book. "It's okay. Never mind. I know. Gio said it was probably pretty bad."

He paused, staring down at the table where they sat. "It's in the past. He can't hurt me anymore. I'm too strong now."

"Okay."

"I don't want you to worry about me."

The corner of her mouth lifted. "You're my dad."

"Exactly. It's my job to worry about you, not the other way round. You were always an old soul, even as a child."

She snorted. "I must have been so obnoxious. Grandma always said she turned grey early because of me."

"You were a joy. Just… headstrong." He grinned. "And frighteningly perceptive for a cute little girl."

Beatrice looked up at her father. She was still struck by how young he looked, frozen in time the same age he had been when she was young. "Was I?"

"What?"

"A joy? Was I? Was it worth it being a single dad when Holly left me with you? I must have been a surprise. And you couldn't hit the clubs with your friends when you were twenty-two, could you? Not with a baby and no one to help you."

"Oh." Stephen shrugged. "I had Grandma and Grandpa. Who needed to go out dancing when I had toothless baby smiles at home? You made things plenty exciting."

She thought of all the Friday nights when she was young when her father had taken her to the skating rink or the movies, instead of spending time with other adults. Though she hadn't recognized it at the time, his whole life had revolved around her. "Thanks, Dad. For not… you know. When I met Holly a couple years ago, she said she knew I'd be better off with you. That you'd take care of me. So… thanks."

His voice was hoarse when he finally replied. "You are completely welcome, Beatrice. Your mom is the one that missed out."

A booming voice came from the hallway. "Agreed."

Beatrice turned when she heard Giovanni. He walked over and sat down next to her, kissing her cheek.

"Hello, Tesoro," he whispered in her ear. "I missed you."

"Sorry, I got caught up here."

"No problem at all. Let me help your father. Baojia is waiting for you in the practice room. More weapons training tonight."

She leapt up. "Oh! He said I could try out the *dao* and maybe some other stuff tonight. Cool." She was halfway out of the room before she turned back. She skipped over to Stephen and leaned down, brushing a kiss across his cool cheek. "See you later, Dad."

"Bye, Mariposa. Have fun with the swords. Don't stab anyone." Stephen paused and frowned. "Well, unless you're supposed to."

"See? You're still such a dad," she said as she winked and darted out the door. She could hear the two men chuckle as she raced down the hall.

"The saber, or *dao*, has a different balance than the *jian*," Baojia said softly as he circled her. "You must learn to carry it in a different way. Your stance will be different. Your thrusts will be different. Remember, the sword is not a weapon; it is an extension of your arm, and you must balance yourself with that in mind."

She took a deep breath, moving slowly through the tai chi forms as he instructed. Painfully slowly. Her muscles were tense and quivering. Beatrice tried to focus on her balance and the weight of the blade in her hand.

"Would it be better if I just stayed practicing with the *jian*?"

"And be limited to one weapon? What do you think?"

"I think it's always better to have options."

Beatrice took a deep breath as her instructor stepped into her line of sight, eyeing her up and down as she moved. "Yes, it is," he said in a rough voice.

Beatrice blushed, not sure if they were still talking about swords.

"So"—she cleared her throat—"after this, do I get to try out the pike? I've been curious about that one spear with the thick base."

"So *many* jokes." She heard him say under his breath. She burst into laughter and stumbled, shaking her head when she saw his eyes dance.

"Okay, I walked into that one."

He laughed. "You, my dear, walk into them all the time." He grabbed the saber from her and hung it back on the wall. "I'm just forcing myself to be on my best behavior."

"Oh really?" She blinked at herself when she heard the flirtatious tone of her voice. What was she doing? She shook her head and turned back to her teacher.

Yes, Baojia was her teacher.

Her instructor.

Baojia was... distracting.

He narrowed his eyes as he looked over the weapons Tenzin had decorating the walls. She saw a devious smile cross his face as he walked to a rack of spears and chose two. He held them up for her.

"So, spears..." He lifted one eyebrow. "European or Asian? What's your preference?"

She rolled her eyes and reached for the one in his right hand. "This is your best behavior? And European, if you're asking."

He shrugged. "Pity. You really should try both."

"I'm sure the European will suit me fine, thanks." She examined the weapon, enjoying the razor-sharp point and smooth wooden grip. Baojia brushed past her.

"Strange that you chose the Asian one, then." He walked to the other side of the practice mat and bowed. "Now, watch, and I'll show you how to handle this."

Harmless flirtation was the furthest thing from her mind an hour later when she finally handed the spear back to Baojia. He had demonstrated the hook swords, or *shuang gou* for her, knocking the long wooden spear from her hands at a distance when he hooked the two lethal weapons together to demonstrate their reach. The spear had splintered in her hands as she held it, and she was more determined than ever to learn to wield the complex weapons, no matter what Giovanni thought.

Baojia was encouraging and smiled a little as they put the weapons away. "You'll be ready within a year after you turn, I think.

Given what you are learning now and your natural aptitude for weapons, you will be ready to wield these as soon as your reflexes catch up with your mind and your amnis."

"What do you mean, 'catch up with my amnis?'"

Baojia shook his head. "It's impossible to explain to a mortal. Even a bright one like you would not understand it."

She grimaced. "Oh, well, I guess I should be flattered you're willing to teach a mere mortal like me anyway."

"Yes." He smiled and walked behind her to stretch her arms. "You should be. I usually don't bother with humans."

"So why me? Ernesto's orders, huh?"

She couldn't see him as he lifted her arms, stretching them before they moved into hand-to-hand combat practice.

"Why you?" he murmured. "What an interesting question…"

That I notice you're not answering.

"Yeah, well, I'm Miss Popular for some reason. Even the bad guy wants to hang out with me."

He lifted her arms, running a hand down her tricep to knead it. His fingers were cool and strong against her sore muscles. "I told you not to worry about Lorenzo. Take a bath later. Soak your arms, or they will be stiff."

She cleared her throat. "Well then, I'll just put all those icky thoughts about murdering him out of my pretty little head, won't I?" She pulled her arms away and walked across from him. They bowed and began practicing. Baojia never *really* hit her. Not like Tenzin. He seemed more interested in teaching her how to attack. If he did manage to land the odd blow, he usually apologized very formally.

"You should leave killing him to Giovanni or Tenzin. Or me, if he threatens you."

"Oh? Why is that?"

He frowned as if she was speaking Farsi, which was on her list of languages to learn after she turned. Come to think of it, she thought, it was entirely possible that Baojia already spoke Farsi.

"Why should you leave killing Lorenzo up to Giovanni, Tenzin, or myself? Because he's a vampire and you're not, foolish girl. Don't kill yourself by being an idiot."

"Now there's the kind of sweet talk I expect," she grunted as she struck his shoulder. She went to land a kick, but he grabbed her leg and held onto it.

"I'm serious, B." He waited until she met his dark eyes. "Don't think you can challenge him. Compared to Giovanni or myself, he's not that strong, but he is *very* smart. He's a survivor, and in our world, strategy counts as much as strength."

She scowled at him. "It's not like I'm going to go hunt him down right now. Let's just say it's… on my list."

He raised an eyebrow. "Does Gio know you have a list?"

Did he? Probably. She often thought Giovanni could read her mind, he knew her so well. Baojia and Beatrice went back and forth for a few more minutes until she heard the practice room door open. His scent reached her nose even before she turned.

"Hey," she said, and a smile spread across her face. *Now there was a distraction.*

Giovanni leaned against the wall of the practice room. He had changed into a pair of loose, black pants and a shirt that hung open at the neck. The sleeves were rolled up, and Beatrice could see the muscles of his forearms as he crossed them over his chest and watched her.

He smiled at her, a languorous, easy grin that made her insides melt. His eyes raked over her flushed body, and she felt her heartbeat pick up. *The things that vampire could do with a single smile…*

He curled a finger, beckoning her. Beatrice walked toward him, making another list in her mind, when Tenzin darted into the room.

"Stop right there." Tenzin held up a hand and nodded toward Beatrice. "You, practice. You"—she glared at Giovanni—"I told you not to distract her. You'll get her back later. She needs to work."

Giovanni narrowed his eyes, while Beatrice scowled. "Tenzin," she said, "I don't like you very much right now."

"Nor do I," Giovanni muttered. "Ignore her. You've practiced enough for one night."

Tenzin pulled his collar. "She has not."

"I really think…" Beatrice pouted when Tenzin shoved Giovanni into the hallway. She turned to see Baojia watching her with a smile. "What?"

"Options," he almost sang as he picked up a long, wooden pole and tossed it toward her. "Always good to have options. Now, let's talk about the staff."

CHAPTER NINE

Mount Penglai, China
September 2010

"The water vampire is interested in Beatrice."

Tenzin snorted. "Which one?"

Giovanni glared at her as they walked through the palace grounds. "You know which one I'm speaking of."

"Well, Baojia is interested in her. Lorenzo is interested in her. I think half the palace is fascinated by the strange American girl, so you might want to specify."

He stopped and watched her as she hopped along the top of a carved stone wall. "You know, I forget how irritating you can be when I don't spend time with you for a while."

She flew over him, stepping on his head once before she lit on top of one of the giant, limestone pillars. "I hate it here."

"I know you do."

"You know how you feel about Rome?"

"Yes, Tenzin."

"That's how I feel here. Everyone looking at me with expectations."

"I know."

"And my father is the worst one."

"He cares about you."

"That is… debatable."

He continued walking as she flitted from one stone to the next. Finally, she set herself down on the grass to walk beside him. "You're not jealous, are you?"

"Of Baojia? Not really, it's just irritating."

"She loves you very much. She wants to be your mate for eternity."

He eyed her tiny form as she walked next to him. "And what of you and Stephen? I confess, that—"

"Stephen and I are none of your business. Just because you confide in me does not mean I confide in you, my boy."

He paused. "Who *do* you confide in, bird-girl?"

It was often hard to imagine how long she had lived, but when Tenzin turned her deep grey eyes on him, Giovanni saw millennia in her stare. "No one. I confide in myself alone."

He had the strange urge to embrace her, which he had never once done in all their years as friends. "Are you lonely sometimes?"

She cocked her head and smiled. "I don't remember."

Giovanni shook his head and continued walking. "I am glad that Beatrice and Stephen have this time together."

"He missed her very much. Family is very important to him."

"It has become important to me, as well."

"Family was always important to you. Why else would you look for your uncle's books for so many years?"

"I suppose that is true."

"You were always looking for a family. Now you have one. It is good for you."

A familiar drift of amnis wafted on the breeze, and he turned his head. Lorenzo was walking with Zhongli Quan and a group of six guards. The Elder nodded toward them with an unreadable expression in his eyes before he turned. Two of the guards followed him while four stayed with Lorenzo as he approached Giovanni and Tenzin.

"If it isn't my father and his miniature companion."

The black-clad guards halted abruptly. They looked toward Tenzin with wide eyes, but she only waved at them and shrugged.

"Lorenzo," Giovanni said, "you're becoming even more foolish as the years go by."

"Why? Is she going to attack me here? I have been promised protection, just like you. Penglai is neutral ground; we both know it."

Tenzin's eyes were impassive as she stared at Giovanni's son. "You are irritating, and it will be good when he kills you."

Lorenzo's fangs flashed in the lantern light. "Do you think so? I think we are a long way from my father killing me. After all, we both know I have information he wants."

How much Giovanni was willing to put up with to get his sire's library back was debatable, but he wasn't in the mood to confide in the blond bastard in front of him.

"Go away and do something useful, Lorenzo," he said. "Never mind, that's probably not possible."

"So sullen, *Papà*. Where is your toy human? Has she taken another lover again?"

With one sweep of her arm, Tenzin blew the four guards halfway across the grounds before she rounded on Lorenzo. She lifted the vampire by the collar and shot into the air.

"Be careful what you say about my friend, little boy. You may think you are safe here because it is customary to respect the Elders, but do not forget that my sire is the oldest of all. And while I may bow to his wishes at times..." She dropped Lorenzo a few feet before grabbing him again. "...in general, I am a *very* disrespectful daughter."

She spoke just loud enough for Giovanni to hear. He noticed that Zhongli's guards were taking their time walking back across the grounds, and Lorenzo's dangling form was beginning to attract attention.

Giovanni smiled and sat on a bench to wait.

"Let me down." Lorenzo was trying to sound nonchalant, but Giovanni could hear the quiver in his voice.

"Fine," Tenzin said and she dropped him. His son landed in a heap at his feet before he shot up and walked back toward Zhongli's guards, never sparing Giovanni a glance. Tenzin flew down and sat next to him.

"You really need to get rid of him."

"I know."

"What were you thinking?"

"It's a long story."

Giovanni watched Beatrice pace their bedroom, recounting in detail the different weapons she had tried in practice that night. It was a few hours before dawn, and he could tell she was exhausted. But still, her heartbeat was jumping.

"—and then I tried the other spear, and it kind of had this hook on the end, too. Like on the side? And it was a lot lighter than it looked, something about the way the shaft is balanced or something, and then there was the *shuang gou*. Oh, Gio, I can't wait to learn those. Baojia said that once I turn—"

"Which may be unnecessary. We don't know yet."

She only rolled her eyes and continued. "Yeah, so once I've turned, I'll pick up the hook swords no problem."

He cocked an eyebrow at her. "Really? He said, 'no problem?'"

"Well, he said something about my body catching up with my amnis… or my amnis catching up with my mind. Something like that, but after that, he said I'd pick it up easily."

Giovanni thought she was probably being optimistic, but he had to admire her enthusiasm. He smiled. "Well, even if it takes some time, it sounds like you're getting a good idea of what options you'll… what?"

She had turned red in the face when he said the word "options."

"Beatrice?"

"What?"

He didn't know what. It was strange, but she almost looked…

"Why are you blushing?"

"I'm probably just… tired. You know, I should take a bath and go to bed, I've—"

"You're not just tired." He frowned. For a brief flicker, she had looked… "Why do you look guilty?" He felt his temperature begin to rise.

Her mouth dropped open, but there it was again. Just a hint in her eye.

"I do not look guilty."

"You do." He sat up. "And your heart is racing. Why? Did Baojia do something inappropriate?" While he knew the vampire was interested in Beatrice, Giovanni could not imagine him acting inappropriately toward Ernesto's favored granddaughter. Nor did he think that Beatrice would be unfaithful, but…

"No! No, Baojia was just… kind of flirting. That's all."

He cocked an eyebrow. "Flirting?"

"Yeah." She waved a hand. "He was joking about 'knowing your options' about weapons and, you know, there's some kind of obvious jokes and… yeah, just being silly."

"Silly?"

"Why do you keep repeating the last word of everything I say? That's annoying."

He couldn't keep the smile from his mouth. "Annoying?"

She picked up a pillow and threw it, hitting him dead in the face as he started to laugh. "We were just joking around!"

"I believe you, so why are you throwing things at me?" He couldn't stop chuckling at her consternation. "You're very cute when you're embarrassed."

"I'm not embarrassed. I'm irritated."

"At Baojia?"

"At you!"

He kept laughing and pulled her onto the bed as she tried to walk past. "Did he ask if you wanted to play with his sword?"

"Stop," Beatrice said as she began laughing, too. Soon, they were wrestling on the bed and he had her arms pinned above her head so she had to stop slapping at him. "I'll have you know," she said, gasping, "I told him that I only liked European spears."

Giovanni burst into laughter again and leaned down to kiss her. His head fell forward as he buried it in the crook of her neck. "Beatrice, I'm not jealous."

"Why not?"

He lifted his head and met her mouth, stealing her breath when he kissed her. "Because no one, *tesoro mio*, will ever love you the way that I do. Of this, I have no doubt."

A sweet smile spread across her face. "No?"

"No."

The next evening, Giovanni passed Baojia in the hallway. The water vampire nodded at him politely. He paused. "Baojia?"

"Yes?"

He turned toward the water vampire. "I just wanted to thank you for all the time you have spent training Beatrice."

"I am at her disposal."

"I have never been able to quell my protective instincts enough to train with her as she deserves, but I know she is progressing, and it pleases me. I also know you usually do not train humans."

Baojia curled his lip. "I'm not doing it as a favor to you, di Spada."

"I know. I appreciate it nonetheless."

Giovanni saw Baojia smirk a little. "And she has good things to say about her weapons practice?"

"*Weapons* practice?" Giovanni nodded. "Oh yes. She quite enjoys weapons practice."

Baojia's eyes narrowed. "Yes… she's very skilled."

Giovanni chuckled and continued walking. "You really have no idea."

CHAPTER TEN

Mount Penglai, China
October 2010

Despite the slow pace of life on the island, time seemed to slip away with a whisper. It had been three weeks since Lorenzo made his appearance, but Beatrice had scarcely noticed. Her nights were occupied training with Baojia, and her days were occupied with Tenzin or her father, who had absorbed Tenzin's ability to stay awake almost effortlessly through most of the day. Stephen scarcely needed sleep, so the long separated father and daughter spent hours hidden away in the library of Tenzin's quarters, getting to know each other again.

Other than her training, Beatrice's nights were spent with Giovanni. He was doing his utmost to keep her occupied during any hours Lorenzo might be active, keeping her away from the practice room, as well.

"Come back to bed."

She rose from the silk pillow, intending to take a quick shower at nightfall before she met Baojia for practice with the sword. She'd taken an afternoon nap and woken to Giovanni's lips again.

"I need to go practice."

He stretched with a lazy smile and hooded eyes, knowing what the slip of the silk sheet did to her as it crept down his sculpted chest.

"*Tesoro mio,*" he purred, "come back to bed. You're not dressed yet; we have time."

His hand crept out, fingers slipping around her thigh as he drew her back to the luxurious bed.

Beatrice allowed herself to be pulled. "I know what you're trying to do, possessive vampire."

"Yes?" he asked as he laid a kiss along her bare hip. "What is that?"

"You're trying"—she sighed and gave in, falling into the curve of his arms—"to distract me."

"How am I doing?"

"Very, very well." She gasped when he ran his fangs along the curve of her shoulder and his hands teased her body, sparking as they pulsed with amnis. Beatrice leaned her head to the side and moaned when his tongue teased her pulse.

"Well, I wouldn't want to disappoint."

They decided to make use of the luxurious marble tub much, much later.

Tenzin watched Beatrice as they practiced.

"You're getting much more limber."

"Thanks." She panted as she executed a complex series of kicks and punches from the wushu technique Tenzin's father had developed hundreds, maybe thousands, of years before. Her legs were aching, but she reveled in the stretch in her hamstrings as her leg lifted in almost a full split.

"Maybe Gio's libido *is* good for something."

"Tenzin, please!" Stephen called from the side of the practice room where he was studying.

"Your ears are just as good as mine!"

Beatrice may have unconsciously held the pose longer than she intended. Tenzin ignored the crimson flush on her face and batted her leg down to the floor.

"Let's work on flips."

"Tenzin." She shook her head. "There's no way I'm going to be able to do most of those until I turn."

"You can still practice. Don't be lazy."

Beatrice heard Stephen snort. "Why don't you give her a break so she can help me with this Latin passage?"

"Lazy De Novos!" Tenzin stormed toward the door. "Fine, take fifteen minutes while I go find someone to eat. And, Stephen, don't pretend you need her help."

Stephen only looked up and winked at Tenzin before she left the room. Beatrice grabbed a towel and a glass of water before she sat down next to her father.

"Do you really need help?"

"No." He grinned. "I'm not even reading Latin. This is a Greek manual on alchemy from Alexandria. Have you learned any classical Greek yet?"

She shook her head. "No, it's so dense."

"You'll learn fast enough when you put your mind to it. Especially after you turn." He glanced up, and a serious expression blanketed his eyes. "You're sure about it?"

"What?" She patted her face with the towel. "About turning? Yeah. I mean, Gio and I... well, you know we're serious, and I wouldn't commit myself to him without being sure about the vampire thing."

"But do *you* want it? Or is it just because of him?"

She leaned back against the cool wall. "Dad, I know you're being the good dad here and looking out for my interests, but you realize that there's no way I can answer that, don't you?"

"Why?"

She frowned, trying to think how she could explain. "I have no idea what my life would be without him. Without all this. I can't even imagine. This is reality now. My dad became a vampire through no fault of his own. I was drawn into it by virtue of being your child. And no." She held up a hand. "I won't allow you to apologize. It's not your fault either."

"I still feel guilty."

She rolled her eyes. "Well, get over it. Life happens. You were taken. I was targeted. I met Gio. We fell in love. We have a family. I wouldn't have said this even a year ago, but... all this happened for a reason. God, fate, destiny. Somehow, it was meant. Our lives are so intertwined, I can't even imagine it any other way at this point. And I want it."

She leaned forward and grasped her father's cool hand in her own. "Do you understand? I know there are sacrifices. I know there are limitations. I still want it. I'm tired of always being the one that needs protecting."

Stephen looked at her for a long moment. "Okay."

"Okay?"

"Tenzin told me exactly what you'd say. She says you'll be an extraordinary vampire. Greater than me, no doubt."

Beatrice smiled and shook her head, still patting sweat from her face. "I have no illusions. I know I'm still going to be the slow one."

"Oh, I don't know about that." He chuckled and flicked his wrist, and she felt a cool spray of water at her back. "There, that better?"

She closed her eyes and grinned. "Much. Thanks."

"Controlling water does come in handy occasionally."

"You're really powerful now, aren't you? From exchanging blood with Tenzin?" She saw him glance away and squirm in discomfort. "I'm not asking about… anything, really. It's none of my business, I know. I just… I'm happy that you're stronger now."

"I am," he said quietly. "I'm very strong. Tenzin has been… well, she's—"

"Back." Beatrice turned when the door opened and Tenzin strode in. "And you need to practice your flips, lazy De Novo."

She wrinkled her forehead and turned back to her father.

"Don't look at me," Stephen said with a smile. "You said you didn't want to be protected."

Beatrice stuck her tongue out at him, but Stephen only laughed.

"You really… I have to…" Giovanni cut her off by sinking into their kiss. They were tangled in bed, and he was distracting her again. He moved over her, his iron arms boxing her in as he kissed down her body.

"Beatrice," he whispered before muttering something unintelligible in rough Italian.

"I really need to learn that language." She sighed as her eyes rolled back.

"Hmm." He lifted his mouth and gave her a wicked smile. "I'll just switch to another language you don't know then."

"I'll catch up with you eventually."

"You don't need to catch up." He moved up her body so he could whisper in her ear. "Just stay. Stay with me. Stay here."

"I can't… oh"—she arched her back in pleasure—"stay here forever."

"Yes, you can."

Giovanni set about proving why staying in bed with him really *was* the best plan, but he was interrupted by a loud knock at the door.

He looked up with a snarl and sped naked to the door in the sitting room. She heard it open.

"Go away," she heard him say before he slammed it shut.

Beatrice sat up in the bed, covering herself with the sheet. He walked back in the room and dove into the bed.

"Who was that?"

"No one," he said before he pulled the sheet away.

"Giovanni!"

He rolled his eyes and lay back on the bed, pulling her on top of him and running his hands through her hair. "That was your fencing teacher."

"Baojia?"

"Yes."

"You slammed the door in Baojia's face?"

"Yes." He obviously didn't consider this rude or unusual as he began investigating the freckles that dotted her cleavage. "He's probably standing out in the hall now if you want to tell him something," he said before his mouth returned to her skin.

She rolled off of him. He only sat up and tried to pull her into his lap.

"Sorry, Baojia," she called loudly, knowing he would be able to hear. "Sorry my... Giovanni is a rude vampire."

"Fine." Beatrice heard his muffled reply from the hall as she hid her face in her hands. "I'll be in the practice room when you escape his clutches."

Giovanni gave a satisfied laugh, but she slapped at his shoulder and pulled away, standing to walk to the bathroom so she could take a shower.

"What?" he called out, still laughing.

"You can't keep me occupied every single hour that Lorenzo is awake. I have things I need to be doing."

"Yes," he said as he lay back on the bed, stretching his legs. "I can think of several right now, in fact."

She shook her head and shut the door, only to hear it open as she stepped in the shower.

"I really need to go practice, love." She felt him run the ginger-scented soap over her back.

"Consider this a warm-up," he said as he ducked under the water.

Her face was still flushed when she finally made it to the practice room.

"Sorry," she said when she spotted Baojia in the corner of the room.

"No need to apologize. We practice on your schedule." He stood and handed her the practice *dao*, which had become her favored weapon for practice. She hadn't switched to the full-weight weapon yet. Soon. The thin steel blade curved wickedly in the lamplight, and she began her regular warm up routine, spinning and thrusting in the style Baojia had taught her.

He made quiet corrections to her form before he grabbed his own weapon and began demonstrating a new series of maneuvers. He rarely spoke, and the vampire's near silent instruction became a kind of meditation, focusing her mind as her muscles memorized the intricate steps.

They practiced almost silently for another hour before she spoke again.

"He'd prefer it if I never left our quarters after dark."

Baojia gave a quiet chuckle. "I can't blame him for that."

"No, really, he doesn't like me being out when Lorenzo might be around."

"Are you sure that's his only motivation?" he teased quietly.

"Haha. Men."

Baojia laughed again. "Like I said, I can't blame him for that."

He came to a halt and she followed his lead, standing at relaxed attention and mirroring his stance. "Were you my woman, Beatrice"— his eyes darted down to her mouth—"I would hardly let you leave the room." He grabbed her *dao*, brushing a finger against her wrist as he took it from her suddenly limp hands. "For safety's sake, of course."

He walked calmly over to the wall of weapons, placing both sabers back in their cradles before he looked over his shoulder with a smile.

"Safety's sake." She gulped. "Right."

He caught her eye and tossed a *jian* in her direction. Her arm reached out instinctively and caught it.

"Switch weapons."

Beatrice straddled Giovanni's lap in the large tub, working a lather up as she shampooed his hair. He just watched her, smiling as his blinks became longer.

"You better not fall asleep in here, old man." She laughed. "There's no way I could carry you to the bed."

"Well, at least you know I couldn't drown."

She smiled and pinched his shoulder to rouse him. He sat up and put his hands on her back, warming them to soothe her sore muscles as he laid his head against her shoulder.

"Thanks, Gio."

"Your back feels tense. Good practice? And did you have dinner with your father this afternoon? I forgot to ask."

"Yep. He hates the food here, too."

Giovanni chuckled. "Just because there's no hot sauce."

"You can take the girl out of Texas..."

He laughed against her neck as she poured the water over his hair, rinsing the soap out and soaking them both.

"I'm still amazed that he can stay awake so well."

Beatrice shrugged. "It must be Tenzin's blood."

"It must be. It's no wonder his amnis seemed so strange when I first met him."

She pulled back. "You never told me that."

"I didn't know what to make of it," he murmured. "It seemed different, but I couldn't pinpoint how. It makes sense now."

"Why?" She stood and reached for one of the towels, handing the other to him when he followed her.

"I would have guessed that he was much older. Easily my own age, but perhaps even more."

"Wow."

"It was definitely odd. And the fact that he can stay awake for most of the day now, it's extraordinary. My sire could stay awake except for a few hours in the middle of the day, but he was over two thousand years old."

She frowned as she patted her hair dry. "So my dad is the equivalent of a two thousand year old vampire?"

"Well." Giovanni shrugged. "His energy feels that way. He doesn't have the life experience, memory, or skills, of course."

"Still… wow."

"Yes." He rubbed the towel across his shoulders before he grabbed Beatrice's, hanging both on a hook by the door. "It's quite a strength."

"I'll say." She grabbed a brush to comb out her hair, but Giovanni picked her up and took her to the bed, tossing her in the middle with a playful grin. He grabbed the brush and settled behind her, kissing her shoulder as he let the heat build on his skin to warm them both in the cold bedroom.

"Gio?"

"*Sì, Tesoro?*"

She leaned back and pulled his warm arms around her. "I feel like this is the calm before the storm."

He took a deep breath and rested his chin on her shoulder.

"I do, too."

"Stupid, stubborn vampire jerk," she muttered under her breath, stabbing the air in the dark garden.

"Focus. You're not going to hurt him, but by all means, visualize that if it improves your focus. Plus, it's just sort of amusing."

Baojia's droll voice drifted across the lawn as she whirled and stabbed the air, focusing on a spot in front of her that had a stubborn, five hundred year old man floating in it.

"Stupid, overprotective…" She thrust into a tall camellia bush that was beginning to bud with white blossoms.

"Please don't kill the shrubbery, my dear. The Elders might get annoyed and not let us practice out here again."

Normally, any kind of sparring was disallowed on the palace grounds, but Elder Zhang had overheard Beatrice whining about feeling cooped up one night and generously offered the gardens for her to practice, promising he would smooth any ruffled feathers in the court as long as she and Baojia were careful.

Beatrice had been overjoyed she would be able to escape the confines of Tenzin's quarters.

Giovanni had not.

"Stupid, overbearing—"

"Beatrice, if you hack that scholar's stone, I will disarm you! Focus."

She shook her head and brought her mind back. The fight with

Giovanni could wait. He had certainly stormed off in a huff, smoke pouring from his collar as he stalked back to the library, ostensibly to help Stephen translate more of some Greek manual for Elder Lu's monks to examine.

The two scholars were sending letters back and forth to the mysterious monastery that no one knew the location of except for the Eight Immortals. Stephen had visited, but had been blindfolded for the journey. Not even the highest-ranking administrators knew the secret site of the protected library where the book was being kept.

Nor did anyone know where Elder Lan had gone. No word had reached Mount Penglai about the strange immortal's whereabouts, so the whole palace was in a kind of holding pattern. Tension blanketed the grounds, affecting everyone.

Especially Beatrice.

Her martial arts were improving exponentially, mostly because practicing was all she could do. She had progressed in her weapons training to the point that Baojia had moved her from dull weapons to sharp and was practicing more aggressively with her. The strange chemistry Beatrice sensed from her teacher had not dissipated in the tense atmosphere, which only added to the overall stress she was feeling. Even the weight of his stare was starting to bother her.

"Again." Baojia's blade slapped hers and she backed away. "Try that combination again, only this time, try not thinking about your boyfriend."

"Shut up!"

He snarled at her, getting in her face when she glared at him. "Do not order me around, little girl. Do you think I care about your hurt feelings? You wanted to learn from me, so pay attention."

She didn't back down, stepping closer as she tossed her blade to the ground. "I'm done. Go bite something, Baojia."

He grabbed her arm and spun her around when she tried to walk away. "You want me to bite something? I'll tell you—"

"Well, isn't this interesting." Beatrice stiffened when she heard the mocking voice. "Whatever would my *Papà* say if he saw this little scene?"

She turned slowly to see Lorenzo sitting on a bench nearby, surrounded by guards.

"Beatrice," Baojia warned quietly. "He's baiting you. Ignore him."

"Gio wouldn't say anything to you, you slimy little bastard." She spit at the blond vampire. "Leave me alone. Or were you going to try to grab me again? Not so brave when you don't have others doing your dirty work, are you?"

Lorenzo's blue eyes narrowed, and a smile flicked at the corner of his lips. In the blink of an eye, he stood before her, leaning down and hissing before Baojia could pull her behind him. Her bodyguard pressed her into his back, standing his ground as the palace guards intervened and stepped between the two water vampires. They pushed Lorenzo back and Beatrice heard a low snarl come from Baojia's chest.

"Back away, Lorenzo." She heard him say. "I have orders to protect this one, and I don't care who your patron is. I will happily end you if you interfere with my assignment."

"Everyone is in love with the little human." Lorenzo laughed. "It's all so amusing. Such a precious little girl. I do hope she wanders in my direction soon."

"I very much doubt that will happen," Baojia said as Beatrice slumped against his back, suddenly exhausted and wishing she could run away. Despite her fear, she didn't want to show any weakness in front of her old antagonist, so she straightened up and stepped out from her protector's shadow.

"Run along, Lorenzo," she called. "No one wants to play with you today."

"I'll just have to see if I can change your mind," he said with a wink and a smile before he jumped across the stream and strolled back to the opposite side of the palace gardens.

They both watched him until he was out of sight. Baojia finally turned to her.

"Don't be brave. Bravado will get you killed."

Beatrice only shrugged and turned to walk back to Tenzin's. "So will fear."

He caught up with her. "I request that you do not make my job more difficult for me, Beatrice De Novo."

"Afraid of my grandfather's wrath if I get hurt?"

"Of course I am. I'm not an idiot. Also…"

"What?" She stopped and turned to him, suddenly desperate to know why he watched her the way he did. It had become more than just the obvious male appreciation she was used to. His dark eyes searched her face.

"I find you… worthwhile. For a human."

She snorted. "Worthwhile?"

He frowned. "I would find it very unpleasant if anything were to happen to you, B."

Beatrice had no idea what to say to him, and her heart was racing in her chest. Baojia looked as if he was on the edge of saying something else, so she turned abruptly and retreated to her room.

CHAPTER ELEVEN

Mount Penglai, China
October 2010

Stephen and Giovanni paged through the books in Tenzin's library, looking for any further connections between Geber's research in the elixir manuscript and existing alchemic practices in the far East. They had been looking for any precedent for the attempt to stabilize vampire blood for human consumption, but had found none.

"Did you see this?"

Stephen handed Giovanni a book. "It was written in the eighteenth century, comparing Aristotle's theory of aether and the traditional fifth element in Indian alchemy. A contact mentioned it years ago and told me it might be worth looking into. This is the first copy I've found. Might be relevant."

"I hadn't seen it, thank you." Something caught Giovanni's attention. "What contact?"

Stephen shrugged. "Someone in Rome."

Giovanni frowned, but continued working.

The two vampires had come to an uneasy truce in the time they had spent together in the library, and Giovanni was forced to acknowledge that Beatrice's father cared for her deeply, even though he had left her for so many years. Stephen De Novo was as open and honest as Giovanni could expect, and he found himself looking forward to seeing the man more with each passing day.

In addition to his deep love for Beatrice, Giovanni could also see how much Stephen cared for Tenzin, though he still could not classify their relationship. Since it was Tenzin, he accepted that he probably never would. Whatever had drawn his old friend to Stephen, they seemed to care for each other, and Stephen had grown immeasurably more powerful as a result. His already keen mind had been sharpened, and the vampire seemed to have a photographic memory for detail. Giovanni wondered if he was seeing a preview of how Beatrice's fascinating mind would develop after she had turned.

If she had to turn. He still held out some hope that the elixir might negate her need to give up her mortal life, though they still disagreed on the subject. He knew, far better than she did, the sacrifices that vampire life called for, and he would spare her if he could.

"Giovanni, have you given any more thought to why Lorenzo might want this?"

He looked up from his book. "What? The elixir?"

"Yes."

He took a slow breath. "Money is the most obvious answer. If this was made viable and could be marketed in the health industry, he could become tremendously wealthy. And since your daughter stole the majority of his fortune, I'm sure that is attractive."

"I still can't believe she did that."

Giovanni smirked. "I can."

"And she still has it?"

He shrugged. "We don't talk about it all that much. She's a very canny investor, and I know she and Caspar cleaned it through mostly legitimate channels, so she's extremely rich now. I believe they invented a wealthy uncle of some sort." He looked up with a wry smile. "Congratulations, you have a dead brother."

Stephen laughed. "She gets that from my father, I think—that deviousness. My father would have been an excellent con man if he hadn't been such a good Catholic."

"She talks about him occasionally. I know they were very close."

A wistful smile crossed Stephen's face. "I deeply regret not being there at the end of his life. I hate that Mom and B had to deal with that alone."

Giovanni paused, thinking about all the friends he had lost through the centuries. "That is the way of the world, De Novo. People die. Their loved ones continue on."

"But my daughter won't die, will she?"

He looked up, meeting Stephen's brown eyes. They hadn't changed when he was sired. They looked exactly like Beatrice's.

"No, she won't."

"Would you stay with her? If she had wanted to remain human?"

His heart gave a quick beat. "I would have stayed with her as long as she would have allowed me."

Giovanni saw Stephen nod. "Yeah, I know what you mean."

They continued working together and Giovanni could hear Beatrice arguing with Baojia down the hall in the practice room. She stormed outside, but he also heard Baojia follow her. He forced himself to remain in his seat, knowing she was well-protected on the palace grounds, even if Lorenzo was lurking. They had argued more than once about what she perceived as his "hovering."

"There could be another reason that we're not seeing."

He turned at Stephen's soft voice. "What? For why Lorenzo wants the elixir?"

"Yes."

"There's much we don't know, so his motivations could be endless."

"I still think there is something we're not seeing about the effects. I agree with Tenzin."

Giovanni leaned back in his chair. "I'm also curious how he thinks he might produce it. He would need reliable immortal blood donors, and he can only create water vampires, so he must have some plan for that."

"And he would need a lab to create the elixir once the formula was decoded. It wouldn't be easy. My contact in Rome—"

"Who is this contact you mention?" Giovanni had noted it before, but now, he went on alert.

Stephen only shook his head. "I don't know, to be completely honest. It's someone that found me years ago when I was still running from Lorenzo. There was a note in my hotel room in Warsaw when I came back from the National Archives. It just said, 'I'm here to help.' I was terrified at first, thinking that someone had found me and would reveal me to Lorenzo, but he always seemed to step in at exactly the right time to help. Since then, he has left me information at hotels, or sent it to my address in Brasilia. Tips about research. Clues leading me to Geber's other work. It was all… rather friendly, to be honest. I came to think of him as a friend, even though I really didn't have any way to contact him. I haven't received anything since I've been here. The last communication was the mention of Elder Zhang's name."

"But how do you know he's from Rome?"

"He mentioned it once. He either lives there or visits a lot, I'm sure of it. I'm assuming it's a man only because the handwriting looks masculine. He's the one that told me when you went to Livia's to negotiate for Beatrice after Lorenzo took her. He's kept me apprised of Lorenzo's movements so I could keep one step ahead of him. He told me you were tracking me. One of his last letters to me said that Lorenzo had been researching private pharmaceutical labs in Eastern Europe."

Giovanni's mind raced. He tried to think who in Rome could be so well-connected that he would have access to all that information. Not only did this immortal know Stephen's whereabouts, but he also seemed to have intimate knowledge of the manuscript.

Stephen's voice broke through his internal reverie. "Has Beatrice been to Rome?"

Giovanni shook his head. "No. I'll not take her until… well, it's not time for that yet."

"Does Livia know about her?"

"I've kept her apprised of the situation."

Stephen smiled. "I'm sure it's a comfort to her to know you have found someone after so long."

Giovanni gave a tight smile. "Yes."

"I'm sure she will love Beatrice. And your father would, as well."

And I'm sure he wouldn't have.

Andros's blanket disdain for women was something that his sire had hidden fairly well, but Giovanni only said, "There are few that meet your daughter that don't love her."

"When was the last time you were in Rome?"

Giovanni chose another book, wishing that Stephen would choose another subject. "When I went to petition for her release. It was a complicated visit."

"I'm sure it was. The two of you should go back after all this is over. I know it has been a joy to me to see the two of you together. We always want our children to find someone that loves them with such devotion."

He flashed back to a memory of his father and Livia, the blanket of manipulation lying heavy over their last visit to Rome in 1506. There had been no joy between them. Any affection Livia had ever had for Giovanni was layered in self-interest.

"I'm sure we will go eventually."

"There have been many times over the years when I wished I could have met your father. His library was an inspiration to me."

Giovanni smothered his instinctual reaction, as he had for over five hundred years. "I'm very pleased Andros's collection has been preserved. Even if it is not in my hands. You have no idea where it is now?"

Stephen shook his head. "When I first discovered it, it was in Ferrara. But after Lorenzo took me, he moved everything to an old villa in Perugia. That was where I was held for the first three years after I was turned. And where I escaped from."

Giovanni's eyes darted up. "Perugia?"

Stephen smiled. "Yes, a beautiful old place. I heard it was the site of a medieval fortress of some kind that had burned down. The villa was built in the seventeenth century."

"Brigands, Livia. Everything was destroyed. The servants fled. If Father had not sent Lorenzo and I to Crotone on that errand, we would have been destroyed, too."

She had sobbed in the middle of the court. "It cannot be! My Andros, my Niccolo! How will I survive without him?"

"I am so sorry."

She had embraced him in front of the throngs, his newly turned son standing behind him. "You are such a comfort to me, Giovanni. Such a comfort. To have Niccolo's beloved son in my court is... such a comfort." Her eyes lit with calculation. "You must stay for a time."

"I—of course I will stay. For a time."

"Yes." She had stroked his arm. "Of course you will, my darling Giovanni."

Had Lorenzo rebuilt Andros's old villa? Giovanni had given him property nearby, but had his son recreated the villa where they had murdered his sire? Giovanni shook his head and focused back on Beatrice's father, who had been staring at him.

"I'm sorry to bring up your father. I forget that some losses can still be painful, even after so many years."

Giovanni cleared his throat. "Yes, I don't think about him much anymore."

"You were fortunate to have had the time with him that you did." Stephen smiled. "Not all of us had such excellent examples of immortal life."

Giovanni forced a smile. "Fortunate. Yes, Stephen. I was very... fortunate."

Hours passed, and it was just before dawn when he heard a commotion in the courtyard. An unwelcome scent hit him, and he rose swiftly to rush out the door. His ears tuned to Baojia's voice.

"Get back! I have her. Just stay back and someone get the Italian, dammit!"

He raced down the hall, flames erupting along his collar when he saw Baojia carrying Beatrice in his arms like a child. She was unconscious. Her face had a grey pallor, and she was bleeding from a cut on her forehead.

"What the hell happened?" he shouted.

"She got away from her guards. I found her in a creek outside the palace grounds. She was face down, but I drew the water out of her lungs. She's stable now."

Baojia handed Beatrice's limp body to him, and he forced back the flames when he heard her rasping breath and steady pulse. She was still unconscious, but the color was returning to her face. He placed his palm on her temple, but her mind felt only as if it was sleeping, and he sensed no damage, so he heated his arms to warm her cold body.

Tenzin came down the hall with Stephen on her heels. "I will kill those guards. How a human could escape them is beyond me."

"Where were you?" Giovanni growled at Baojia. The water vampire glared at him.

"I thought it best to let someone else protect her for a few minutes so we didn't kill each other, di Spada. Trust me, she was in a foul mood. Someone would have been injured."

"Someone was injured, you fool!"

Giovanni strode to their room, laying her on the bed and covering her with the thick blankets before he turned on Baojia, Tenzin, and Stephen, who had followed them.

"All of you, go away." He spotted Nima in the corner. "Nima, can you bring her some broth, please?"

Tenzin only cocked her head, examining Beatrice's limp form. "You're lucky it was Baojia that found her. If there hadn't been a water vampire around—"

"I'm well aware of the consequences, Tenzin."

"I'm just saying you shouldn't be so mad. She was lucky this time."

"Tenzin, get out."

His old friend didn't leave. "You need to get over this attachment to her pulse, my boy. Her mortal life—"

"Out!"

Stephen grabbed Tenzin's arm and pulled her to the door, but not before sending his daughter one longing glance over Giovanni's shoulder. Fortunately, he didn't try to approach the irate, territorial vampire who hovered over her. Baojia followed them, and Giovanni knelt down beside Beatrice and stroked her forehead. The cut was oozing blood, so he pierced his tongue and healed it, cleaning the wound and the blood that was smeared on her forehead. His hands framed her face, and he could feel her start to wake.

"Gio?" Her voice was rasping.

"You're in bed, Beatrice. You fell. Or were pushed. You almost drowned. Do you have any memory of it?"

He suspected she wouldn't. The water had washed away any scent on her, but her mind bore the telltale smudge of amnis. A vampire had attacked her. His son, probably, but there would be no proof. Lorenzo had been waiting for his opportunity, and Beatrice's stubborn and independent nature had provided it.

"I was… taking a walk in the forest."

"By yourself?" He tried to tamp down his anger.

"Yes, by myself." She must have seen his expression and she scowled. "Do you know what it's like to go weeks with people hovering around you? I was going crazy."

"So you left and palace grounds and left yourself open to attack?"

She winced and brought a hand up to her forehead. "Can we not argue about this right now? Can we just… I have a headache."

He glared at her. "We are talking about it now, because you might have been killed. How could you be so foolish?"

She curled her lip. "How could I be so… you know what? You try having people hovering over you twenty-four hours a day and see how you do." She sat up in bed, color rushing to her face as her temper built up steam. "You try being the one constantly protected! Having your mind open to anyone that can get their hands on you. Being constantly under the threat of manipulation from any vampire who even brushes your skin. Have you thought about that?"

"Beatrice—"

"Have you ever thought about the fact that one touch from anyone untrustworthy would make me their puppet? Let them discover any of the secrets I know? And I'd have no way of protecting myself or the people I love! I might not even remember telling them."

His stomach churned at the thought, but his mind fought against the words she threw at him.

"I'm sick of it! I'm sick of all of this." Giovanni knew what she was going to say before her mouth even opened. "Gio, I'm ready."

He sat back on his heels, as his heart began to thump. "No."

"What is your problem? What?" She leaned toward him. "You wanted me to have a choice? Well, this is my choice. I want to be a vampire. And I don't want to wait. This vulnerability—"

"Beatrice, you have no idea—"

"I have a very good idea what I'm giving up. I'm ready."

He shook his head and began pacing the room. "No."

"Why?"

"Because you're not ready."

"I am."

He tugged at his hair as he paced. "No!"

"It is not your choice."

Giovanni knelt by the bed, placing both hands on her cheeks. He could feel her pulse pounding in her neck, and his desperate heart raced along with it. "Don't I have a say in this? Haven't I earned that? Why does it have to be right now?"

She shook her head, her eyes pleading with him. "You know why," she whispered.

"I don't! If you would just stay with me—"

"I can't do that, love." She shook her head, tears building in her eyes. "I can't live my life under constant protection. I want to be able to protect myself. I don't want to be vulnerable anymore. I don't want my mind to be someone else's open book!"

For a brief moment, he panicked at the thought of Beatrice being forced to give up the secrets she held. His conversation with Stephen had reminded him that if his and Lorenzo's secret were ever discovered, their lives would both be forfeit to a very powerful immortal. Only one human knew the truth about his father's death.

Only Beatrice.

And her mind *was* an open book.

Her eyes pleaded with him. "Jacopo, you know I'm right. You know—"

"There has to be another way." She still had no idea what she would be giving up, and the tears fell down her face.

"There isn't!"

They were interrupted by a quiet knock at the door. Nima came in, bearing a bowl of broth with a soft smile and a gentle pat on Beatrice's cheek. She looked between the two of them before she slipped out the door.

Giovanni walked over and secured the room, twisting the locks closed as he heard Beatrice go to the washroom. He heard the shower start to flow, but he stayed in the bedroom, listening to her as she washed the attack from her body.

She thought she knew so much, but as mature as she was, he knew she didn't truly understand how much her life would change. It was impossible.

He was still sitting in the armchair when she came out, wrapped in a soft white towel. There wasn't much time before dawn. Beatrice walked over and sat on his lap, curling into his chest.

Giovanni stroked her hair. "How do you feel?"

"Other than a sore throat, I feel fine."

"Baojia had to pull the water from your lungs."

"But he did. And I'm fine."

"You might not have been. This is Lorenzo, please don't underestimate him."

"I know who my enemy is." She didn't. Not really. She only thought she did. "Don't be angry with me," she whispered as she kissed his neck.

His brow furrowed in frustration. "I love you. More than you can imagine. Don't put yourself at risk. Do you have any idea what it would do to me?"

"I need to do this."

"You need to wait."

"I know you think that."

He gritted his teeth and remained silent. The full force of her attack suddenly hit him, and he clasped her to his chest.

"I need you," he whispered, peeling off the towel she wore. He needed the pulse of her heart against his chest. He needed the smell of her blood as it rushed through her body. He wanted to see her skin glow in the lamplight as he moved in her.

She met his kiss with equal fervor, gripping his shoulders as she straddled his lap. They made love frantically, face-to-face in the low light of the oil lamps, and she pulled him to her neck, asking without words for Giovanni to bite her and send her over the edge.

"You're injured."

"Please," she whispered. "Please." With a low growl, he gave in and bit, her warm blood coursing over his tongue as they both climaxed. He held her wrapped in his arms, rocking back and forth as he sealed the tiny wounds and pressed his ear to her pounding heart. He held her and walked to the bed, tucking her into his side as he began to feel the pull of day in his limbs.

Beatrice stroked a hand over his heart, feeling the slow thump as his body warmed with the rush of her blood. His hunger sated, Giovanni's eyes began to droop, and she sat up, watching him as he fell into his daytime rest.

"I love you, Jacopo."

He struggled to stay awake. "*Ti amo.* Stay. Stay with me today. Don't leave."

"I will stay." Beatrice stroked his hair, and their eyes met. He recognized the familiar look of resolve. "I'll never leave. I'm going to be with you forever."

Giovanni's lips tried to form the words of protest, but they lay silent in his mind before he blacked out, her flushed face the last thing he saw before he closed his eyes.

CHAPTER TWELVE

Mount Penglai, China
October 2010

Beatrice watched Giovanni for a few minutes before he ceased breathing, and she knew he would not rise until just before dusk. She left his scent on her skin as she dressed in a pair of loose pants and a T-shirt. Then she left the room, locking it behind her. She ignored the chill in the air when she walked out to the garden and sat in the sun, closing her eyes as the warm rays touched her skin for the last time.

She let her mind drift to the night before. She had been practicing with Baojia, frustrated with her own fumbling attempts to best him.

"Deflect, girl!" He slapped at the blade of her dao *with an open palm. "Where is your mind tonight?"*

Her mind was on Lorenzo, who she had seen walking across the garden as they left earlier to practice outside. As soon as her heart began to race, Giovanni had rushed to her side, arguing with Baojia until the vampire had relented and taken their practice back to Tenzin's rooms.

"I'm just… my arm is really sore; can we take a break? This full-weight sword is kind of killing me."

He frowned. "You didn't take this long switching from the practice jian. *What's your problem?"*

She lost her temper. "Maybe I'm not an immortal, badass vampire,

Baojia! Maybe I just need a fucking break for once. Is that too much to ask?"

He curled his lip in disgust. "You're acting like a child. I should send you to your room until you have improved your attitude."

She threw the sword on the ground. "Go to hell! I am not a child, and maybe I have a bit more on my mind than just your dumb sword practice. The last thing I need—"

"You will not treat your weapon in that manner," he hissed.

Beatrice gasped when Baojia rushed to her. He stood, glaring into her eyes as he flipped the dao up with his foot, grabbed her hand, and slapped the handle into her palm. As the sword flipped in the air, it caught a finger, and she winced as she felt the blade slice her skin.

Baojia grabbed the sword from her hand immediately and brought her palm up to his face, his eyebrows furrowed in alarm.

"Beatrice, I..." Immediately, he brought her finger to his mouth and licked at the blood as it trickled down her hand. She saw his tongue flick out, piercing a long fang, and he sealed the wound in a matter of seconds.

As soon as he had, he froze. His eyes lifted to hers, and she saw his fangs grow longer in his mouth. Her breath rushed out of her body as she felt the soft caress of his amnis spread over her palm and tease the skin of her wrist.

"Stop," she whispered. "Let go of my hand."

But he didn't, nor did he move. Baojia stood inhumanly still, and his eyes never left hers. For a brief moment, she could imagine falling into them, and she pulled away, stunned by the rush of her own pulse.

"Stop." She wasn't sure whether she was talking to him or herself.

"I'm sorry, B."

"Forget about it."

"I most certainly will not."

She flushed in embarrassment, furious at the idea of Giovanni or Tenzin walking in and seeing them in such proximity. "Really, forget about it. All of it."

"Beatrice—"

"I'm done practicing for the night."

"We're not finished here."

She huffed out a breath. "Yes, we are." She reached down and grabbed her dao, then tried to walk past him, but his arm shot out and grabbed her wrist. She felt the creep of his energy again when their skin met, and she wrenched it away.

"Don't! Don't touch me."

"B, just listen—"

"I'm done. Got it? You..." She was still blushing, and she couldn't forget the intimate feel of his tongue and the teasing caress of his amnis. "Just forget about it."

"You cannot deny that there is something—"

"Shut up!" she shouted. "What? You getting tired of the donated blood? Need a little refreshment? I'm not a fucking appetizer."

He blinked in surprise, but anger quickly overtook his features. "You arrogant little—"

"Leave me the hell alone! I'm going for a walk." She continued toward the door. "Don't worry. I'll take my precious sword."

"Get back here, girl!"

Beatrice turned, gave him a bitter smile, then flipped him off, noting absently that the finger he had healed was the one now raised in ire. She continued walking backward, straight out the door. She turned down the hallway and out to the gardens, ignoring Baojia as he called her name. She heard him call for Tenzin's guards, so she ducked down a corridor she had seen the servants using.

She followed it toward fresh air. With the lack of windows in the palace, it was hard to tell which way led outside, but she felt a gust of cool air waft across her heated face, so she followed it, eventually opening a door that led to the outer perimeter of the palace grounds.

She saw a path leading through the forest that surrounded the compound, and a few monks were walking in the grey hours before dawn. She followed them, but soon got lost in the dark maze of the shifting bamboo. Following the sound of water, she came upon the creek that fed the streams that cut through the gardens. Heaving a sigh of relief, Beatrice began to follow it back to the palace gardens.

"A beautiful woman carrying such a weapon. What is the world coming to?"

She whirled, gasping when she heard his voice. She immediately raised her sword. Lorenzo only smiled and stepped into it. Lifting a hand to prop the heavy dao on his shoulder, he laughed.

"There, now you're quite safe. You can chop off my head if I threaten to harm a hair on yours. Feel better?"

"What are you doing here?" She debated whether to try chopping off his head, or at least trimming the hair he seemed so fond of.

"Do you think you could? Chop off my head?" His full mouth

pouted in concentration. "I'm not sure you could. You might not realize how much strength that actually takes. There are all these pesky bones and tendons. It's harder than it looks. I should know."

"Would you like to be my test subject? What do you say, you bastard?"

"I just want to talk. Since you seem to be the most rational of your little group, I thought I'd give you a try. You see, my attempts to reason with my father have failed."

"Gee, I can't imagine why."

Lorenzo shrugged. "I can't either. I tried to explain that I no longer wished Stephen any harm, or you for that matter, and he just ignored me. I think he's still blinded by his desire for our father's books. That vampire is quite single-minded when his attention gets focused on something." Lorenzo gave a lascivious smirk. "Of course, you probably know that by now."

She swallowed, struck by something Lorenzo had said. "What do you mean? You've said over and over that you wanted to torture and murder my father. And me. Why would I believe that you no longer want to hurt us?"

He cocked his head. "You're a very perceptive woman, Beatrice De Novo. Look into my eyes, and see if you believe me. I do not wish any harm to come to you. Nor do I have any interest in your father. All I want is—"

"The book."

He smiled. "I knew you would understand. All my interest in you and your family will cease if I get my books back. That's all I want. Well —" He smiled. "I'd be lying if I said that was all I wanted." He let his gaze rake over her body.

She snorted. "Right, like that's going to happen."

"I deeply regret not tasting you… really tasting you the night I had you on my boat. That was foolish of me. Tell me, do you plan on turning, Beatrice?"

She couldn't help the smile that flickered across her face at the thought of being as powerful as the monster across from her.

"Ah, I see you smile. Excellent idea, if you ask me. And refreshing. So nice to see a human that's not attached to breathing or breeding. Very forward thinking of you."

"I don't really give a shit about your opinion. I really doubt that comes as a surprise."

He chuckled. "Enough chatting. It's quite addicting talking to you, you know. I do love good banter. But I'll return to my original point, I promise to leave your father and all your relations in peace as long as I get that manuscript and the journals."

"And what about Ioan? What about him?"

Lorenzo merely shrugged. "Was he your lover? Your father? Your child? Leave Ioan's vengeance to his family; it is no concern of yours."

"But Gio would never—"

"Giovanni"—he stepped closer and let the blade run along his skin, drawing a line of blood—"will do what you want. You know you could persuade him to give it to me if it meant he could go back to his quiet, uneventful life. He can bury himself in his books and research again, just like you know he wants to."

Beatrice would have been lying to say the idea was not tempting. On one level, she knew she could probably convince Giovanni if she really tried. But...

"I don't make deals with the devil, Lorenzo. Even when the devil looks me in the eye." She stepped forward and let the blade cut deeper into his skin. His lip curled in disdain.

"Fool." And she gasped when his cold hand reached up and grabbed the back of her neck.

The next thing she remembered was looking into Giovanni's tormented green eyes.

It was the idea of mental manipulation, even more than physical harm, that Beatrice feared the most. The period of her teenage years when she was afraid she was losing her sanity had been the most frightening of her life.

Until she was immortal, Beatrice knew she was vulnerable.

The morning sun poured over the garden, lighting the gleaming limestone pillars and flashing across the streams that cut through the grass. The air was lush with the sound of morning birds, and brilliant fall leaves lay scattered along the lawn as servants spread across the silent grounds, raking the paths in their orange robes.

Beatrice sat on the damp ground under a weeping maple and watched the sun rise in the East. She sat for hours, watching it track across the garden and memorizing the way the shadows shifted and the light danced on the rippling water. She let her mind roam to the waterfalls of Cochamó and the rainbows in the mist. She let herself remember the sunset over the Pacific and the searing heat of hiking in the desert with Dez as the light painted the rocks red.

She spent hours staring into the bright garden and never closed her eyes.

When she felt the soft touch on her shoulder, she turned to see Nima standing with a cup of cardamom tea. Though she had hardly spoken to the woman in the weeks they had been at the palace, her quiet human company was welcome. She sat next to Beatrice on the ground, surprisingly flexible for one with such a wrinkled face. Her dark eyes looked over the sun-lit grounds.

"I have painted many gardens for Tenzin over the years," she said in quietly accented English, "but it's never exactly the same."

"There are photographs."

Nima nodded her silver-grey head. "Yes."

"Still not the same, though."

"No."

Beatrice sniffed, swallowing the lump in her throat, before she gave up and let the tears fall down her cheeks.

"Sorry," she sniffed again.

Nima just smiled. "I understand the grief."

"But I know I'm ready."

"Tenzin said you would be. That was one of the reasons she asked me to be here. I don't usually like to leave the mountains."

Beatrice frowned, curious why Nima's presence was important, until she looked into the old woman's eyes and understood the quiet sadness that lived there.

"You said no, didn't you?"

"Yes."

"Oh," she breathed out.

"And I regret it every day."

"But why—"

"By the time I really understood the regret, my body was old. I would not choose it now. It is not vanity, simply... not what I wish for eternity."

"Was she angry?"

"Yes."

"But you are still together."

Nima smiled and nodded. "Yes."

"Someday, she'll watch you die."

"And that is the sadness I live with."

Beatrice swallowed the lump in her throat. "So I'm making the right decision?"

Nima smiled. "I can't tell you that, but I think you already know."

Beatrice looked over the sun-washed garden again and closed her eyes. "Yes, I know."

"It is still understandable to grieve."

"Thank you for being here."

"You're welcome."

Nima tucked her feet under and sat next to Beatrice as the sun rose to the apex of the sky. The two women sat silently in the sunlight, listening to the chirp of the birds and the buzzing bees. They watched the wind tease the orange, red, and purple leaves from the trees, and the clouds drifted across the sky, their slow-moving shadows falling across the earth.

It was close to three o'clock when Beatrice rose, helped Nima to her feet, then walked inside, shutting the door to the sun for the last time. She walked down the hall to the practice room to find Tenzin sitting there with her father. She looked into the storm-grey eyes of her friend.

"Are you ready?"

"Yes."

"I can't." Stephen shook his head. "I can't drain her, Tenzin."

"It has to be you. That's what needs to happen. Her fate lies with water, not air."

"I can give her my blood. I just can't *drain* her."

Tenzin scowled. "You'll be very weak if you don't."

Stephen still shook his head. "I can't do it."

Beatrice put a hand on her father's arm. "Tenzin, is it that important who drains me? As long as I have Dad's blood to turn, right?"

"Yes, but his amnis will be drained from giving you his blood. I don't like the idea of him being so weak."

"Then you can give me some of yours later. And I'll feed after," Stephen said, "but you cannot ask me to drain my daughter to the point of death."

"Fine," Tenzin rolled her eyes. "I'll probably need the strength when he wakes, anyway."

Beatrice shuddered at the thought. "He's going to be furious. Tenzin, I'm sorry for anything Giovanni—"

"Please," she snorted. "It's not like he can hurt me. This is one of those situations where it is better to ask forgiveness than permission. Besides, he knows it's coming."

"That's not going to make him any less angry." She felt a churning in her gut as she remembered his plea before he fell asleep. She felt like she was betraying his trust, but she also felt as if she had no other choice.

Tenzin grabbed her arm. "Are you ready? Really?"

She nodded. "Okay, dirty details time."

"Fine. I'll drain your blood, you'll probably pass out, but your father will feed you his. It won't be instinctive for you to drink from him at first, but don't worry, we'll make sure you get enough. He'll be able to use amnis to make you swallow the blood until you latch on."

She bit her lip. "And I won't remember any of it?"

"Probably not much. I'll use my amnis to keep you from struggling. Your body will fight the blood loss instinctively, so it's better if I use it to keep you calm."

Beatrice hated the thought of that, but agreed it was probably for the best. "Okay. What happens after that?"

Tenzin and her father exchanged a look. "Your body will go through quite a few changes at first. The first couple of hours it will expel anything from your digestive system. But you won't be awake for that."

"Oh, *ew*." She took Tenzin's hand. "I want you to promise me that you will not let Giovanni be here when all that stuff is going on. One, gross. Two, he'll freak out."

She shrugged. "I'll be able to keep him away. Once it's done, he'll understand."

Beatrice thought Tenzin might have been a bit overconfident on that one, but she didn't have much choice but to trust her. "Okay. Then what?"

"Your body will shut down for about twenty-four hours, or until first dark. Then you'll wake up and be a vampire."

"Am I going to be hungry right away?"

"Not immediately, but definitely the first night." Tenzin just shrugged like it was no big deal.

She sighed a little and saw her father's mouth quirk into a small grin.

"And?"

"What? We'll find someone to feed you. It's not a big deal. There are lots of bowing people around."

"Um… that's not exactly… can I have donated blood at first? I don't want to drain anyone."

Stephen was quick to reassure her. "We won't let you kill anyone. We'll make sure you have some fresh blood, but you will need a lot."

"How much?"

Tenzin said, "About a person's worth."

Her mouth fell open. "That much?"

"Just at first. The first year or so, you'll have to drink a few cups every night and then you'll need much less."

She began to feel her heart rate pick up. "Don't let me kill anyone. I… I can't—"

"You won't." Tenzin reassured her. "We'll have you fully stocked with fresh blood that hasn't been preserved. No preserved blood for a while. You need the fresh stuff to be strong. Animal will do if you must, but human is always the best."

"Okay." She nodded. "Okay."

"Any other questions?"

"What will it be like? At first?"

Tenzin frowned. "I don't really remember. It's been a long time. Stephen?"

Stephen took a deep breath. "You'll feel very overwhelmed. All your senses will be heightened. Your hearing will be better. Your sense of smell. You'll feel the electrical currents almost like a web around you. This place is ideal because there is so little electricity, it won't be as overwhelming as—"

"Oh!" Beatrice gasped.

"What?" Stephen looked at her in panic. "B, you can change your mind at any time, you don't have to—"

"Yes, she does!"

He glared at Tenzin. "No, she doesn't."

"She really does."

"Stop." Beatrice held out a hand. "Don't fight. I'm just… It's silly. I just realized I won't be able to use my computer anymore."

Tenzin rolled her eyes. "Is that all?"

"Yeah," she frowned and felt her father reach over to squeeze her arm. "That's all."

For a moment, the unexpected grief welled up again. She felt childish to feel grief about something that seemed so inconsequential, but it wasn't. Then she remembered the feeling of helplessness she'd had again when she woke the night before, weak and shivering from another attack. She thought about her conversation with Nima in the garden and about the flicker of grief she saw in Giovanni's eyes every time he looked at Casper.

She didn't want to be vulnerable. She didn't want to leave Giovanni.

She was ready.

"I'm ready."

Beatrice looked up and realized they were waiting for her. Her father stood and pulled her into a fierce embrace.

"I love you, kiddo. It's going to be fine."

"I'm glad you're here, Dad. This is the best thing. Right? I mean, you're my dad."

"Yeah," he smiled, and his eyes crinkled just like she remembered as a child, "I'm your dad."

She whispered, "And you always will be."

"Yep."

"Sentimental De Novos," she heard Tenzin call. "The very angry, territorial fire-vampire will be waking up very soon. If we want this to happen, we need to do it now."

Beatrice nodded and went to sit on the grouping of low cushions in the corner of the room. Stephen sat across from her, and Tenzin sat to her left and pulled her hair to the side. She gave her a full, fangy grin. Beatrice cocked her head at an angle.

"Okay, drink up."

"I have to say, you do smell delicious. I kind of get why he wants to keep you."

Beatrice frowned. "Tenzin, please don't make me feel any more like dinner than I already do."

Her friend laughed long and hard. Finally, Beatrice did too. Then Tenzin reached over and stroked Beatrice's hair back from her face, and the soft look she occasionally allowed herself peeked through.

"It will be all right. Relax." Beatrice could feel the amnis start to creep across her skin as she stared at Tenzin. Her father held her hand

and she allowed the soft brush of her friend's influence in her mind. She closed her eyes and listened to the hypnotic voice.

"Meditate. Just like we practiced. Calm. Let yourself relax."

She drifted, focusing on a picture of Giovanni she held in her mind. It was the single-minded look he gave her sometimes. When he was angry. When he made love to her. When he killed for her. It was the look that told her she was the center of his world.

"I am your balance in this life," she whispered to him, even though he was not there. "In every life."

Her eyes flew open when she felt Tenzin's fangs strike.

Beatrice could feel her body jerk once at the attack before Tenzin's influence drifted over her limbs and caused her to fall still. She could still feel her father holding her hand, and her senses were on alert, but she couldn't speak, nor could she move.

She was paralyzed. Cut off from reaction to the fierce attack her mind fought against, but her body was powerless to stop. Tenzin's bite wasn't painful, but her vicious, curled fangs buried themselves in her artery and Beatrice felt her heart race at the unwelcome intrusion. It was as if her body had been forced into a whirlwind, and she knew there was no escape. The blood rushed to her head as she felt the hard draw of Tenzin's mouth at her neck.

Drums beat in her mind. It was nothing like the soft, drugging bites that Giovanni took. It was hard. Violent, no matter how Tenzin tried to reassure her. Her mind began to scream '*No*' as she felt the life drain out of her.

It wasn't quick.

'*There are an average of ten pints of blood in the human body,*' she heard the echo of her high school biology teacher in her mind as her thoughts scattered.

Ten pints.

Twenty cups.

How long it would take to drink that much water?

But blood was thicker than water.

Or whiskey.

How long had he known he would sire her?

Did he know?

Who knew?

Was that why?

Her heart pounded. A ringing grew in her ears.

Her mind began to flash, and the lights danced across the room.

A sunrise.

Her grandparents slow dancing in the living room.

Her father reading her a bedtime story in a purple-painted room.

Hiding in a tree to read *A Little Princess*.

Sunset on Galveston Bay.

The pictures flashed like an old film reel.

Her father. Webs in the living room. Grandma's swollen eyes. Hands twisted in rage. A knife at her leg. His pale face in the streetlamp. Grasping hands.

Books lined the walls of her mind, all falling open to different pages.

"There's a position open at the library."

A pair of vivid green eyes.

"What's your real name?"

The taste of whiskey filled her mouth.

"That was for me."

A thundering silence washed over her.

She heard nothing but his voice.

Her heart.

His voice.

"My name is Jacopo."

Thump.

"I'm here for you."

Thump.

"I will always come for you."

Thump.

"Don't you know how I adore you?"

Thump.

"You are my balance in this life."

Thump.

"In every life."

There came a force of wind in her ears.

"Forever."

Thump.

Forever. Forever. Forever.

The wind grew louder, filling the room as she felt the first falter of her heart.

She dimly heard her father say something as Tenzin's mouth

pulled away. Her body was passed from one set of arms to another, more familiar, pair. The wind still roared through the room.

Forever.

Forever.

Forever.

The shriek grew. There was a banging and clamoring as the whirlwind took over, and she heard a door burst open. The roaring filled her ears as she felt the drip of blood at her lips.

Her eyelids fluttered closed.

Her heart fell silent.

His inhuman roar was the last thing she heard before the black void took her.

CHAPTER THIRTEEN

Mount Penglai, China
October 2010

Giovanni was engulfed in flames. His roar shook the room.

"*Beatrice*!"

Tenzin held his shoulders against the wall as the fire unfurled around him.

"No!" he raged as the smell of her blood filled the air.

He couldn't hear her heart.

He couldn't see her eyes.

Giovanni was trapped in Tenzin's iron grasp as his lover's blood flooded his friend's body and turned her cheeks red. The blue fire burned his clothes and spread up the wall behind him as he continued to struggle.

"Let me go!"

He couldn't hear her heart.

"No."

The snarl ripped from his throat. "Release me, or I will kill you."

"Her father is feeding her."

Giovanni's roar was inhuman. Stephen looked up in horror as he pressed his wrist to Beatrice's mouth. Her lips weren't moving.

He couldn't see her eyes.

"You need to calm yourself."

"I will kill you both!"

He heard another vampire enter the room, but his eyes never left Beatrice's crumpled form. She lay lifeless on the cushions as her father forced his blood in her mouth.

He couldn't hear her heart.

"Well, this was stupid."

"Shut up, and help me hold him."

He felt the pinch of a metal pike pierce his shoulder and the wall behind him, holding him as Tenzin's wind forced the flames up the side of the practice room. The air was filled with smoke and fire.

"A little help with the flames, please."

He saw Beatrice's throat move once before Baojia blanketed him with a sheet of water drawn from the stream that cut through the room. He relaxed slightly when he saw her lips begin to move and latch onto Stephen's wrist. Her father cradled her in his arms as Beatrice began to drink.

Giovanni slumped against the wall, Tenzin holding his shoulders while Baojia tugged the spear out of his flesh. He could not tear his eyes from her.

"Tenzin, let me go."

"No."

"I won't kill Stephen."

"I don't really trust you right now."

The flames flared again on his torso.

"Let me go!"

Baojia doused him again, but he still struggled against Tenzin's hold.

"Calm down, my boy."

"Let me go to her."

"Her father is feeding her. Let him take care of her."

"Tenzin!" He took a deep breath and closed his eyes. "Please, bird-girl. Let me go." When he opened his eyes, he stared into her grey ones, trying to ignore the flush of her cheeks, rich with Beatrice's blood.

"Are you calm?"

He finally heard her heart give a faint thump, and a new trace of amnis began to drift across the room as Stephen's blood entered her system. A familiar honeysuckle smell reached his nose.

"Please," he begged. "Let me go, Tenzin. Let me go to my wife."

She drew back in surprise. "What?"

"My wife," he pleaded. "Let me go to Beatrice. I need to go to her."

Her hands released him. "I did not see that."

Giovanni rushed over, taking her limp hand and pressing it to his cheek as she continued to drink from her father's wrist.

It was cold. The human warmth gone from her forever.

He pushed down the instinctive rage and grief to focus on Beatrice.

The new whisper of her energy comforted him, and he put his hands to her temples, searching for the familiar signature of her mind. Her scent was the same; fainter, as he knew it would be. Giovanni brushed her cheek with soft fingers as her father took his wrist away, biting it open again before he put it back to her mouth. Beatrice's lips were stained with blood and rivulets dripped down her neck, mingling with Tenzin's angry bite marks. He resisted the urge to heal her, knowing that any of his blood mingling with her own before she was fully turned could be tragic.

Stephen looked at him cautiously. "Did you say 'my wife?'"

"Yes." He brushed the hair away from her face. She was deathly pale.

"When?"

"We were married in Santiago months ago."

Silence blanketed the room. The only sounds came from the new vampire suckling at her father's wrist. Giovanni watched her with a single-minded focus, memorizing the rhythm of her lips and throat as she drank.

"Why didn't you tell anyone?" Tenzin asked.

He shook his head, continuing to stare at Beatrice. "Her idea. She wanted a more formal ceremony after all this was over. I thought it was silly, but she insisted. Why are we talking about this?"

"Because they are waiting for you to erupt again." He heard Baojia's stiff voice from the edge of the room. He could feel the vampire leave, but Tenzin remained, moving closer to him and placing a hand on his shoulder.

"I'm very, very angry with you both, but now is not the time for that." He continued to stroke Beatrice's hair, tucking it behind her ear so it wouldn't fall in her face.

"It was her idea."

He whispered, "I'm angry with her, as well."

No one said anything. All three were focused on Beatrice as she drank. He could feel her amnis begin to pulse, and he knew she was almost finished feeding. She would not wake until nightfall the next day. He finally tore his eyes from her and looked at Tenzin.

"Have you informed your father?"

"Stephen and I told him months ago."

He just shook his head, stunned by her audacity. He shoved her hand from his shoulder.

"Get away from me."

"You need to leave her with us and go to your room."

"I'm not leaving her," he scoffed.

"Giovanni." She sat next to him, but he refused to look at her. "You know what changes her body will be going through as she turns. She didn't want you to see that. You know this. There is a reason a sire takes care of his child."

He swallowed once. "Don't ask me to leave her."

"I didn't ask it. She did."

A new ache pierced his heart, and Giovanni looked at Stephen, who only nodded before he returned to watching his daughter, cradling her as if she was an infant. As much as he wanted to stay with Beatrice, he knew her father was probably telling the truth. He would honor Beatrice's wishes, even if she hadn't honored his.

Watching Stephen hold her, he realized he felt more at ease leaving Beatrice in the care of her father than with his oldest friend. Tenzin tried to touch his bare shoulder again, but he brushed her off.

"My boy—"

"I'll go," he whispered. "Bring her to me before dawn. I don't want her waking with anyone but me."

Stephen nodded. "Fine."

Beatrice stopped drinking and curled instinctively into her father's arms. Giovanni gave one last brush to her cheek, leaned over to kiss her temple, then stood to go with clenched fists. He turned at the door to watch Tenzin crouch beside Stephen and Beatrice, guarding the room with watchful eyes. Then, he forced himself to walk back to their room and wait.

Tenzin knocked on the door hours later, and, without a word,

Giovanni took Beatrice's sleeping form from Stephen's arms. They had bathed her, but a faint human smell still clung to her body. She seemed lighter than normal, and he was reminded how small she was beneath her bravado. He kicked the door closed before he walked to the bed and nestled her in the silk sheets. He secured the room, double-checking every safety measure, before he lay down with her. He took the sheet from her body and wrapped her in his arms, pressing her cold skin to warm her.

When Giovanni touched her, her energy twined with his, reaching out even in the black void of the deepest sleep. The touch of her amnis flooded him, and it was as if he could feel the brush of her small hands over his body. He lay utterly still, closed his eyes, and waited for her to rise.

When he opened his eyes an hour before dusk, Beatrice was pulsing with amnis, her senses already heightened though she wasn't yet conscious. The hairs on her body stood on end and her skin was damp, the water in the air drawn to her as she rested. There was no question, she was most definitely her father's daughter. And with Stephen drinking as much of Tenzin's blood as he had been, she was going to be very, very powerful. He could read her energy signature already.

He rose, threw on a robe, and went to open the door. Nima was sitting on a bench outside.

"Nima?"

She looked up. "Yes, Gio?"

He paused, unsure of what to say.

"Has Tenzin informed you—"

"I know. I talked to Beatrice yesterday morning."

He blinked. "You did?"

"Yes." She smiled. "She was very peaceful about her decision. Only a little worried how you would react."

"Of course." He didn't know how to respond to her. He was angry. Relieved. Furious. Unavoidably excited. He shook his head. "Is there blood available?"

"Tenzin has already arranged fresh donors. Beatrice was quite concerned about not draining anyone."

"She would be."

"It's taken care of. We will keep it warm for her." She motioned to one of Zhang's younger vampires who he saw standing at the end of the hall. "Send for someone when it is needed."

"Thank you, Nima."

For the first time, he was grateful he was in Penglai, that she had made her change there. No other place in the world was more of an island for immortals. Everything in the palace revolved around their particular needs and foibles.

"And please let Beatrice know that all the human staff has been moved to another part of the quarters, so she doesn't need to worry about them. I'm leaving now. I just wanted to speak to you before I left."

"Thank you again."

"We are at your disposal. It is our honor to help." She gave a nod and walked down the hall, giving quiet instructions to the young vampire at the end of the hall.

Giovanni shut the door and checked the clock on the wall, before he walked back to the bedroom. He paced for a few minutes, determined to push back his anger and frustration. It was not something she could deal with her first night. Taking a deep breath, he peeled the sheets back to really look at her for the first time since her change.

He had been right. She was stunning.

Her skin was smooth and pale, a luminescent pearl that glowed in the lamplight. Her hair was the same, a thick, shining wave of brown that would hopefully still match her eyes. It wasn't uncommon for eyes to change, but her father's had not, so he hoped Beatrice's wouldn't, either.

He pulled her lip up to see the delicate fangs peeking at him. For the first time in days, he smiled. They weren't fully extended yet, but he could imagine them gleaming in her mouth, and he shuddered in anticipation.

Her body was the same, preserved for all eternity as it had been on her last day of human life. The marks in her neck from Tenzin's bite had healed, but he could still see the tiny scars left on the rise of her right breast where he had bitten her while they made love on their wedding night. She had asked him not to heal that bite, wanting the tiny reminder that only they would see.

The small scar on her knee remained, a token of childhood that he kissed, along with the small, sad scars that marked her thigh. She could have had them removed, but she had chosen not to. He traced over each mark on her body that remained unchanged.

"*Tesoro mio*," he murmured as he stroked her face. "So stubborn. How I love you."

If there was one thing he remembered from waking, it was the pain along his sensitive skin. Every nerve ending was heightened in a vampire, particularly a new one who hadn't fully mastered their amnis and the shield it could provide. It was that sharp, overwhelming pain that had first caused the fire to bloom on Giovanni's skin as a newborn vampire. He would never forget the look of fascination and glee in Andros's eyes when he saw it.

He knew she would be most comfortable surrounded by her element, so he left her in bed and drew a warm bath in the large, marble tub. Then he walked back to the bedroom and gathered her up to wait.

He could feel it in her skin first, the twitching, shuddering sensation that rippled wherever his fingers touched. It started on her arms, then traveled down to her fingers, which twitched under the warm water. His arms encircled her as she lay against his chest. He felt her rouse, and she took a deep, gasping breath.

"Ah!" she cried, scooting away from his arms and turning as the water sloshed out of the bath. She put her hands over her ears to shield them from the sound of her own voice, but winced at the movement. "What's wrong with me?"

He held his hands up, soothing her as her eyes darted around the room. He almost sighed in relief that they were the same deep brown.

"Shh," he whispered, conscious of her newly keen hearing, "what is the last thing you remember?"

Her eyes finally settled on him, and she stared rapt at his face.

"Your eyes are different. Why are your eyes different?"

He smiled. "You're just seeing more light, Beatrice. I'm the same."

She shivered, and blood-tinged tears fell down her face. "It hurts. Why does it hurt everywhere? I'm sorry, are you mad at me? Please, don't be mad at me."

His heart ached at her confused plea, and he swallowed the last of his anger in the face of her need. "Take a deep breath. It will calm you, even though you no longer need the oxygen. It's habit."

She took one, a look of confusion coloring her face when she realized she didn't need to breathe it out. "Now let it out." She did, then took another. "Your skin hurts because the nerve endings are much more sensitive. Your whole body is like an exposed nerve."

"Yeah," she moaned. "No kidding."

He continued to make soothing noises, humming quietly as she took a few moments to compose herself.

"Why are we in the bathtub?"

"It should help with the sensitivity. Does it feel good?"

"Yeah." She breathed out. "Really good."

"Do you feel the water around you?"

"Yes," she said, looking down in fascination. "It loves me."

He smiled. "Yes, it does. Water will always be your element now. You will have more control over yourself when you are surrounded by it. Do you feel your amnis?"

Beatrice wasn't paying attention. She had lifted a hand out of the water, drawing rivulets of it up to meet her fingertips where she made them dance like puppet strings. Giovanni was amazed by her control. The mere fact that she could be sitting in the water and not have it rushing uncontrollably over her body was remarkable.

"Water loves me."

"Yes, it does."

"I love water."

Giovanni chuckled. Her mind was probably so flooded with new sensory information, she was focusing on the one thing that seemed to make sense. He remembered the same feeling looking into a candle on his first night of immortal life.

"I love you," she said. She was staring at him again.

"I love you, too." As if it was even a question.

"You're mad at me."

As if it was even a question.

"We'll talk about it another time. Now is not the time."

"I can agree with that."

He saw her staring at the lamps, probably fascinated by the new light spectrum she could see. "Can I kiss you?" he whispered.

She cocked her head. "Will it hurt?"

He leaned forward, tentatively reaching for her. "I'll try to be very gentle."

She nodded, still staring at him. He braced himself on the sides of the tub and bent down to give her a whisper of a kiss.

"Oh." She breathed out with a small smile. "Wow."

"Didn't hurt?"

"No." She blinked back more tears. "Kiss me again."

"I love you," he said before his mouth met hers in another soft kiss.

"I can feel your amnis," she whispered. "It's like another layer of skin. All over. Moving."

"Do you feel yours?"

He could see her eyes narrow as she filtered through the flood of senses. Then, she smiled and looked up. "Yes."

"Soon, you'll learn how to make it cover your skin like me. That's what will let you heat your skin, keep your senses manageable, all of that. Your amnis is both a weapon and a shield. A second skin is an excellent way of thinking about it."

Even as he spoke, he could see her close her eyes and furrow her eyebrows in concentration. When he reached out to touch her hand, she didn't flinch. A layer of amnis already covered it and she knit their fingers together, palm to palm.

"Do I look different?" Her eyebrows shot up, and she lifted fingers to her mouth. "I have teeth!"

As soon as she touched them, her fangs descended even more, and it took every bit of control he owned not to lean over and lick them. He wanted to pierce his tongue on her teeth and let his blood flood her mouth. He wanted her to sink her teeth into his neck. Into his chest. He wanted her to feed from him as he had fed from her. Giovanni pushed back the growl in his chest and focused on her eyes.

"Ith kin' of hard to talk with theeth," she mumbled, speaking around her descended canines.

Her strange lisp broke him out of his trance, and he laughed. "You look the same, Beatrice. Just… paler skin and longer teeth. You'll get used to the teeth."

He kept chuckling, and she flicked her fingers at him. A splash of water rose from the tub and hit his face.

"Okay," she grinned. "Thath's going to be awthume."

He couldn't stop laughing. "And you'll be able to save my shirts if I lose my temper now."

She swallowed and her fangs seemed to retract. "Just… all sorts of benefits to controlling water, aren't there?"

Giovanni smiled as she leaned back against her side of the tub. He reached for her foot underwater and touched it. She flinched for a moment before her toes relaxed and he set both her feet on his lap.

"Are you really mad at me?"

He stared. He didn't want to argue with her on her first night as an immortal. She would be far too volatile. "There's no use in anger toward you. It's done." He paused. "And I know it was your decision."

"Are you mad at Tenzin and my dad?"

"Yes," he growled.

"Why?"

"Because they were planning this and they didn't tell me. They went behind my back."

"So did I."

He sighed and let his head fall back. "Maybe I just don't want to be angry with you. It's easier to be angry with them. I don't like it when we fight."

She smiled and reached a hand over to pat his as it lay on the side of the tub.

"Just as long as you realize it's not logical. I'm more to blame than they are."

"Tesoro, I realized long ago that logic departs me when it comes to you."

She grinned again, which exposed her fangs. He couldn't help himself. He leaned over and cupped her face gently before he kissed her. His tongue delved into her mouth and searched for them. When he found the slick lengths, he flicked the tip of his tongue against them and purred when he heard her moan. She moved into the kiss, and her fangs fell more. They were long, sharp, and slick with the taste of his blood as he cut himself.

He recognized the moment the blood touched her tongue. She tried to pull him closer, but he pushed him away gently. "Hungry?"

She nodded, still eyeing his mouth.

Giovanni wanted to take her right then, but he knew she needed to feed. Plus, the minute she left the tub, her senses were going to overwhelm her again. It would be days before she was even partially in control of her body. He certainly hoped there were no emergencies they would have to deal with. He rose from the tub, feeling her hungry eyes on him as he wrapped himself in a towel.

"Stay here. I'm going to find you some blood."

"No people!"

He smiled. "I've already made arrangements with Nima. She has fresh donors waiting. Nothing to worry about."

Her mouth fell open as she stared at him. "Oh, blood sounds so damn good."

Giovanni cocked an eyebrow at her. "Well, Beatrice, that's hardly a surprise. You're a vampire."

She grinned with two gleaming white fangs. "Yes, I am."

CHAPTER FOURTEEN

Penglai Mountain, China
November 2010

"When are you two going to start talking again?"

"Well," Tenzin blocked a kick that Beatrice aimed at her left knee by taking to the air. "There was a time about two hundred years ago that he stopped talking to me for five years because I killed one of his servants."

"You what?" Beatrice's mouth dropped open. Tenzin landed a few yards away and rushed her, sliding to her side along the mat as she pulled Beatrice's legs out from under her. The two women fell into a heap before Tenzin shot up again.

She shrugged. "He was a very dishonest human. He'd been stealing from Gio. And he was taking advantage of a servant girl."

"So you killed him?" Beatrice shook her head as she jumped to her feet, continually amazed by Tenzin's rather interesting take on morality.

"He was diseased anyway. And the servant girl was pregnant. He was trying to beat the baby from her by striking her stomach. An entirely worthless human. I'm not sure why your husband was so upset." Tenzin landed a blow to her shoulder and Beatrice stumbled back and grimaced.

Tenzin had been slipping the "your husband" phrase into

conversation as often as possible. Always with a smirk or a snort. "I'm not sure why he was angry, either."

Tenzin dodged a quick blow she aimed at her head. They had been practicing Zhang's style of kung fu that evening and Beatrice was still amazed that the movements came so naturally.

"He started talking to me again when I explained why I killed the human. He wasn't completely unreasonable."

Beatrice rolled her eyes. "So you took five years to tell him why you killed his servant?"

"Yes."

"Well, that kind of explains it, Tenzin."

The small woman shrugged one shoulder before her hand reached out and landed a jaw-shattering blow to Beatrice's face. Beatrice winced, but shook her head and continued to fight, feeling the water in the air automatically draw to her skin as her bones knit together.

"I hate talking to your husband when he gets self-righteous and flame-y. I gave him a few years to cool off, then I had a rational conversation with him. It's not my fault he always assumes the worst."

"Stop it."

"Stop talking to your husband?" Tenzin grinned. "Not really a problem at the moment."

"Stop with the 'your husband' thing, all right?"

Tenzin burst into laughter. "I think it's hilarious."

"What?" Beatrice asked as she ducked down to avoid another blow. "That we didn't feel like sharing personal news that was really no one's business but ours?"

"No," Tenzin snorted, "that you two participated in an arcane human ritual that was completely unnecessary. It's not like you need a piece of paper. You're mates."

Beatrice frowned. "Do you have to make it sound quite so scientific?"

Tenzin laughed so hard that Beatrice managed to land a blow to her torso that knocked the vampire to the ground. She skidded and came to a stop near the stream in the practice room, still laughing. Beatrice went to sit next to her and lay on her back, staring out the open ceiling, the roof drawn back to show the sparkling night sky.

"Was it his idea or yours?"

Beatrice sighed, knowing she wouldn't get out of answering.

Tenzin was fascinated by the whole situation, for some odd reason.

"Getting married was his idea. Keeping it to ourselves was mine."

"That doesn't surprise me. He's remarkably sentimental for a vampire."

"He's a five hundred year old Italian Catholic, Tenzin. Of course he wanted to get married. He's just annoyed that we only had a civil ceremony. Among other things."

Tenzin was silent, and Beatrice finally looked over to see her staring at her with a sympathetic look. She reached over and tucked a strand of hair behind Beatrice's ear.

"He adores you. You must know that."

Beatrice bit her lip and tried to keep the bloody tears from her eyes.

"It'd be nice if he started acting like it again, you know?"

The first nights after Beatrice had turned, Giovanni had been perfect. Strong, tender, supportive, he was everything she had needed him to be as she made the awkward, often painful, transition from human life to immortal.

He had helped her to master her amnis so she could walk around the room without cringing from a gust of air. He stayed by her side as she saw her father and Tenzin again, supporting her through the roller coaster of intense emotions that seemed to be her constant companion. He had been quick to make sure she never had to wait when hunger struck her and made sure that all humans were kept at a safe distance. He had been the steady, quiet presence Beatrice had needed him to be.

But as the days passed and she grew more confident in her body, as she regained her composure and her control, Giovanni had drawn away, sinking into a shell of polite resentment. They slept in the same bed every night, but he had not touched her in weeks, and he refused to speak to Tenzin. He conversed only in the most polite way with Stephen and Baojia. And only when it was strictly necessary. He was most often in the library, still searching for the key to the elixir formula, or in the Great Hall, strategizing with Tenzin's father and his allies.

"Do you think it will be five years before he forgives me?"

"Please, you're his wife. He'll get horny. You'll fight. The two of you will make up. We won't see you for a few days. You'll be fine."

She glared at Tenzin. "Thanks, that's reassuring."

Tenzin shrugged. "It should be. I've been alive for over five thousand years. If there's one thing predictable about the male of the species, it's their sex drive and their fascination with fire."

Beatrice snorted. "That's it, huh?"

"Most advances in technology occur because they're either trying to impress women or blow things up. It's as predictable as the sunrise."

The two women stared at each other for a few seconds before they burst into laughter. Even Tenzin was wiping blood stained tears from her eyes.

"I'm being mostly serious, my girl. He really does adore you. He's angry right now. He feels like you went behind his back. That we both did—"

"We *did* go behind his back."

"But it was for the best."

Beatrice fell silent, wiping new tears from her eyes. "You sure?"

"I'm positive." Tenzin sighed. "Some things just have to happen a certain way. He will understand that in time. And he hates being angry with you, I can tell."

"I'm not a big fan of it, either."

Tenzin waved her concerns away. "You'll both be fine. You love each other too much to be angry for long. Plus"—she held a finger up—"you didn't kill anyone. That's a definite point in your favor."

Beatrice sighed and looked back up at the stars, gleaming and multi-colored in the night sky. How had she ever thought the night was black? It was a million shades, none of them as dense or unyielding as she'd thought.

Eternal night was a million swirling shades of grey.

She was drinking a large mug of warmed blood the next time she saw him. Giovanni passed in the hall, stopping when he saw Beatrice and Stephen at the large dining table.

"Good evening, Beatrice, Stephen. How are you tonight?"

The mouthful of blood stuck in her throat.

"We're doing well," Stephen said. "Thank you. Tenzin said Beatrice's kung fu is becoming quite exceptional."

"That's excellent."

She forced the blood down, almost choking on the thick liquid as it slid down her throat. He was wearing a pair of grey slacks and a white oxford shirt, open at the collar so she could see the rise of his

143

chest. She tried to read his eyes, hoping that their brilliant green depths might have softened to her since she had risen that evening.

They had not.

"I… I'm practicing later with Baojia," she said, looking down at the small plate of food in front of her. It looked even more unappetizing than it had a few minutes before. "You should come by. We're doing weapons and water practice."

"I'll try."

"Gio, are you hungry?" Stephen offered. "The cooks prepared a very mild—"

"I'm fine, thank you." Giovanni glanced at her briefly. "I've already fed this evening."

A thick spike of jealousy cut through her. Beatrice wondered who he had fed from. It was just as likely Giovanni was making use of the donated blood in the palace as she and her father were, but a small part of her wondered whether he would be spiteful enough to drink from a human without telling her.

Stephen was speechless, looking between the two of them awkwardly.

"I have a meeting with Zhang in a few minutes. I'll see you both later."

Her father said, "Have a good evening."

"Bye," she said, never looking up and holding in the tears that wanted to escape. She heard his steps retreat down the hall, and she gripped the mug so tightly that it cracked, leaking blood over the ebony table before it dripped to the floor.

Beatrice rose and rushed to her room, never having finished her meal.

She regretted skipping her ration of blood later that night when she sparred with Baojia.

"Shit!" she yelled as he sliced through her arm with the razor-sharp *dao*. She had been distracted by the burning in her throat.

"Pay attention before I put another slice in you," he yelled. "Where is your head tonight?"

"I've got a lot on my mind," she spit at him as she walked to the wall to replace her *dao* in its scabbard. "Can we do water practice for a while?"

"Fine. But only because I'll probably take your head off at some point for pissing me off. Then I'd have to deal with Giovanni trying to take mine."

"Doubt he'd even care at this point," she muttered as she took off her outer shirt to reveal the black tank underneath. It was skin tight, but since water practice usually involved both of them getting soaked from head to toe, the last thing she needed was to have wet practice robes flapping around while she tried to move.

"Let me count the ways I'm completely uninterested in your lover's spat with your husband, Mrs. Vecchio," Baojia sneered. "Don't waste my time."

She swung an arm at him, reaching out with her amnis to fling the water from the stream to his face. "Don't call me 'Mrs. Vecchio.'"

"Fine." He spat out the water from behind bared fangs. "Let's play."

With a quick flick of his hand, she was soaked by a thin wall of water that materialized behind her. She rolled closer to the flowing stream, avoiding the charged air he aimed at her face. Since her change, Beatrice could sense the amnis in the air almost like floating currents that filled the room. And on each floating current, she could send her element. While she was only beginning to understand the force of it, Baojia was an expert.

The water vampire, though relatively young among his kind, was an expert fighter, and his mental control, along with his control over his amnis, was masterful. He could send a thin stream of energy anywhere in the large room, almost beyond her detection, and the water in the air was drawn to it. If the stream was solid enough, he could send a bolt of electricity through it, rendering her useless until she could manage to throw up a shield of her own to counter the attack. He had shocked her in this way countless times, though she was beginning to get a better handle on detecting the trace of his amnis brushing against hers.

"Now," he lectured as they moved through the room, circling each other and trying to use the water in the room to their own advantage, "water tricks are a waste of time. That is Lorenzo's problem; he's too showy. Don't bother with showing off. Over seventy percent of the Earth's surface is covered in water. It suffuses the air around you. It makes up a portion of every living being on the earth. And you are that element's master. You can control it. You can manipulate it, Beatrice."

"Does that mean I can manipulate bodies?" She had never even considered it.

"That's more difficult, because there is muscle and will involved, but eventually, yes, you will."

"Even vampires?"

"Only if they let you." A whip of water wrapped around her legs, throwing her to the ground as he answered her. "Remember, we all have amnis. If a vampire is protecting himself, your amnis will not break through unless you are far, far more powerful. It's almost unheard of. Humans, on the other hand, are your toys to play with." She rolled away and climbed to her feet.

"That's kind of creepy." Beatrice attempted to trip him with a thin strand she drew from the tip of her bare foot. He caught it in the corner of his eye and jumped over it with ease.

"Clever one."

"Thanks."

They spent another half an hour trying to best each other with water, combining it with kicks or punches as it benefited the fight. Baojia dominated her, and she spent most of her time on the defensive, but slowly, Beatrice began to predict his movements.

"You're a fast learner," he said with a playful smile. She was embarrassed by how that smile affected her. It had been weeks since anyone looked at her with that kind of approval or admiration.

"That's good to hear, considering how completely inept I feel most of the time."

"You're not inept," he said with a sudden scowl, as he almost knocked her over from the right. The water splashed her eyes, and she struggled to blink it out. "You're just young. And you're far more powerful than I was at less than a month old."

"Did you really leave China to work on the railroads?" She had been curious about the vampire's history from the beginning, but he was even more secretive than Giovanni.

"What? You think because you are a vampire now, I will confide in you?"

If she could have blushed, she would have. He knocked her back with a punch to her shoulder. "No! I'm just… sorry, I was just curious."

"Curiosity killed the little water vampire, you know." He smiled and she wondered what, exactly, he was referring to.

"I may be immortal now, but I don't think I changed *that* much."

"I don't think you did, either." She was distracted by their conversation and blinked in surprise when she twisted instinctively to dodge a kick to her midsection. "Sadly, Mrs. Vecchio, you have lost none of your... unusual appeal."

"What's that supposed to mean?"

His lips curled into a smile, but it wasn't a lighthearted one. "You'll give me a run for my money one of these days... Mrs. Vecchio." His arms lifted, calling the water from the stream into a thick coil that wrapped around her torso and spun her before knocking her over.

"Stop." She spat out the water that slapped her face as she fell. "Stop calling me that."

"Stop calling you 'Mrs. Vecchio?' But that's your name, isn't it?" He circled her, and his dark eyes held a trace of bitterness.

"My name is Beatrice."

"Not 'B' anymore, huh?" he said softly. She stood and they eyed each other, continuing to circle, each looking for any sign of weakness. The hairs on the back of her neck stood on end. "You are what he calls you?"

She narrowed her eyes, confused by his shifting moods. "What the hell is your problem?"

She felt the thin brush of amnis stroke the small of her back a second before he sent the shock. She winced and instinctively blocked it with a surge of her shield.

"Didn't fall over that time, did you?"

"No!"

"Stop thinking so damn much, B. You're stronger when you're angry."

Suddenly, Baojia came at her, a fury of fists and kicks that she tried to block, but even with her new speed, his blows knocked the air from her lungs. She couldn't keep up. He was aggressive; and, despite his iron control, she sensed an edge of anger in his blows.

"Hey—"

She was cut off by a fist.

"Defend yourself."

"What—"

A slap hit her cheek.

"Don't think about it. Hit me."

She stepped back, shaking her head to clear it. It didn't hurt the way it had as a human, but it still hurt. She could feel the cut on her lip closing even as he landed another blow.

"Hit me!"

"What are you—" A flurry of water pounded her. Beatrice tried to block each surge, but they soon knocked her to the ground. In a flash, Baojia had grabbed a sword and had the edge pressed against her neck.

"And you're dead."

She shoved the blade away, ignoring the bite of the blade against her skin, crawling to her knees and glaring at him as the blood rushed through her veins. Anger reared up and her fangs descended. "What do you want from me?" She felt her amnis swirl along her skin, out of control as her fists clenched. The water in the air quivered around her.

"You're more powerful than they realize, but you're not using it."

"What?"

"Instinct," he spat out. "You're still a human in vampire skin. Your muscles know these patterns, but your mind hasn't caught up. If Lorenzo attacked you tomorrow, he would kill you. Let your instincts take over and fight!"

"You want me to fight?"

"Yes!"

"Fine!" She hopped up and took a deep breath. She stood in her normal ready stance, but Baojia only sneered.

"Such a cute little girl, Mrs. Vecchio."

A thin red veil fell over her eyes, the fangs grew long in her mouth, and she felt her amnis pulse. Her heart beat its own unique rhythm, no longer bound by the trappings of biology. She felt the water in the air around her. Beatrice stopped concentrating on moving her limbs deliberately, as she had in *tai chi,* and just felt.

Baojia was crouched across from her.

"Hit me."

She let the amnis flow down her arm. Her fist landed in a blur, and Beatrice grinned.

He wiped the trickle of blood from the corner of his lip and smirked.

They started circling faster. She bent over, weaving back and forth, ready to strike. The amnis took over her limbs, and she began to move even faster, dipping and bending. In the back of her mind, she realized she was moving in ways she never would have attempted as a human, but there was no pain.

"Faster," he whispered.

She spun faster. Punching. Kicking. Flips and rolls did not challenge her immortal body.

It was effortless, she realized, as she took a deep, unnecessary breath. Her body was made for this. Her limbs moved without thought, the long practiced muscle memory colliding with her amnis as she moved in her own lethal ballet. Her amnis crackled as the water in the air was drawn to her, creating a thin sheen over her skin.

She flipped toward him, and her foot struck his face before she rolled away and shot up again. He sent another stream of water toward her, but she lifted a hand and blocked it with ease. Beatrice crouched down and swept his legs from under him before she rolled away. Then Baojia leapt on her shoulders. She bent back, nearly folding in half until he lost his grip and rolled away.

He reached out and grabbed her wrist, pulling her back to his chest. She could feel his cool breath at her neck.

"More," he whispered.

A swift hunger rose in her, and she thought of the blood dripping to the ground from her cracked mug. She wanted more.

More blood.

More fight.

More...

She bared her fangs, hissing as he shoved her away.

Beatrice stumbled for only a second before she was on her feet, spinning into a kick that landed near Baojia's ear. She smiled as her heart raced. She heard the door to the practice room swing open and was distracted for a second when she saw Giovanni enter. Baojia's kick landed on her jaw, knocking her back as she heard a snarl rip from her mate's throat.

A heartbeat later, she had been shoved back, and Giovanni pounced on Baojia, rolling across the floor in a tangle of limbs as the fire flared on his back and arms. She sent a wave of water over the two vampires, who were twisted in a growling heap.

Baojia pulled away and the two immortals began to circle each other. The water vampire's shirt was half torn from his body, and Beatrice could see burns healing at his neck. Giovanni eyed him, snarling as he placed himself between Beatrice and the perceived threat.

Beatrice knew instinctively that Baojia had triggered Giovanni's most territorial instincts, and she shook her head, trying to clear her mind so the practice session didn't end in death or serious injury. With her blood roiling, she was having difficulty focusing on anything other than the rippling muscle that spread over her mate's back, bared through the burned shirt and dripping water from the shower she had thrown at him. She could already see steam rising from his skin as his ire spiked.

Giovanni was magnificent. Pulsing energy and raw power. Beatrice could sense the amnis surge over his body. She could see the low flames licking along his chest. She could hear his blood roaring in her ears and smell the smoke pouring off his skin.

"Gio," she breathed out.

His head lifted and his eyes darted toward her voice and scent. Baojia leapt on him, but Giovanni only batted him across the room before he moved toward her, nostrils flared and fight forgotten as the blue flames swirled along his arms.

Not a word passed his lips when she pounced on him. Beatrice heard the hiss as her damp skin met his burning arms. He grabbed her, his fingers digging into the soft flesh of her hips and burning through the cloth that covered her before he strode toward the doors. As they sped down the hall, she saw Baojia, watching them with bared fangs from the door of the practice room. He narrowed his eyes and glared before he ran in the opposite direction.

They reached their chamber door, and Giovanni kicked it open.

"Fight later," he growled before he slammed it shut.

CHAPTER FIFTEEN

Penglai Mountain, China
November 2010

"Fight now," she panted as her fingers clutched his neck. Their mouths crashed together as they stumbled through the room. She felt his fangs run along her neck.

"Later."

"Now!"

He reared back, glaring at her before he threw her on the bed. Giovanni paced, silent and furious around the room. Finally, he spoke in a tightly controlled voice.

"How could you do it?"

"You know how!"

"No, I don't." He bent down and grabbed her chin, forcing her face to his. "Why don't you explain it, Beatrice? Explain why my *wife* would conspire with my best friend to turn herself without even telling me or letting me be involved!"

She rose onto her knees. "You know why. And I told you over and over again, you just didn't listen. You weren't the vulnerable one. You weren't the weak one. I was done with it. I was *ready*."

"You were not! You have no idea what you're giving up."

"I do, too. Don't be so arrogant. Do you think I don't know my own mind?"

He paced, still glancing over his shoulder toward her. She could see him struggling to extinguish the swirling flames that covered his torso.

"I can be your equal now," she continued, peeling the wet clothes from her body. "I'm not weak anymore. Look at me. My mind is my own. My body is my own. He can't make me do anything anymore."

Giovanni pounced on her, rolling in the sheets as he trapped her under his body. She reached out with her amnis, throwing a layer of cool air over his back as they were enveloped in a cloud of steam.

"Your body is mine," he growled through clenched teeth, "as mine is yours. You are my wife. My mate. We are *one*. And you shut me out." His angry eyes suddenly furrowed in pain. "Did it hurt? Were you frightened? Who held your hand as the life drained out of you? Whose eyes did you see before your heart stopped?"

She had no answer.

"That should have been me, Beatrice. Even if I could not turn you, it was my right to be there to care for you."

Bloody tears filled her eyes, and she lifted a hand, the cool water meeting the burning skin of his cheek. Tendrils of steam rose from the contact.

"I'm sorry," she whispered. "I'm sorry I shut you out." She reared up and captured his lips with her own, rolling them over with inhuman strength so she was straddling his hips. "But I'm not sorry I did it. I'm not sorry that I'm a vampire. And your anger is worth being with you forever."

He shook his head, fury still swirling in his eyes.

"And even if it takes years for you to forgive me, I'm not going anywhere. I have eternity now." She swallowed the lump in her throat. "But, please don't make me wait that long."

Giovanni lay motionless as she splayed her hands across the thick muscle of his chest. Both watched in fascination as the vapor rose where they touched. Their room was like a sauna, and thick clouds hung around them, making the lamps glow in the dark room. She could feel his heart pound beneath her hands, and she closed her eyes, arching her back in pleasure when his burning fingertips traced the bite scars that marked her breast, slowly swirling over her preternaturally sensitive skin.

Her fangs grew longer in her mouth, cutting her lip as they descended. She felt him rear up, tasting the trickle of blood that fell from her lips and down her throat. Giovanni licked up from her collarbone, locking his mouth with hers before his tongue invaded. She gasped when he stroked along the length of her fangs.

"Yes," Beatrice hissed as the hint of his rich blood filled her mouth. She pulled him back, fusing their lips as she traced along his own sharp teeth. The taste of their mingled blood seeped down her throat.

Smokey.

Sweet.

Hot.

Cool.

His blood reminded her of the rich taste of the whiskey they had shared before their first kiss, years before when he was hiding and she was human. The memory gave her pause, and she drew back, licking the last of their blood from his lips before she looked at him.

Giovanni's eyes were closed, and he seemed to sway in her arms. She peeled the scraps of his shirt away and pressed their skin together. His chest burned against hers. Their hearts pounded together, the usually slow movement of their veins excited by blood and anger. His eyes were still closed as she began to rock against him, trailing her fangs across his chest until he shuddered.

"*Beatrice…*" His voice was rough, his hands smoothed down her shoulders, kneading the small of her back as she pressed their hips together and he loosed a low moan. Her fingers threaded through his hair and she brought her mouth to his in a whisper of a kiss, flooding her lips with amnis. Their energy twined, and Giovanni took a deep breath, arching his back and opening his eyes, which finally met hers with tenderness.

"I missed you," she whispered.

"You are my balance in this life," he said before he pierced his tongue and kissed her again. She pulled back and drew blood in her own mouth.

"In every life," she finished.

Their lips met, and they drank the other in, their amnis twisting and melding so that Beatrice couldn't feel where she ended and he began. Giovanni picked her up and pulled at the thin leggings she wore to practice. She pulled at the buckle on his belt, struggling as he held her.

"Beatrice…" He finally stood up to rid himself of the last of his clothing as he eyed her in the center of the bed. The urgency returned, along with her hunger, and she eyed the thick vein in his throat.

"Gio?"

"Yes?" She heard the low growl in his throat as he stalked toward her.

"I need…" She swallowed the burning in her throat.

Giovanni braced himself over her as she backed against the headboard. "Tell me what you need."

"I need…" She eyed his neck.

"*Sì, Tesoro*," he purred, and his tongue stroked the fangs that peeked from her mouth. "Feed from me; I have only one request." He caught her lower lip between his teeth, biting down as her heart raced.

"What?"

When he whispered, his fangs nicked her ear. "*Do not be gentle.*"

Beatrice hissed before she reached up, pulled his hair to bare his neck, and struck.

Giovanni roared, pulling her close, and fusing their bodies as she drank. He rolled them over and she lay on top of him, drawing the thick blood from his neck as he writhed beneath her.

He grasped her hips, sheathing himself deep in her body. She pulled away and arched back with a gasp of pleasure. He reared up and Beatrice clutched his arms before leaning down to sink her fangs into him on the other side, piercing the curve where his neck met his shoulder.

"Yes." He hummed in pleasure before he bared his own fangs and lifted her arm, biting his teeth into the soft flesh above her elbow as she gripped his hair. He felt her shudder for a moment before her mouth returned to the thick muscle at his shoulder. They drank from each other, their blood fueling the heated release they both sought. The room began to fill with steam as her skin touched his, each pushing the other closer to ecstasy.

Beatrice pulled away and searched for his mouth. He met her kiss, both of their lips wet with the other's blood. Fire and water, they met each other as equals as they reached their release together.

They lay together for what could have been days. Nothing else existed for them. Lost in each other, they drifted, their energy spinning them in a thousand silken threads. He lost count of how many times she drank from him, but his hunger for her bite was never sated. Again and again, he pressed her closer, his amnis seeking hers as his blood traveled through her body.

The room filled with clouds as they moved together, only to gather on Beatrice's body as she rested, an endless cycle of heat and release coalescing around them. Giovanni drank from her, her energy swirling and pulsing in waves. She fell into daytime rest, but he woke her, a cup of fresh blood near the bed and his mouth traveling over her body. He had no idea how much time had passed.

It didn't matter, he thought, as they moved together.

They were eternal.

"I feel... drunk."

Giovanni chuckled as she lay boneless across his chest, her arm draped across his waist in their bed. The steam had finally dissipated in the room. "I'll take that as a compliment."

Beatrice blinked, but didn't make a characteristic smart remark. He smiled. She did sound drunk.

She asked, "Is it the blood?"

"I have no idea. I've never shared blood with anyone before. It's probably a combination of that and our amnis combining."

She stretched out next to him, and her energy flowed over his body, touching each corner of his skin like a feather.

"You feel so good," he breathed out, shivering at her touch. "Is that what my amnis always felt like to you? Soft? Like feathers or silk?"

"Hmm," she mused. "Kind of, but hot. Your energy is always hot, even when your skin isn't."

He frowned. "Not painful?"

"No." She shook her head. "Just warm. I've always loved to feel you. From the beginning, I've loved that."

"I love it, too," he whispered, brushing the hair from her face, in awe of the startling creature next to him. It was Beatrice, but stronger. Delicate, but not breakable as she had been.

"Beatrice?"

"Hmm?"

"I understand." She looked up at him, her eyes wide at his quiet declaration.

"You—you do?"

He gave her a small nod. "It still hurts that you chose to go through that without me. And I still think there are reasons you should have waited, but I understand why you did it. And I understand why you wanted to do it here."

She shook her head. "I never wanted to hurt you, Gio, but you're so stubborn. And I was so worried—"

"Shhh," he whispered, leaning over to kiss her. "I know I can be stubborn." He lifted an eyebrow. "But so can you."

She smiled. "You're stuck with me now."

"And I am *eternally* grateful," he whispered.

Her hand began brushing over him again, combining with the current to arouse him. Giovanni had little hair on his body, most of it burning off when the fire took over, but what little there was lifted and followed her fingers, as if pleading for attention.

"I had no idea you liked biting so much," she murmured as her lips trailed down his chest.

He took a deep breath, releasing it as he enjoyed the feel of her mouth and the scrape of her teeth. "I had no idea I did, either. Maybe I didn't until it was you doing the biting."

She gave a throaty laugh and looked up, her fangs gleaming in the candlelight. "I like it."

"Good," Giovanni said with a hoarse voice as she bent her head, sinking her fangs into the V of muscle that ran from his waist. He arched his back and gave a low hum of pleasure. "What do I taste like, Beatrice?"

"Your blood?"

"Yes."

Her tongue lapped at the punctures in his skin, licking the blood before the wounds closed.

"Like smoke. Spicy. Rich."

He smiled. "Like your favorite foods."

She cocked her head, smiling at him. "Yeah, I guess so. That's convenient." She grinned, then leaned down to taste again. "You're like… my own hot sauce."

He burst into laughter. "That's what I get for marrying a Texan."

Giovanni pulled her up to kiss her lips and taste his blood on her tongue. It was startlingly arousing.

"And I think I discovered why the food here is so bland."

"Yes," he brushed a hand through her hair. "When they cook for vampires, it's very mild. Your taste buds will be heightened for quite some time. I think it was ten years before I tasted any food that didn't seem too strong. Like everything else, you will adapt."

"Gio?"

"Hmm?" His lips moved along her neck, nipping and testing the soft skin.

"What do I taste like? Is it different now?"

"The same," he breathed out, "except perhaps a little stronger, sweeter."

Giovanni had always loved the flavor of her blood and had worried about taking too much for that reason alone when she was human. Now, it wasn't an issue. What they took from each other couldn't harm them when they were exchanging blood. He could already feel his energy swirling inside his mate, heightening their connection and their pleasure.

Beatrice slid down and nibbled across his waist before she sank her teeth in the other side of his waist, her fang marks mirror images in his perfect, sculpted body.

He pulled her up to meet his mouth again, as his fingers fluttered along the crease of her thigh.

"I'm keeping you locked in our room for the next several nights. Just in case you had any plans, cancel them. No working. No training. You're *mine*."

"Oh?" she gasped as he rolled her onto her back. "Are you sure that's a good idea?"

"Yes. I'll have them deliver some blood to us. That's all we need."

Her fingers traced the arch of his brow. "I just need you."

Giovanni pressed his hips into hers, and she wrapped her legs around his waist. They kissed leisurely for what could have been minutes or hours. Time had lost all meaning to him.

"I want to stay with you forever," he whispered, looking into her eyes. "I want the world to go away."

Beatrice lifted a hand to his cheek, stroking it and igniting another surge of desire. "I do, too." She closed her eyes and arched up. "Love me now."

"I will love you always."

It was a quiet knock on the door some days later that finally roused them out of their safe cocoon. Tenzin stood in the hall with a solemn look on her face. Giovanni wrapped himself in a sheet and stood silent in the doorway, listening, but still refusing to speak to her.

"I have a message from the Elders."

He cocked an eyebrow.

"Lan is on the way home."

His heart dropped in his chest, and he finally spoke.

"How long?"

"Two weeks."

Giovanni nodded and shut the door. He walked back to the bedroom, wrapping Beatrice in his arms as she drifted in her daytime rest.

CHAPTER SIXTEEN

Penglai Mountain, China
November 2010

"I need to talk to you about something."

Beatrice looked up from the bowl of noodles. She was eating a light meal after rising for the evening. "What's up?"

She had discovered she was better able to eat some mild foods and was more comfortable with a little in her stomach. Between that and all the blood she had been drinking, both his own and human, Giovanni was satisfied Beatrice was as strong as she could be. Her control was impressive, her amnis was surprisingly powerful, but she was still young. He only hoped she could avoid any sort of serious physical confrontation for some time, though her intense training with Tenzin and Baojia seemed to be paying off.

"Tenzin came to the door as you were falling asleep this morning. Elder Lan will be back in two weeks."

She didn't look frightened, only resigned. "I guess we have two more weeks of what I'm considering our honeymoon, then."

Giovanni laughed. "*This* is our honeymoon?"

She shrugged. "Well, we did spend time in Cochamó, but that just feels like home. And with the move and everything, we didn't really get to take one after we came back. Then we came here and I started training so much... so, yeah."

"I would like to point out that if you had let me tell anyone we were married, they might have been more understanding and allowed us some time away."

"You *did* tell a few 'someones' we were married." She rolled her eyes. "Apparently when I was unconscious. I haven't heard the end of it."

Giovanni only laughed and came to sit next to her on the chaise. He pulled her feet into his lap. "I want to take you to Italy when all this is over. I'd like to take you there for a long trip. Maybe that can be our real honeymoon."

"Can't be too long. Ben's going to forget about us one of these days. We are the worst fake aunt and uncle in history."

"I very much doubt that he'll forget us. He'll be fine. Maybe…" He cocked his head. "Maybe if we go, we could take him with us."

"Huh?" She curled her lip.

He laughed. "Not as much of a honeymoon, but we could make it a group trip. Maybe Kirby and Dez would want to come with us and help with Ben. I don't know that Caspar and your grandmother would want to leave home for that long, but if Kirby and Dez come, we could go for the summer. They could look after the boy during the day. We'd still get plenty of time to ourselves, but we'd be able to spend time with them, too."

Her face suddenly fell, and tears sprang to her eyes. "I'm not gonna be able to see any of them for a while, am I?"

Giovanni shook his head when one of the harsher realities of her new life struck her. She set her food down and crawled into his lap. He wrapped his arms around her and kissed her temple. "My grandma," she whispered. "Caspar."

"They are both in very good health. And you're very strong for a new vampire. Very strong, Beatrice. After a year or so…"

She nodded her head, still tucking herself into his chest.

"I need to talk to you about something else. Something I should have spoken to you about years ago." Giovanni took a deep breath. "Speaking of Italy… of Rome, that is, I need to tell you about Livia."

"Livia? Your friend in Rome?"

He shook his head. "I wouldn't call her a friend. Livia is… well, it's complicated. You remember"—his voice dropped to a whisper and he murmured in her ear—"you remember about my father. Don't say anything, remember there are many sensitive ears in the palace."

Beatrice nodded again, pressing closer.

"You must know, you and my son are the only beings on earth that know the truth about Andros. And it *must* stay that way."

She drew back and looked at him, the question evident in her frown.

"What we did... what *I* did... it is a very grave crime. To kill your own sire is a very grave crime."

"So, everyone thinks—"

"Lorenzo and I told Livia that the villa was burned by marauders. That Andros was killed in the fire."

They were still speaking in whispers, but his ears were alert to the sound of any passerby in the hallway. They had been left alone, for the most part, but he could take no chances.

"But really, Lorenzo killed him, right?"

"He sent all the servants away and dragged Andros into the sunlight when he was in the depths of daytime rest. I saw the ashes in the courtyard when I woke. Paulo was sitting in the corner, weeping and shaking. I took him to Crotone the next night and turned him. We burned the villa before we left."

"And the library?"

"That is more complicated. And I don't know what happened to all of it, only Lorenzo does. It's one of the reasons I'd like to take him alive, if possible."

"But your uncle's books were safe, so your father's—"

"Paulo told me that after my uncle's collection was burned in Florence, Andros became paranoid. He kept some of his books in Crotone. Some of them at the villa my uncle left me near Ferrara. Some at the property in Perugia. It was scattered, and since Lorenzo was the one who oversaw the property and the human servants, I did not keep track of it as I should have. When he told me later that most things had been lost, destroyed or stolen, I believed him. He must have been planning for some time."

"Wouldn't Andros have noticed?"

"I don't know what he told Andros. After he died, I was focused on survival, and I foolishly trusted that my father would have kept track of Paulo. He had been with Andros since he was a child and my father trusted him, possibly even more than me."

"Why?"

"Andros thought he could control Paulo. He thought... my father had little respect for humans, Beatrice. He didn't really understand them anymore. He thought Paulo adored him. He couldn't see the resentment because he didn't really look. And Paulo was very good at presenting a front, just like Andros."

"So, everyone in the vampire world thinks your father was... a good guy?"

Giovanni shrugged. "Define 'good.' Andros was highly respected. Feared. Admired. Most never saw his madness or his cruelty. He was the consummate politician, a master manipulator. Even adored in some circles as the highest example of learning and culture. If it was ever known that we killed him..."

"What would happen? And why hasn't Lorenzo told anyone in all these years?"

Giovanni snorted. "Paulo would be killed first. He was human when he killed Andros."

"But you—"

"My life would also be forfeit."

She spoke in an angry whisper. "To who? You're the one he tortured. You're the one he kidnapped and held captive for ten years. Who has the right—"

"Livia," he whispered, leaning so his lips brushed her ear, "is not just one of the most powerful vampires in the Old World. Not just the vampire who helped me to get you back. Who spoke for me with the council in Athens. They never would have allowed me to attack Lorenzo the night I took you unless she had intervened on my behalf. But Livia has always had a strange sort of affection for me, because Livia..." His breath caught for a moment, and he pressed Beatrice closer. "Livia was my father's wife."

A few nights later, Tenzin, Stephen, and Baojia joined them in the living area to talk about Lan's return and what it would mean when the council met.

"It's a sort of trial, but not one you would recognize, Beatrice." Tenzin was sipping tea and looked bored. "They do it mostly for their own amusement. Everyone knows how they will decide before they go in; it's all worked out ahead of time in private negotiations."

"Well," Stephen added, "except for Lan. In this matter..." He only gave a shrug.

Beatrice looked around, confused. "What? What does that mean?"

Giovanni leaned forward. "No one knows how Lan will vote, and he's the most unpredictable."

"Or she," Beatrice whispered. The whole table laughed. "Really?" she asked. "No one knows?"

Tenzin smirked at Giovanni. "Have you ever seen Lan get angry?"

"Only once," he grimaced. "Not pleasant."

"It doesn't happen often." Tenzin's eyes danced toward Beatrice. "Try to imagine an extremely old and powerful fire vampire having a temper tantrum. It takes a lot to get Lan truly angry, but when she does, numerous vampires usually end up dead. Lots of humans, too."

Giovanni saw Beatrice's eyes grow wide. "But that doesn't happen often, right?"

"No, Tesoro, it takes much to provoke Lan. Despite his playful appearance, he's one of the canniest vampires on the council."

"I'm not going to lie, the whole he or she thing is kind of annoying."

"Agreed," Stephen added quietly.

"He," Baojia smiled, "or she doesn't feel the need to inform anyone. Are you going to be the one to ask?"

"No," Stephen and Beatrice said together.

"Getting back to the trial," Tenzin said, "the council is fairly evenly split. My father and Elder Lu are firmly our allies. The Immortal Woman will side with Giovanni, because he's a fire vampire, and she's like that. Royal Uncle Cao will go along with Lu because he doesn't want to disagree."

"What about Elder Li?" Stephen asked.

Giovanni shook his head. "You know how the earth vampires tend to be. It seems that he will most likely follow Zhongli Quan since they are typically allies and he won't want to disrupt that. Since Zhongli is the one who invited Lorenzo to Penglai, we can assume he'll vote with him."

"Han Xiang?" Baojia asked after the second water vampire on the council.

"He'll vote with Zhongli," Tenzin said. "He always does, just to spite Lu."

"But," Stephen directed himself to Beatrice, "Earth vampires also tend to be the ones most amenable to compromise, so if a reasonable one is offered, Iron Crutch Li and Royal Uncle Cao would probably go in that direction."

"What kind of compromise could there be?" Beatrice asked. "Lu's monks have the books. Lorenzo wants it. Giovanni wants it. Someone has to win." No one spoke, and Beatrice looked around the table. "So, by my calculation, that leaves four elders on our voting side and three on theirs. And no one knows what Lan will do."

Giovanni said, "He could vote for us."

"She could vote for Lorenzo, too." Tenzin shrugged. "I've known Lan for years and I don't even know how she'll vote."

"Again with the he and she thing…" Beatrice muttered under her breath. "So, if Lan votes against us, that leaves it at a tie. What happens then?"

Giovanni's eyes darted to Tenzin's and both of them smiled.

"What was that look?" Beatrice asked. "That was a look."

"A tie means that your husband could challenge Lorenzo," Baojia said.

"I don't like that option!"

"Neither would Lorenzo," Tenzin snorted. "Giovanni would put an end to him quite easily. It's really the best thing that could happen."

Beatrice leaned forward. "But then we'll never know what happened to the books. Or why he wants the elixir. I think we need to know that stuff, don't you guys?"

"You aren't worried, are you?" Tenzin looked scornful. "Have you ever really seen your mate fight? He's ruthless. Lorenzo wouldn't have a chance. I trained him myself."

"And he has that irritating habit of bursting into flames," Baojia said.

Stephen raised a hand. "I have to agree with Beatrice on this. As much as I'd like to see my sire dead, I think he has information we need. Lorenzo wants this elixir for a reason, and I think it's obvious at this point that there are others involved in his scheme. We need to know who they are, or we're back in the same boat of not knowing who may be after us."

"Lorenzo said he had made promises to people. When he had me on the freighter, he said he had 'made promises to people who were starting to doubt he could deliver.' There's obviously someone else involved. At least one other person, maybe more."

"And," Stephen added, "if my contact is correct that Lorenzo was researching pharmaceutical labs in Eastern Europe—possibly to produce it—then he must have someone who can fund him. That wouldn't be cheap, and B stole most of his money."

"You did?" Baojia turned to Beatrice with a look of amusement. "I always wondered why a college girl had that much cash. Ernesto never said. How clever of you."

"Thanks!" She smiled.

Giovanni swallowed a growl, but he caught Baojia's eye and threw an arm around the back of Beatrice's chair.

Tenzin crossed her arms over her chest. "So, killing the annoying one is not the ideal outcome. But, if it happens, it happens. If there's a tie, Gio has to challenge Lorenzo; that is what's done. And if he challenges him, he *will* kill him."

"He can't just like… take him captive or something?"

Tenzin shook her head. "Nope. All or nothing. Only one of them would be allowed to leave the island."

"Great." Beatrice sighed.

Giovanni was torn. He wanted to find his father's books so badly he could taste it, but the prospect of killing Lorenzo was also rather alluring. Since it was out of his control, he chose not to torment himself. He would do what he needed to do. Soon after, the group split for the evening; Beatrice kissed him goodbye before leaving with Tenzin and Baojia for more training. He and Stephen went to the library and dove back into research again.

A week and a half flew by, and the five of them stayed barricaded in Tenzin's quarters except for one brief trip to the open ocean for Giovanni and Beatrice. She was ecstatic, ebullient in her joy and surrounded by her element. She dove under the surface, playing for hours. She wasn't as strong as she might have been, and Giovanni suspected that, like her father, she would draw more elemental strength from fresh water, though she could easily manipulate both.

Late on Friday night, Tenzin, Beatrice, Stephen and Baojia were playing a game of poker by the fire while Giovanni read a book. He saw Beatrice's nostrils flare a second before a knock came at the door. She burst up from the table, rushing toward the door, but Stephen quickly caught her, holding her back from the human servant someone had foolishly sent.

Giovanni walked over and took Beatrice's arms, braceleting her wrists with one hand before he grabbed her around the waist and took her from her father, carrying her to the corner. She snarled at him, baring her teeth and whipping around in an attempt to get away and hunt the human. He waited patiently for Tenzin to send the servant away.

"Order some blood, at least a liter," he called over his shoulder to Stephen as Beatrice cursed at him in Spanish. Baojia stood behind him, ready for her to break away. Giovanni was reluctantly grateful. A newly turned vampire in the midst of bloodlust could be surprisingly strong. When he could hear the human's steps receding, he shoved her into the corner, braced his legs around hers, and brought his wrist to her mouth. She tore at it, biting hard into the flesh as she glared at him with narrowed eyes.

"Shhh," he murmured. Soon, she was calmer, and he let go of her wrists, bringing his hand up to stroke her hair. "Drink what you need, my love. Your father is getting you more blood."

He could tell when reason grabbed hold of her again because her eyes cleared and bloody tears leaked from the corners. She let go of his wrist and wrapped her arms around his waist, leaning into him.

"I'm sorry," she whispered. "I'm so sorry. That was the first time I've smelled a live one. Their blood—"

"I know. Don't apologize; it's perfectly natural, and we were unprepared. It's fine, Beatrice." He still stroked her face as he heard Stephen enter the room and Baojia faded back. Giovanni could smell the warm blood from the corner. "Go, drink. You hadn't fed tonight. We've been too casual about it, being isolated like this. You'll need to be more prepared in the future."

"What about the trial?" She sniffed and wiped her eyes as she sat at the table. "There are usually humans in the hall. I don't want to hurt anyone."

Tenzin came to sit next to her, holding a folded piece of paper. "There won't be any during the trial. It's vampire only. If you were still human, you wouldn't be allowed in." Giovanni caught the quick gleam in Tenzin's eye.

"What is it?" he asked.

"Lan's back. They're meeting tomorrow night."

Giovanni nodded. He had no sense of nervousness, only a grim kind of resolve. Whatever happened, he would be getting his way.

Either the council could vote with him, or he could kill Lorenzo.

Giovanni tried to ignore the pervasive sense of foreboding when he rose next to Beatrice the following afternoon. By nightfall, they were both fed and dressed in the formal clothing that Zhang provided them. They wore the soft blue-grey robes and pants that the scholars of the court wore. Their collars were adorned with a single jewel indicating their element, deep blue lapis lazuli for Beatrice and a blood-red jasper for Giovanni. Beatrice tied her hair back into a subdued knot at the nape of her neck.

They met Tenzin, Stephen, and Baojia in the front room. Stephen also wore the grey scholar's robes, but Tenzin wore a silver robe similar in style to her father's formal white, which was decorated with an ornately jeweled Mandarin collar with dotted moonstones and pearls. Her hair, which she usually tied back, flowed around her shoulders in a long, black sweep. Baojia looked severe in the plain black robes worn by the palace guards. They were met and escorted by one of the green-clad administrators who worked for Zhang.

"Gio?" He heard Beatrice speak softly as they crossed the gardens.

"Yes?"

"My dad was explaining all the color meanings to me. If yellow is supposed to be the most beautiful color, why do the servants wear it around here? Wouldn't that be reserved for the Elders or something?"

He smiled. Trust Beatrice to be curious instead of nervous on the way to meet an enemy. "Many of the servants here are monks, Beatrice, so they wear their yellow or saffron robes. Most of the other humans dress in brown. But the ones you have seen tending the gardens are almost all monks. It is considered a great honor to serve in the palace of the Eight Immortals."

"Oh, I guess that makes sense."

"The elders wear white because it is the symbol of death."

"That… doesn't make much sense."

He smiled again. "But they are the masters of death, aren't they?"

They climbed the stone steps leading to the great hall, even Tenzin was oddly subdued as they made their way to the front of the room and took their place in front of Zhang's leather throne.

The elder was already seated, looking calm and fearsome, his hair loose and long as his daughter's. At times, it was easy to forget that Tenzin and her father belonged to a far less civilized past than the one represented by most of the sophisticated vampires of the Chinese court. With his hair flowing around him, seated on his saddle-like throne, Elder Zhang Guo looked like the ancient warlord he was. Tenzin stood behind her father, playing the loyal daughter for appearance's sake. Even the most powerful of immortals would tremble to challenge the pair.

Giovanni glanced at Beatrice, who was taking in everything with her perceptive eyes, measuring each Elder and the people who scurried around them. Baojia stood behind her, watching, always watching, anyone that came too close. Once again, Giovanni found himself reluctantly grateful.

"Baojia, will you be able to translate for Beatrice?" he asked quietly. "I'm sure this will all be in Mandarin, and I will have to speak at some point."

"Not if you want me to be able to concentrate on protecting her."

"I can translate," Stephen whispered.

"Anything you don't want overheard, say in Spanish," Giovanni said. "It's not widely spoken here and will be the most secure."

Stephen nodded as Zhongli's guards entered the hall. The Elder was already at the front of the room, but the guards ushered Lorenzo between them. Giovanni scoffed when he saw his son wearing scholar's robes like their own. Though the pursuit of knowledge was far from a priority with him, Lorenzo was nothing if not a master of appearances. In that way, Giovanni supposed Lorenzo truly *had* become Andros's heir.

Giovanni was curious about the company he was keeping. There were eight guards around Lorenzo, all wind vampires from the look of their robes, which bore the milky moonstone associated with the wind element. Eight. A lucky number, particularly when associated with business. He had a feeling that the selection was not without calculation. All the Elders were superstitious, but none more so than Lorenzo's host, Zhongli Quan.

Little by little, the hall filled, until eventually, every elder was on his or her throne and their entourages filled the room in front of them. Energy buzzed, the collision of electrical currents charging the air. The torches and lamps that lit the room flickered, and a soft wind brushed through the crowd. Everyone was there and waiting.

Except for Elder Lan.

Giovanni exchanged a look with Baojia, who only shrugged. "No one's surprised, are they?"

Suddenly, every head turned when a laugh rang from the back of the room, and a high-pitched voice called out, "Are you all waiting for me? How amusing!"

The childlike elder tripped into the room with a huge smile adorning his or her face. Just as Lan passed them, Giovanni saw the elder pause for only a fraction of a second. Lan caught Beatrice's eye as she stood next to Giovanni and gave her a playful wink.

Giovanni looked down at Beatrice, then back to Lan, who had already moved up to the throne at the front of the room. Beatrice looked up at Giovanni with an expression of equal confusion.

"What the hell did that mean?" she murmured in Spanish between clenched lips.

"Tesoro… I have no idea."

CHAPTER SEVENTEEN

Penglai Mountain, China
November 2010

"There's still something I'm not getting about this," Beatrice whispered to her father in Spanish as the formal greetings of the court began. Each elder was standing to greet the assembled vampires and most of them seemed highly impressed with their own voices.

"There's a lot about this that I don't understand," Stephan whispered back.

"Why did he agree to this?"

"Who?"

"Lorenzo," she said. "Why did he agree to this? Everyone seems to be sure that the Elders will either vote for Gio or tie, both of which leave Lorenzo at a disadvantage, so why did he ask for this trial?"

Stephen shrugged. "Perhaps he didn't plan for it. When he made the request, it was right after Lorenzo discovered he had no claim over me. Maybe it was not well thought out."

"I'm not buying it," Beatrice whispered as the Immortal Woman began to speak. Like Lan Caihe, He Xiangu was not as long-winded as the rest of the council. Thinking about her own terse mate, Beatrice wondered if it was a characteristic of all fire vampires. "Lorenzo plans everything. He may be totally different from Gio in a lot of ways, but not that. They both plan for every contingency."

"Beatrice, I don't know what to tell you."

"Shhh," Giovanni turned to them and made a shushing motion as Tenzin's father stood to speak.

"Immortal brothers and sisters of the council, I would take this opportunity to introduce an immortal sired in my household these past weeks. Most of you know the dear friend of my only child, Tenzin, was turned by my daughter's mate in my home. We welcome you to our honored company, Beatrice De Novo. Daughter of water, mated to fire. Kinswoman of Don Ernesto Alvarez of California. Honored friend of my house and learned scribe."

Though Beatrice had been briefed on the importance of her formal introduction, she still felt like blushing, even though she couldn't. Her heart began to beat as she stepped forward, nodding deeply to Zhang, then turned to the rest of the room and gave a slight nod. She stepped back next to Giovanni, with her father standing behind her. Her eyes scanned the room, searching out Lorenzo to gauge his reaction.

She finally spotted his blond curls in the middle of a group of Zhongli's guards. Far from the anger she had expected, Lorenzo looked positively gleeful, and his eyes looked her over with clear interest and approval. She knew Giovanni had spotted him when she felt his hand brush hers. His amnis reached out and wrapped around her waist.

Stephen leaned over once Zhang had stopped speaking. "Why do they call us scribes, B? It makes me feel old."

She snorted a little under her breath. "Because it sounds cooler than assistant professor and librarian?"

"Laugh if you want," she heard Baojia say as his eyes scanned the room, "but Zhang gave you that title deliberately. It is now part of who you are here, and it's not something this court takes lightly."

"Come to think of it, B, I've never been named a scribe in any formal way," Stephen said. "That is significant."

"And I was not informed of it," Giovanni muttered. All four were speaking in Spanish, and Beatrice could see the curious looks from the few vampires around who could hear them.

"I think we need to shut up now," Beatrice said.

"Quite right, Tesoro."

Zhongli was speaking. "It is my guest, Lorenzo, who has brought this petition to us. He claims the right of ownership on a certain book that is in the possession of Elder Lu Dongbin's monks." Zhongli nodded toward Lorenzo, who stepped forward.

"The book in question belonged to the sire of my own father, Giovanni di Spada of Florence, Giovanni Vecchio to the company here. Though it was intended for my father, the great library of Nikolaos Andreas was scattered five hundred years ago. It is only with great care and much time and expense that I have managed to find a few valued pieces from my grand-sire's collection."

"Liar," Beatrice whispered.

Giovanni shot her a look. "Shh."

"Imagine my dismay when those same books were stolen by my own son when he ran from my home. He took this manuscript, along with several others that were worth a considerable amount of money. I'm sure he has sold many of them." Lorenzo shook his head sadly. "But this one in particular was very dear to Andreas and it is my hope that it may be returned to my rightful ownership."

Royal Uncle Cao, the earth vampire, leaned forward. "But if it was intended for your sire, then why do you have a claim on it?"

It was Zhongli that responded. "Surely the Elder must recognize that my guest is the one who found the book. If Giovanni Vecchio wanted it, surely he would have been the one to find it."

"Perhaps he would have," the Immortal Woman spoke, "if he had known it had survived the destruction of Andreas's library."

"Indeed," Elder Lu added. "It seems to me that the original intentions of the owner, the scholar, Nikolaos Andreas, should be honored in this matter. He intended it for his only son; it should belong to his son. I'm sure Giovanni Vecchio would reimburse his child for any expense he incurred while searching for the book."

"Indeed," Giovanni spoke up, "I would be happy to reimburse Lorenzo for any expenses, though I sent him into the world with wealth, as is the custom."

"I was wondering," Elder Zhang spoke, "why your son took these books, Lorenzo. You imply that it was for money. Did he not have an allowance from his sire?"

"Why would you?" Beatrice whispered.

All eyes turned to Stephen as he spoke to the hall. "Sadly, my father did not send me into the world with anything, Elder Zhang. I had to fend for myself."

A low murmur of disapproval filled the room. Beatrice looked at Giovanni. "What? What's the big deal? I mean, not every vampire is turned by their choice, right? It's not always friendly. Why would Lorenzo give my father anything?"

"Even in cases where the vampire is unwilling, Beatrice, it is still customary after a certain number of years to send a child into the world with some degree of independence if they want to leave. Since I was Andros's only child, he would have given at least a quarter of his wealth to me if he had sent me away."

"What? Really?"

"Yes, I wouldn't have gone—he had far too much influence over me—but when I sent Lorenzo out on his own, I sent a third of my wealth with him."

"It is the custom among our kind," Baojia whispered. "If you send a child away from your care, out of your aegis, it is considered very shameful to send them away with nothing."

"But Dad escaped."

The room was still milling, and Beatrice could see a sour expression on Lorenzo's face.

"My son," Lorenzo spoke over the crowd, "Stephen, ran away from my aegis. If he had told me his desire to leave, I would surely have given him gold, as is proper."

A few vampires on Zhongli's side nodded, as if that explanation was satisfactory, but Beatrice could tell by the subtle frowns and veiled expressions of the vampires in the hall that the mood of the room had shifted against Lorenzo.

"Perhaps he took these books out of spite," Elder Han, the water vampire, said. "Why should we honor the actions of a spiteful child?"

"Why should we deliberate at all?" Elder Lan finally spoke, and the attention of the room swung toward the previously silent vampire. "Why shouldn't it remain with Lu's monks? I'm sure they are taking good care of it."

More nods were seen among the Elders, and Lorenzo pursed his lips.

Beatrice didn't like the idea. They needed to find out more about the book, and currently, it was being held at a monastery of unknown location, and they couldn't even examine it. If they were ever going to find out what the secret of Geber's elixir was, they needed the manuscript.

"What is this book that we deliberate over? What makes it so valuable that it warrants the time of the council?" Iron Crutch Li asked.

Lorenzo stepped forward, confident again. "It is an unfinished manuscript of the alchemist, Jabir ibn Hayyan, or Geber, as he is known in the West. It is not among his published works, but Geber was an acquaintance of Andreas, and it was given to him for safekeeping. It had… sentimental value to my grand-sire."

Beatrice asked. "Is that true?"

Giovanni shook his head. "I have no idea. It's possible, but my father had little regard for alchemy when I knew him. He considered it more superstition than science."

"This claim seems very straightforward to me," Lorenzo's ally, Zhongli, said. "The book is clearly Lorenzo's."

"Of course it is," Beatrice muttered.

Elder Han spoke. "This book may have been intended for Andreas's son, but he forfeited his rights by not pursuing the manuscript when it was lost. I see no claim here by Giovanni Vecchio."

"I see no claim here by Lorenzo," the Immortal Woman spoke up. "Can we not honor the intentions of the great Andreas and give his property to his only child? Let this conflict be between sire and child. The book belongs to Vecchio."

At that point, whispers began to circulate the room, and Beatrice looked around. The hall seemed to be split exactly as Tenzin had predicted, and Beatrice's eyes sought out the one elder that no one seemed to be able to predict. When she found Lan, the enigmatic vampire was looking straight at her. Lan scanned the crowd, propped herself up on her knees, and addressed the gathering of immortals.

"Brothers and sisters," Lan said with a smile. "I feel at a disadvantage after my travels. It seems that so much has passed in my absence. May I be permitted to ask a few questions?"

Lu Dongbin leaned forward and nodded to Lan. "Of course, Elder Lan. The hall is yours."

"Oh good!" Lan clapped and grinned. "Dr. Vecchio, did you send your son into the world with wealth?"

"Yes," Giovanni answered respectfully. "I sent him with half of my gold, and I gave him property in our homeland, as well. It is what my own sire would have wanted."

"You honor your father, Dr. Vecchio. And did you send him with any of your father's library?"

"It was my own son that had the care of my father's books when he was human," Giovanni said.

Careful, careful, careful. Beatrice's heart raced.

"After my father's home had been raided, and Andros died in the fires, Lorenzo gave me the grave news that my father's property near Ferrara had also been ransacked by brigands and the majority of the library lost. Rumors abounded for many years that this piece or that had survived, but there was little fact. My own business now centers on finding lost books and antiquities, in part to find what I can of my father's collection. But I had no knowledge of this manuscript until a few years ago. I have been searching for it since I learned of it."

"So you *were* searching for it?"

"Yes, Elder Lan."

"And found it here?"

"In the stewardship of Elder Lu's monks." Giovanni nodded at Lu. "I have full confidence they have handled it with care and respect."

"And do you ask for it to be returned now?"

Giovanni paused, as if considering. "Though I would prefer that the book return to my own library, I ask only to be able to examine it. I am willing to leave the book in the care of Lu's monks if that is what the council desires."

It wasn't the ideal outcome, but if they were allowed to examine the manuscript more carefully, Beatrice realized that Giovanni would probably be able to memorize it enough for their purposes.

"Lorenzo?" Lan turned to Giovanni's son.

"Yes, Elder Lan?" Lorenzo stepped forward with an ingratiating smile.

"How many children have you sired?"

Beatrice blinked at the unexpected question.

"What does that have to do with anything?" she whispered to Stephen.

"Canny vampire," Baojia murmured.

"Why?"

"The Eight Immortals have been outspoken against those who sire many children, Beatrice." Giovanni looked at her with a subtle smile. "They consider it irresponsible and unwise."

"Oh."

Lorenzo didn't look pleased. He looked nervous. "I… I have had the joy of siring many children in my life, Elder Lan. I cannot give you an exact number at this time."

"Or he doesn't want to," Baojia said.

"You have sired so many children that you can't remember the number?" Lan said with a raised eyebrow. "That is… unusual."

"Is it?" Beatrice whispered.

"How many children does Carwyn have, Beatrice?"

"Um… eleven, right?"

Giovanni nodded. "Eleven in over a thousand years. And that is considered a very large family."

"Oh… so Lorenzo—"

"Is not making himself look very responsible if he can't even remember the number of humans he has turned."

Lan still questioned Lorenzo. "Have you ever taken a mate to help care for all your children?"

"What? Are we questioning his family values here?" Beatrice asked between clenched teeth. "Is Lan going to ask if he uses corporal punishment next?"

"Well, the answer to that is yes, but I have no idea where Lan's going with this," Stephen said.

Lorenzo looked confused, as well. "I have never taken a mate, no."

Lan broke into a huge smile. "But your father has!"

Lorenzo returned a tight smile of his own. "Yes, he has a mate now."

"I have met her. She is a scribe. She spent many years training to care for books in her university. I like her very much. Do you?" Lan leaned forward with a dancing smile. "You must like her, too! I heard she was a guest of yours for some time. Is that true?"

Lorenzo spoke carefully. "Yes, Miss De Novo was a guest at my home in Greece for some time."

Beatrice's ire spiked, and she whispered, "Why do people keep forgetting the whole kidnapping and murdering thing?"

"Calm down, B," Stephen said behind her. She could feel the water in the air drawn to her, and her skin became damp.

"She's very intelligent, is she not?" Lan continued. "And your own child, Stephen, sired her. You must be pleased since you like having a large family."

"Of course, I'm very pleased." Lorenzo didn't look pleased; if anything, he looked a little green.

"And so Mistress Scribe is part of your family and mated to your own father, as well. It's all so wonderful, is it not?" Lan clapped again, seemingly delighted by the happy circumstances. The rest of the council looked either confused or disinterested, most of them accustomed to Lan's odd outbursts.

"Yes, it's... very wonderful," Lorenzo forced out.

Just then, Beatrice caught a strange light in Lan's eyes. "It is, isn't it?"

She was bewildered, and Giovanni looked as lost as she did. Her father placed a protective hand on her shoulder, and Baojia seemed to stand at attention. Beatrice glanced at Tenzin and Zhang, but both wore completely impassive expressions that were impossible to decipher.

Beatrice looked back to Lan, who had sat back on her throne and seemed to be thinking. Finally, the elder piped up, "I have no idea which vampire should have the book! It's all quite confusing."

A collective breath seemed to leave the crowd. Everyone had been waiting for Lan's judgment, but if none came...

She looked around. "Does that mean Gio and Lorenzo will fight?"

Stephen leaned forward. "If the council cannot come to some agreement, that is the only option."

Even as he said it, Beatrice sensed a buzzing from the crowd. What had been anticipation and interest was slowly building into a more heated energy. The vampires that surrounded them seemed to be preparing for a confrontation. She could see some silently moving to the edges of the hall, slowly shifting position as a new current swept the room.

Giovanni was tense, and she could feel the heat building on his arms. Beatrice reached a hand out for him, only to hear the hiss of steam when their fingers touched. Her own body seemed to be preparing for a fight without her mind thinking about it; she felt damp air at her collar.

"What's happening?" Stephen asked.

Through it all, Beatrice kept watching Lan. She sensed, somehow, that the small vampire had not finished, though the crowd's attention had left the elder. Lan lounged in her throne, examining her fingernails and playing with the ends of the hair that had slipped out of her topknot. Suddenly, the innocent-looking vampire took a breath and Beatrice tensed.

Lan murmured, almost under her breath. "Unless…"

Every eye focused on Lan as the small vampire spoke. Lan's eyes lifted and sought Beatrice again.

"Perhaps there is some sort of compromise we can reach, after all."

CHAPTER EIGHTEEN

Penglai Mountain, China
November 2010

Giovanni blinked. Though he tried to remain impassive, the unexpected statement from Lan startled him. His mind raced, trying to predict and plan around the unknown.

"What kind of compromise could there be?" Zhongli asked. The wind vampire was looking around the room with suspicion. "Either the book belongs to Vecchio or Lorenzo. What compromise—"

"Perhaps the book belongs to the world." Lan sat up on his knees again. "It sounds very important. A book of universal knowledge? Wisdom to be preserved and shared? I don't know..." Lan flicked his wrist carelessly. "Perhaps it needs only a caretaker. Someone"—Lan's eyes swept the hall, landing briefly on Beatrice before he looked at Lorenzo—"who both parties can agree is a learned and able steward. A scribe who could care for the book. One that has a connection to both Lorenzo and Dr. Vecchio."

Giovanni's eyes flicked to his wife. *They wouldn't...*

In a flash, Lan's peculiar questioning made sense. He had constructed the trap perfectly, and Lorenzo would be forced to walk in. Giovanni's heart began to race, though his face remained blank.

"A scribe?" Elder Zhongli asked with a slight smirk. "Who could..." His eyes fell on Beatrice and grew wide. It was only a fraction of expression, but the whole hall began to stir. Furtive glances were directed at Giovanni's wife, who still stood next to him, apparently clueless to the web she was being drawn into.

"Now that's an interesting development," Baojia muttered.

"What?" Beatrice whispered. "Who are they talking about?"

Lan smiled and clapped. "There is a scribe present who has a connection to both the parties! She has even been acknowledged by the Elders. The daughter of Lorenzo's son. The mate of Giovanni Vecchio. She has even studied book science at a modern university. Beatrice De Novo is clearly able to care for the book. It is the perfect compromise."

"What?" Beatrice whispered. "Not... not me. It's not my—" Giovanni reached over and clutched her hand, willing her to be silent as the Elders deliberated.

Lorenzo looked livid. "And where exactly would she keep this precious book? Has she a monastery like Elder Lu? A library of her own?"

"As a matter of fact," Giovanni stepped forward before Beatrice could speak, "Miss De Novo has an extensive library in Southern California, in the territory of her grandfather, Don Ernesto Alvarez, a noted scholarly and artistic patron. While the facilities do not have the history of Elder Lu Dongbin's monastery"—Giovanni nodded toward Lu and the Elder nodded in return—"they are extensive and modern, the very finest in the New World." He could feel Beatrice squeeze his hand. If he was a mortal man, his fingers would have been crushed by the pressure.

"See?" Lan clapped again. "It's perfect! She can take care of the book and then both of them can see it."

Zhongli leaned forward, his tight smile the only evidence of his discomfort. "It is a most excellent compromise, Elder Lan, but can Miss De Novo truly guarantee that Lorenzo would remain safe when he is examining this book? Surely you are aware that Lorenzo and his sire have a... complicated relationship."

"I am sure that Miss De Novo would guarantee Lorenzo's safety in her library. After all"—Lan's eyes darted between Lorenzo and Giovanni—"are not places of knowledge sacred to those immortal? As are places of worship? They are the outer reflections of our inner wisdom." Lan rose to his feet and turned toward Beatrice. Suddenly, the childlike elder did not look like a playful boy or girl; and the wisdom, power, and amnis of the ancient vampire swept over the room.

"Beatrice De Novo," Lan said in a deeper voice, "if it is the will of this council, would you keep this book? Would you guarantee safety to these two parties who wish to claim it? Would you guard the knowledge therein with honor? What is your answer, Mistress Scribe?"

Giovanni could hear Beatrice's heart pounding, and her fingers still clutched his. He turned toward her as all eyes in the room searched her out. The air was still, but alive with energy. When their eyes met, Giovanni's heart soared in pride and respect. Far from the panic he had expected, Beatrice looked calm, peaceful even. She met Lan's eyes with confidence.

"I will, Elder Lan. It would be my honor to do this for the Elders of Penglai. I would guard this book and guarantee the safety of all those who examined it while in my library."

Giovanni could almost hear Carwyn in his mind. *Clever, clever girl...*

Though part of Giovanni rebelled at the thought of Beatrice guaranteeing Lorenzo's safety in any way, his more practical side realized that he would likely kill Lorenzo long before his son ever had the chance to examine Geber's manuscript. As long as Lorenzo wasn't killed while trying to examine the book under Beatrice's care, no one could challenge her honor.

"What a truly excellent compromise, Lan," Tenzin's father stated with a wide smile. "How fortunate that you were here to present such an amiable resolution to this issue. I wholeheartedly support giving the book into Beatrice De Novo's care. I can vouch for her excellent character and wisdom, and the honor and wisdom of her kinsman, Don Ernesto Alvarez, whose own son accompanies her. Though she is young, Miss De Novo spent her mortal life preparing for this role, to be a caretaker of knowledge. It is only fitting that she take the role of scribe and steward in her immortal life, as well."

Elder He, the Immortal Woman, leaned forward. "I, too, like this compromise. It respects both parties, as Miss De Novo has connections to both Lorenzo and Vecchio. Indeed, we have just heard from Lorenzo's own testimony how much he admires his father's mate."

"Yes," Iron Crutch Li smiled from the opposite side of the room as he sat between Zhongli and Han, both of whom wore sour expressions. "It is always best to compromise so both parties feel that they are treated fairly. I will support this as well."

Brilliant Lan. Giovanni would never underestimate the savvy of the odd immortal again. By presenting a compromise to the council, Lan had practically guaranteed the outcome they wanted without bloodshed. Both earth vampires on the council were known to support almost any compromise that avoided taking a clear stand. This decision would not only be acceptable to all those who had taken their side before, but would also sway Zhongli's former ally to their seemingly moderate solution. It would leave the council voting six to two in favor of giving the book to Beatrice. A clear victory for Giovanni with the appearance of moderation.

Clever Lan. His eyes darted back to his wife, whose eyes were glowing with victory. She wore only a hint of a smile, and Stephen watched her proudly. *Clever Beatrice.*

Finally, Giovanni sought out his son, and he blinked in surprise. Far from the anger or bitterness he had expected, Lorenzo seemed placid. He wore a pleasant expression that revealed nothing of his thoughts. He whispered with the wind vampire closest to him, one of Zhongli's guards. Giovanni narrowed his eyes in suspicion.

Elder Lu stood. "Lorenzo, Giovanni Vecchio, are you amenable to this compromise? Will you abide by the terms set out by Elder Lan and agreed to by the scribe, Beatrice De Novo?"

Giovanni stepped forward. "I will, Elder Lu. I respect the will of the council."

He looked at his son. Lorenzo looked at him and smiled for a second. A calculating glint came to his eye. "I will abide by the decision of this honored council, as well. I am most pleased by this resolution." He bowed deeply, then stepped back, melting into the crowd of grey and black-clad vampires on the far side of the hall.

"Very well," Lu continued, outlining the agreed-upon plan. Lu would send for the book by one of his guards, who would bring it to Mount Penglai to be given to Beatrice, who would then take the book back to her library in Los Angeles, where it would supposedly be accessible to Lorenzo and safely preserved.

Giovanni stepped back and motioned to Baojia. The vampire stepped toward him.

"See what you can find out. I don't trust Lorenzo."

"Agreed. This was too easy. He already has a plan to take it from her, I can almost guarantee it. I'll call Ernesto and let him know what has happened." Baojia's eyes danced for a moment. "I'll tell you right now, my father will be crowing about this honor to his granddaughter for a hundred years, at least."

The corner of his mouth lifted. "As will I."

Baojia's smile fell a fraction, and he leaned closer, speaking in Mandarin. "I hope you realize what a fortunate bastard you are, di Spada."

"I do."

"Feel free to piss her off, though." Baojia smirked. "A lot can happen in eternity."

Giovanni couldn't stop the reluctant smile. "Go check in with Ernesto, then find out what the gossip is among the guards. I'll take care of my wife."

Baojia smiled and stepped back, vanishing into the crowd in a heartbeat. Giovanni turned to Beatrice, who was surrounded by Stephen and Tenzin. For a second, he saw Tenzin's eyes examine Beatrice with a pride and care he had rarely seen. He wondered if Beatrice even realized how deep her connection to the wind vampire was. With the blood Tenzin and Stephen had shared, almost as much of Tenzin's blood ran through Beatrice's immortal veins as Stephen's. If Beatrice had been sired to wind, it would have been unexpected, but not unheard of.

"Tesoro," he murmured, and she immediately turned to him, reaching out a hand to grasp his own. "I am…" He smiled, at a loss for words, overwhelmed by love and pride.

"I guess I'm still a librarian, huh?" She gave a crooked smile. "Thanks for giving me the library, by the way."

Giovanni shook his head. "It's yours. Of course it's yours."

She pulled him closer, but only squeezed his hand, mindful of the attention of the milling vampires around them. "It's ours."

They both spoke to Lu Dongbin for a few minutes. The elder was sending a group of guards the next night to retrieve the book, which would then be given into Beatrice's care. Giovanni urged him to send more guards than he thought necessary, but Lu seemed confident that, though Zhongli was disappointed, he would control Lorenzo while he remained on the island.

Beatrice was pulled away by one of Zhang's administrators, as Giovanni tried to persuade Lu. "I have confidence in the excellence of your guard, Elder Lu, but I do not trust my son. I do not doubt the honor of the Elders, but it is not like Lorenzo to give up like this."

Elder Lu only smiled. "I do not wish you to worry. I will send double the guards. The book will be quite safe."

Giovanni was not satisfied, but knew he could not press the issue without offending the elder. He nodded and retreated to Beatrice's side. She was still speaking with Zhang's administrator.

"—a most excellent resolution, Miss De Novo. Elder Zhang considers it an honor that one so close to his aegis, and a close friend of his daughter, has been given this distinction."

"Please tell Elder Zhang thank you for all the help. I'm really glad I could be part of the resolution in this situation. And I'm very pleased to assist the council."

Ever the politician, Giovanni thought. Though it all seemed very casual, Beatrice continued to amaze him with her instincts. She seemed to have a gift for knowing exactly what people were looking for and how to offer them what they wanted while still getting her own way in the process. He congratulated himself again on persuading her to become his wife. He felt a tug on his arm and turned to speak to another administrator, this one belonging to the Immortal Woman, Elder He.

When Stephen, Tenzin, Beatrice and Giovanni finally returned to their quarters an hour later, all pretenses dropped.

"Shit! I am *not* happy about this." Beatrice pulled at her collar. "I know he has a back-up plan. What the hell is Lorenzo up to?"

"Agreed," Tenzin said. "That was far too easy; he is planning something."

Giovanni said, "We all agree Lorenzo is going to try to steal the book, correct?"

Every one of them nodded.

"The question is," Stephen asked, "is he going to try to intercept Lu's guards? Or try to take us on directly?"

Tenzin said, "He'd be a fool to take us on directly unless he has a private army we don't know about."

Beatrice asked, "Is there any way he could find the monastery?"

Tenzin shook her head. "I don't think so. All the Elders know where it is, but if anyone revealed the location, their life would be forfeit. I can't imagine Zhongli taking that chance."

"But *you* know where it is, don't you?" Stephen asked.

Tenzin snorted. "Of course."

Giovanni rolled his eyes and sat at the table, pulling Beatrice onto his lap and tugging at her collar while Stephen and Tenzin argued about something under their breath.

He felt his wife relax a little bit. "You're very covered up in all this, Tesoro."

"Watch it now," Beatrice said as she snuggled into his chest. He could feel the tension begin to drain out of her shoulders. "Don't start getting handsy with the honored scribe."

He chuckled and nipped her ear with his fangs. "Do I have to call you Mistress Scribe now?"

"Only if you're really good," she whispered.

He smiled before he captured her mouth in a kiss. "I sent Baojia out to see what he could learn from the guards. They gossip like old women."

"They do, huh? Do—" She broke off, and they both turned toward a commotion in the hall. Baojia stormed into the room carrying four swords and scabbards. He tossed Tenzin her curved scimitar, a *jian* toward Stephen, and a *dao* to Beatrice. She stood and caught it instinctively. Giovanni could already feel the fire teasing along his collar.

"What's happened?"

"Lorenzo left the island over an hour ago with a large group of Zhongli's guards. They were flying and left fully armed. We need to go. Now. It's already getting close to dawn. They will have a head start because they are only carrying one and the rest are flying, but we may be able to catch up if we take the plane. We can have the pilot fly us to..." Baojia looked at Tenzin, who actually looked speechless.

"Nanping," she whispered. "How could he... The monks. All the monks are there." She reached back and grasped Stephen's hand.

"The word from the guards is that Zhongli has a human mistress who has refused to turn," Baojia said. "He will do anything to keep her, including fund Lorenzo in his search for the elixir. Including revealing the location of Lu's monastery."

Giovanni's fangs burst forth along with the fire that he smothered along his neck. He rose to his feet and began to pace.

Beatrice sent a cooling mist toward him. "So Lorenzo is going to take the book from the monks?"

"He is on his way to the monastery right now. Hurry up." Baojia tossed the odd straps toward Giovanni, who caught them. "I've adjusted these so we should be able to swim with them fairly easily."

Baojia walked over and began to buckle the scabbard around Stephen as Giovanni helped Beatrice with hers. "We have to—Tenzin!"

The small immortal had rushed out of the room.

"She's gone to tell Zhang," Stephen said. "He must be told of Zhongli's treachery. And Lu will need to be told, as well. Zhang can send some immortals to help."

Baojia shook his head. "They're going to be too late. *We're* going to be too late unless we can get on that plane before dawn."

Giovanni walked down to the library to call the pilot of the plane in Beijing. He and Tenzin would fly while Baojia, Beatrice, and Stephen swam to the mainland. They would just be able to make it to Beijing before dawn; then they could fly during the day and land in Nanping by nightfall. With any luck, they would make it to the monastery within a few hours. When he returned to the meeting room, Tenzin was speaking.

"—and they have already taken Zhongli before the council. They found the mistress, as well. My father has sent out his guards in pursuit of Zhongli's, but even he admits they are not as fast, and they will have to rest during the day. We are even farther behind."

"We won't be by evening," Giovanni said, striding into the room. "I've already contacted the pilot. He can have us in Nanping in six hours. Where do we go from there?"

Tenzin paled at the mention of the plane, but straightened stoically. "Up the Nine-Bend River. I will fly you, but the rest will have to go by river."

"Shouldn't be a problem," Baojia said. "I haven't spent much time with Beatrice in the water, but—"

"I'll be fine," Beatrice said. "I'll keep up."

Giovanni nodded. "So we'll fly to Nanping today while we rest. By nightfall, we'll be headed upriver. If we're lucky, we'll beat them there."

Baojia snorted. "I don't think we'll be *that* lucky, but we may just get there in time."

At that grim statement, the room fell silent. Giovanni could only imagine what Lorenzo would do when he arrived at the monastery. He had little respect for vampire life, and none when it came to humans. If he would defy the council of the Eight Immortals to retrieve Geber's manuscript, he was capable of anything. Giovanni felt for Beatrice's hand, and she looked up at him with frightened eyes.

"We have to go *now*," she said. "We're running out of time."

CHAPTER NINETEEN

Nanping
Fujian Province, China
November 2010

Beatrice woke with a burning in her throat. She rose from the bed in the plane, baring her fangs as her eyes darted toward the door. In a heartbeat, she had the handle half turned and Giovanni at her back. He locked an arm around her throat and threw her on the bed.

"You're up early." He fell on top of her, pinning her to the mattress and pulling her mouth to his neck. She struck hard and fast, the thick taste of his blood slaking her instinctual hunger, though it didn't kill it completely.

"Shhh," he soothed her, stroking Beatrice's hair until she was calm again. As soon as she was thinking rationally, she took a deep breath, only to be hit with the unremitting scent of sweet human blood. She could even hear the pump of the pilot's heartbeat, though she realized, for the first time, that the bloodlust was not overpowering.

"Where are we?" she grunted out after she took one last draw from Giovanni's vein.

"A small airfield outside Nanping. Tenzin says it's the closest to the monastery, but we will have to go upriver. It's an hour and a half until sunset, so we can't leave the compartment."

She felt like weeping. "So I have to smell the pilot for another hour and a half?"

"Shh," he whispered again. She buried her face in his neck, sealing the bite marks she had made and trying to block the smell of human with her mate's own, smoky scent. "If it helps, Tenzin is more miserable than you. This is her first time in a plane, and I'm surprised she hasn't peeled the walls off yet, despite the threat of sunlight."

She tried to laugh, but it only exacerbated the burning.

Giovanni continued, "You're beginning to wake earlier and earlier. Just like your father and Tenzin. You're awake ten minutes earlier than last night, and that was ten minutes earlier than the night before."

"What does that mean?"

"It means that unless something changes, soon you will need as little sleep as Tenzin and your father. Maybe only a few hours."

"But that's less than you!"

"I know." He did not sound displeased. "That's means your amnis is already very strong, and growing stronger by the day. This is good. Eventually, you won't need sleep at all."

It also meant that for a good portion of the day, she would be without the support she had come to depend on from her husband. If Giovanni was not awake to distract her or stop her, Beatrice feared what she was capable of.

As if reading her mind, he spoke in a soothing voice. "Don't worry. We'll figure something out. Perhaps your father can stay with us for a time, or Tenzin. One night at a time, Beatrice. Don't borrow trouble."

"Okay," she whispered, burying her face in his skin again.

"Let me up, and I'll get you some blood. That will help your thirst. We have some in the main cabin, I was just about to get it when you woke."

"Have someone block the door."

"Of course." He rose and paused over her, examining her eyes, which were still hazy with hunger.

She gripped the sheets and nodded. "I'm fine. Go."

Giovanni rose, pulled on a pair of pants, then darted out the door in the blink of an eye. In a few seconds, he was back with three pints of blood, cool, but still smelling fresh. He tossed one to her and she caught it with one hand, piercing it with her fangs before she sucked it dry. By the time she was finished with the third bag, she realized that, though the pilot's blood still called to her, with some effort, she could think around it.

"How long?"

"Will the bloodlust last?" He took the bags from her, placing them on the small bedside table before he slid next to her. He wrapped a steadying arm around her waist. "If you progress the way I expect you to, within a year, you'll be able to be around people with ease as long as you feed when you wake."

She took a deep swallow, still distracted by the burning sensation at the back of her throat, though the ache in her gut had been satisfied. "That's not too bad."

"It will pass more quickly than you can imagine."

Beatrice closed her eyes and bit her lip. "Unfortunately, the next hour and a half is going to be torture."

"Well, we can't leave the secured compartment until the sun falls, which means we have no way of making the pilot leave until then. I'm afraid there no escaping the scent, but…"

She looked up to see a smile teasing the corner of his lips.

"What?"

He leaned down to nip at her ear.

"Let's see if I can't distract you, hmm?"

Though she had to admit Giovanni did an excellent job distracting her, there was also a hint of desperation to their coupling. She knew they would be plunged into the most dangerous race she could imagine as soon as the sun crept below the horizon, and she had no idea what to expect. Her *dao* sat propped by the door in the sling that Baojia had fashioned that would allow her to carry it while swimming.

She lay across his chest in the last minutes before sunset. "Am I going to be distracted by humans while I'm in the river?"

He frowned as he ran his fingers up and down her back. The water had been drawn to her skin as they made love, so his hot fingers left trails of steam where they touched.

"You'll be fine. The water will help your control. And I doubt there will be many humans in the river after dark. I'll tell your father and Baojia to watch out for you. Any animals should be fine, they won't smell as appealing."

"I don't want to slow anyone down."

"The key is to let your amnis connect with the water the way it wants to, then allow it to move you upriver. It will be instinctual, so don't try to control it too much. Just let it happen. The way you move already and the way you fight, I think you'll be very fast as long as you allow yourself."

"Okay."

"But I'm going to tell Baojia to swim as fast as he can. If you fall behind, Stephen will stay back with you. I'm sorry, Beatrice, but the priority—"

"Is the monks." She nodded. "I understand, Gio. They're defenseless against Lorenzo. Of course they're the priority."

They both fell silent then, and Beatrice's eyes darted to the clock that hung on the wall. They had ten minutes till sundown.

"We should get dressed," she whispered.

He held her tight to his chest for a moment before he pulled her up and kissed her. They stared at each other for a few more minutes before she rose from the bed. Beatrice focused on the task at hand, pushing the still-present scent of the human to the back of her mind. Giovanni watched her dress in a slim pair of jeans and a tight T-shirt that would not drag in the water.

"Beatrice."

She looked up. "Hmm?"

"I love you."

Her breath caught, and her heart gave a quick thump. "Don't say that like you're saying goodbye."

He frowned and shook his head quickly, but she could see him blink away a red gleam in his own eyes. He rose and dressed in the black combat pants he wore when fighting and nothing else. Though the pants were fire treated and would usually stand up to his element, any other clothing would be nothing but ash, so he did not waste time with it. Giovanni strapped a curved dagger to his thigh and he was ready. He helped her buckle her sword onto her back, making sure she could easily draw it to fight.

Five minutes.

She began to feel a pressure in her chest. "I love you, too," she whispered.

He moved to stand in front of her. "This is no longer sparring. These vampires will kill you, and you must not allow that to happen," he murmured. "There will always be war. It is your job to survive it. No matter what. That is your victory, do you understand?"

Beatrice nodded, staring at his chest and wishing she could bury her face in it to avoid the coming bloodshed. Giovanni grasped her face in his hands and forced her to look at him. He did not look at her with the soft eyes of her lover; he wore the fierce expression of a soldier.

"You must survive, Beatrice. Do you understand? Do *not* sacrifice yourself for any other. Do *not* be meek in battle. Do *not* hesitate to kill anyone that threatens you. Eliminate them swiftly and without remorse. Do you understand?"

"Yes."

A desperate light came to his eyes and his hands tightened on her jaw. "Do you understand?" he asked again.

She reached up and put her hands over his as she stared into his eyes. "Nothing will keep me from you."

They stared at each other for a minute more before Giovanni pressed his lips to hers in a single, fierce kiss before he drew back and reached for the door. He pulled it open and everything seemed to happen at once.

They rushed into the main compartment. Tenzin had the door open and waiting for them. Baojia streaked out, followed by Stephen and Giovanni carrying Beatrice in a headlock as they passed the human in the cockpit. As soon as they reached the deserted runway, Tenzin sealed the door, eliminating the alluring scent of blood; then she grabbed Giovanni and took to the sky in one sweep. Giovanni and Beatrice's fingers touched for only a second before he disappeared into the night.

Beatrice turned to Baojia, but the vampire had already bolted toward a thick stand of forest calling, "This way!" as he ran.

Stephen grabbed her hand, and Beatrice ran at full speed for the first time in her immortal life. Her heart pounded in excitement. The wind rushed around her and, if she had been human, it would have stolen her breath. She squinted her eyes, closed her mouth and ignored the swarm of insects she swam through as she and her father rushed to keep up with Baojia. She could only assume he had been briefed during the plane trip and knew where they were going.

They darted through the thick stand of trees, dodging around tree trunks and skipping over rocks with a swift grace she tried not to think about. The less she allowed her mind to analyze how fast she was going, the easier it was. Her heart pumped, but not with effort. It was pure excitement.

Later, Beatrice would realize she had never truly understood instinct until the moment the scent of the river hit her nose. The rushing water called to her, and when she saw Baojia leap into its depths, she followed without hesitation, her father close on her heels. She had no need to hold her breath; she simply closed her mouth and let the water envelop her, keeping Baojia's murky form in front of her as they sped up the rushing stream.

Beatrice struggled for a moment to keep up with him, trying to force herself forward under her own preternatural power until she remembered what Giovanni had told her.

"...let your amnis connect with the water the way it wants to... allow it to move you... it will be instinctual..."

She forced the thought of kicking from her mind and focused on the rush of amnis over her skin. The moment she did, it was almost as if her energy unfurled into a thousand long tendrils, spreading out in the water as it reached to push her upstream. She had no conscious thought of maneuvering around rocks or the odd raft she came across, she had only to think of where she wanted to go and her amnis reached out to bring her there.

After a few moments, she was fully enveloped in the ecstasy of the river, moving with a single thought just under its dark surface as she tracked Baojia. She barely registered her father trailing behind her or the bends and creases of the river as it wound up and through the deep river valleys of the Wuyi Mountains. She could feel the energy signatures of the fish and small animals that darted away from her, but their blood did not distract her as human blood did. She felt the water shallow out before it grew deeper again.

They sped upriver for miles, and Beatrice had little sense of time. She knew only the water, her amnis, and Baojia's faint shadow in front of her as she followed him. After what could have been hours or minutes, she felt him slow, and she moved silently behind him along the edge of the river. Her eyes broke the surface as they approached the bank where a long bamboo raft was pulled up.

Baojia held a hand out for silence as they walked to the edge of the riverbank. Beatrice could feel the mud between her toes and fought the instinct to remain in the safety of the water. She felt Stephen pick up her hand and tug her along when she hesitated.

None of them said a word as they walked along the muddy bank, finally stepping onto the soft grass that lined the clearing on the edge of the forest.

Baojia smelled it first, and his gaze lifted toward the rise of ancient stone stairs and the scent of blood and smoke. Both hit Beatrice's nose at the same moment, and her eyes darted around, looking for danger. The smell of blood and fire surrounded her.

"The monastery is in flames," Stephen whispered. He looked over her shoulder to a set of stairs buried in the hill. They led up into the dark forest and Stephen started for them before he was pulled back by Baojia.

"We need to find the source of the blood. Di Spada and Tenzin are already up there, I'm sure of it."

Stephen shook his head. "Of course."

Beatrice's nostrils flared. "It's not human."

"No."

They walked cautiously toward where the scent was strongest. As they breached the laurel trees on the edge of the riverbank, she saw them. A mass of twisted bodies and rolling heads, Zhongli's guards were piled into a low depression just beyond a clearing. Their blood sprayed across the dead leaves and detritus that layered the forest floor, and Beatrice gagged at the tangled bodies of the dead vampires.

"Lorenzo must have had men following them," Baojia said.

"But how?" Stephen looked up in confusion. "They flew."

"I don't have any idea, but we'll talk about it later. Take Beatrice back to the river, and I'll go up to the monastery."

"I don't want to wait by the river!"

His eyes cut toward hers. "Too bad. You're not going up there unless there's no avoiding it. It's already a bloodbath from the smell of it, and I'll not have you distracting di Spada with your presence and endangering lives. You're not ready yet. Stay here and keep your head down, little girl."

Baojia turned to Stephen. "And you stay here, too. Keep her away and out of trouble."

"The monks—"

"Are probably already dead. By the smell of them, these bodies have been dead at least an hour. Stay here and keep her out of it. That's the most you can do."

"Baojia," Beatrice still protested. "I'm not going to stay down here when—"

He tackled her and bared his fangs as he gripped her around the neck. "Stay here! I do not have time to argue with you. I shouldn't have come here. I shouldn't have let *you* come here. So don't make me regret it. Stay here and keep your head down, or you'll get someone killed. Probably yourself."

She opened her mouth to protest, but he bared his fangs again and she shut up. No matter how much she wanted to help, she knew much of what he was saying was true. She had little experience in actual battle and would probably only hurt herself.

"There will always be war. It is your job to survive it. That is your victory..."

She nodded tightly and Baojia leapt off, racing up the stone stairway and toward the growing cloud of smoke. Stephen gripped her hand and pulled her up. He drew Beatrice away from the bodies of Zhongli's guards and toward the riverbank where they crouched in the shadows to wait.

"Do you worry about Tenzin?" she asked.

Stephen paused before he answered. "Yes. I know I probably shouldn't. She's lived for five thousand years, right?"

"Yep."

"Right."

"I still worry about Gio," she confessed in a whisper. "Even though he's survived more than I could even imagine."

"You're very lucky, Beatrice." Stephen looked at her in the dim light of the crescent moon. "You're lucky to have found each other. You know that love that I was talking about in my journals? The kind Grandma and Grandpa had? That's the way he looks at you. Like you're the most important thing in the world to him."

She blinked back tears. "He's everything to me."

Stephen gave her a soft smile. "You're very lucky."

They waited in silence as the smell of smoke only grew stronger. Every now and then, Beatrice thought she could hear a shout from the top of the stairs, but nothing was clear. Stephen explained that the majority of the old stone temple was hewn into the side of the mountain, and the hallways were like a puzzle.

"Even if Lorenzo gets there, there are many false corridors and passageways. It was designed as a defensive fortress, so there are escape routes and dead ends; the monks know all of them. It would take him hours to find his way to the library alone." She wasn't sure whether he was convincing her or himself.

But she nodded anyway, even though Beatrice had a hard time feeling very reassured as the smoke grew thicker, blotting out the stars in the night sky. She had little concept of the passage of time, and she sat up straight when she heard a whistling tune.

It was the children's song about a cricket that Giovanni would often sing to her, but as the sound of the whistle grew louder, she shrank back, dreading its approach. It was not Giovanni.

Lorenzo's blond hair shone silver in the moonlight as he bounced down the stairs carrying a wrapped package clutched to this chest. Three guards followed him as he descended. He still sported the grey scholar's robes he had worn in the Hall of the Eight Immortals as he stepped toward the bamboo raft.

Beatrice turned to her father in panic.

"The book," Stephen breathed out as he watched his sire with wide eyes.

Lorenzo's steps halted immediately, and he turned and eyed the bushes where they were hiding. Beatrice heard a taunting laugh come from his throat.

"A book in the hand," he called as he stepped toward them, "and it sounds like *two* De Novos in the bush."

Her father rolled to the right and into the clearing, drawing his sword in one swift movement. Beatrice drew her own and darted around the trees behind Lorenzo's guards as Stephen rose to face his sire.

"Well," Lorenzo chirped, "this night just keeps getting better!"

CHAPTER TWENTY

Wuyi Mountains
Fujian Province, China
November 2010

Giovanni threw fire into another whirlwind that Tenzin tossed his direction, the scent of blood and ash thick in his nostrils. The bodies of Lu's monks lay scattered in the courtyard as he and Tenzin eliminated the last of Lorenzo's water vampires who guarded the outer gates of the monastery.

"One more!" Tenzin swung her arm around, tossing the vampire toward him.

The dark-haired guard fell in crumbled heap, only to rise and run toward Giovanni. These were not the ineffectual spawn that Lorenzo had been creating; these vampires were far more formidable and bore European features that were further confirmation that Lorenzo had allies that remained a mystery. Allies with deep resources to hire or inspire the loyalty of such fierce opponents.

It was taking longer than he'd planned for Tenzin and him to work through them.

Giovanni sidestepped the guard, who tried to spray him with water to extinguish the fire that coursed over his body, but Tenzin drew the wind from the attacking vampire, sucking the water toward herself and allowing Giovanni to light his opponent on fire. He screamed and ran toward the stairs to escape, but Tenzin caught him up in a gust, pinning him to a stone wall as he turned black and flaked away.

"This is taking too long!"

"That's the last one."

"I smell blood in the monastery." He tried to suppress the flames on his body. "Let me just…" He took deep breaths, forcing the fire back so he could enter the stone rooms without harming Tenzin or any remaining monks.

They had seen the crumpled bodies of Lu's monks from a distance as they approached. The journey through the mountains had gone swiftly, but not swiftly enough to beat Lorenzo's men. At least twenty human bodies littered the courtyard and five vampires had patrolled the gates.

"Are you ready to go inside?" Tenzin asked with cold eyes.

He nodded, taking a deep, calming breath. "Yes."

They stole silently through the doors, searching, but quickly bypassing the meeting hall where the monks had met to pray. He forced himself to ignore the lifeless bodies that lay in the shadows. Giovanni followed Tenzin, who quickly wound her way back into the mountain, following tangled corridors and dark passageways that always seemed to end with more bloodied corpses. The sheltered monks of Lu Dongbin's order had been decimated.

Finally, at the end of one corridor, Tenzin's eyes darted to the right. She took a deep breath before she ducked under a thick tapestry that hung on one wall. There was a small stone door, no bigger than a gravestone, that she pulled back before she ducked inside.

Giovanni followed. He heard a scuffling in the chamber and quickly lit a flame that shot to the top of the small room. A young monk, no more than sixteen or seventeen, stood, spreading his arms to guard the clutch of small boys behind him. The young monks wore saffron robes and tears in their eyes.

"We are not here to hurt you," Tenzin said softly. "Where have they gone?"

The young monk examined them before he seemed to decide they were trustworthy. "I do not know. Master Fu-han woke me and told me to gather the young ones here to hide them while he went to the library. I only did what he told me."

"And you have not seen the strangers?"

"I saw no one. But many have come through the halls before you.

What has happened in the monastery?"

"There has been an attack. You cannot stay here—" Tenzin's eyes darted toward the door in panic before she relaxed. "It is Baojia." She turned to Giovanni. "I will find a safe place for these boys, and then we search for Lorenzo."

Giovanni nodded and stepped into the corridor where he found Baojia waiting for them. "Where is Beatrice?"

"At the riverbank with Stephen. It was deserted. All of Zhongli's guards were there, dead."

The boys filed into the passageway and began following Tenzin down the corridor.

"I wondered what had happened to them. There were others in the courtyard," Giovanni murmured. "We killed them."

"I saw the ashes."

"They were not Asian. European."

Baojia cocked an eyebrow. "Interesting."

"I thought so."

They ducked under another tapestry that led to a narrow earthen passageway lined with unlit torches. Giovanni quickly lit one and handed it to the young monk before he turned back to Tenzin.

"I don't feel anything here," she said. "You?"

"I feel nothing in this direction," he said, looking down the dark corridor. "No vampire has been here tonight."

She nodded. "Excellent. This one is very old, I was hoping they would not know of it." She turned to the young man. "This tunnel leads to a river landing. There is a cave at the base. Continue down the corridor and then wait at the riverbank. Take shelter in the cave if you feel danger. Elder Zhang is sending his guards, they will find you and keep you safe."

The young monk nodded.

"Go. We must return to the monastery and continue searching."

"If you find Master Fu-han—"

"Do not worry about your master, worry about these boys. Keep them safe."

She nodded to the young man and then ducked back under the tapestry and ran in the opposite direction from where they had come. Baojia and Giovanni followed her.

"Where are we going?" Giovanni asked.

"There is an older part of the monastery," she yelled. "That is where the library is. Your senses are better than mine in the mountains. Open up and look for them, my boy."

Giovanni tried to focus his amnis to detect any latent energy traces, but the stone walls, along with the mass of blood, adrenaline, and old tangled signatures were confusing.

"They've been all over, it's almost impossi—"

He broke off and swerved to the right, drawn to a clutch of energy in a large empty space.

"Here!"

Giovanni burst through an old wooden door to see three vampires huddled over a group of bodies, feasting on the blood of Lu Dongbin's monks. They looked up in surprise, snarling at the three vampires who entered the stone courtyard that looked like an outdoor kitchen.

Baojia, Tenzin, and Giovanni spread out, surrounding the vampires before they attacked. Baojia drew his sword, immediately cutting off the head of one while Tenzin took to the air and swooped down over the group, hacking at another with her scimitar. Giovanni grabbed the third by the neck, twisting it until the head came off and the three vampires lay in a bloody heap over the bodies of the monks.

"Where the hell is he?" Giovanni said as he scanned the courtyard.

Baojia began to shake his head. "There are more. More than I had imagined. It was a bad idea to leave Stephen and Beatrice by the river. If Lorenzo's not here, he may be anywhere."

"Go," Tenzin said. "He's probably still in the library somewhere. It's a maze. We'll search the rest of the monastery. We weren't in time to stop their murder, but let's hope the monks might have saved the book."

Baojia nodded and ran back out the way he had come, while Tenzin and Giovanni ran deeper into the mountain fortress, searching for Geber's manuscript.

Stephen stood with sword drawn, tense and ready. "Give me the book, Lorenzo."

Lorenzo rolled his eyes. "And why would I do that? I finally got it back, and I had to get rather messy doing so."

Beatrice could see the blood spatter on Lorenzo's robes, even in the darkness. The smell of human blood covered her father's sire and the three guards that surrounded him. She was having trouble concentrating. She gritted her teeth, gripped her sword, and tried to focus on the two vampires that stood across from her in the small, grassy clearing.

"What are you doing, my Stephen?" Lorenzo laughed. She heard him draw his own sword. "Do you actually think you and your little girl are going to stop me? My friends and I just killed all of Zhongli's guards—they were a bit squeamish about killing all the monks, you see —and ransacked a very valuable library to get this book back. I'm certainly not intimidated by you and the girl." He glanced over his shoulder at Beatrice. "Though I do find her very attractive when she's bloodthirsty like this. Nicely done, Stephen. She turned out beautifully."

"Dad?" She didn't know what she was asking. She shifted back and forth on her feet as her eyes darted between the two guards who licked their lips and grinned at her. She had never faced two opponents before.

"Tenzin and Giovanni will be here shortly, Lorenzo."

Lorenzo only laughed. "I very much doubt that. We left… well, a bit of a mess, really. I was worried about her Chinese dragon, but he seems to have run off and abandoned his post."

Beatrice glanced at Stephen again. They were separated on opposite sides of the clearing with four vampires between them.

Her father still spoke calmly. "Baojia will be coming back soon, as well."

"I'm sure you hope so."

Beatrice was starting to panic, and the scent of the human blood covering the guards was flooding her senses, causing her head to swim. There was too much going on. She could see everything, hear everything, smell everything. Far from making her more aware, the flood of sensory input was only confusing. Her fangs were long in her mouth, and she could taste the blood where they had pierced her lip.

Beatrice saw one guard curl his lip and move to attack, and she reacted automatically, cartwheeling to the side. As she hit the ground with one hand and popped up, she brought her *dao* down on the back of the attacker's neck.

Her sword sliced through the thick muscle and bone with a sickening, wet sound, and the head fell to the grass with a soft thunk. Beatrice stared for only a second before she fell to her knees and regurgitated what was left of the blood in her stomach over the headless corpse. She saw the other guard come toward her and rolled to the side, standing in a ready pose.

Lorenzo must have been watching.

"Well, that was fun." She heard him say. "And somewhat disgusting. Must have been her first. She's better than I would have thought for a young one. Looks like those lessons paid off, Beatrice."

"I try." She hoped she sounded braver than she felt.

"I won't make the mistake of underestimating you."

Stephen was still speaking calmly. "Give me the book and no one has to get hurt, Lorenzo. Zhang's vampires are already on their way." Stephen began circling his sire. "Zhongli's treachery has been revealed. The council knows what you are doing."

"As if I care about the council!" Lorenzo scoffed, and she heard the clang of swords. She glanced over and saw Lorenzo and her father parrying. A breeze wafted the scent of blood toward her, and her throat burned. Her opponent only grinned.

"Hungry, little one?"

"You're not really my flavor, thanks."

He chuckled and his fangs ran lower. "But I think you might be mine."

"Yeah?" She feinted to the right before she swept her arm back to slice his thigh. "I really don't agree."

She took a second to find her father. Stephen was facing Lorenzo and one other vampire. He had his sword drawn on Lorenzo's guard and Lorenzo was looking on in amusement. She blinked and missed the quick thrust and parry of her father and his opponent before she turned her attention back to her own fight. The blond vampire she faced had used her distraction to sweep her leg with his own, and Beatrice was thrown off balance as she stumbled back. She quickly regained her footing and returned thrusts as he grinned with bared fangs in the moonlight.

It was all so quick. And yet everything seemed to happen in slow motion. She saw a head with short, dark hair roll near her feet and realized that her father must have killed the vampire he was fighting. She was distracted by the gaping mouth and empty eyes that stared at her, and her opponent took the opportunity to leave a deep gash in her right arm.

"Argh!" Beatrice cried out when she felt the sharp clank of his blade against her bone. She lost her grip on the *dao* and rolled away from the vampire, scurrying toward the bushes as her opponent turned and joined the fight between Lorenzo and her father. Stephen was once again facing two attackers.

"No!" She stood again, clutching her arm as she tried to dive toward her weapon, but Lorenzo saw her. He stepped back and ran toward her sword, snatching it up and tossing it into the river.

"Look who lost her sword!" he gloated. "Didn't Giovanni teach you better? Never lose your weapon, girl. That was beaten into my brain more times than I could count. He must be getting soft not to have trained you as well."

Beatrice's eyes darted around, looking for help from any direction. She had no sword. She was ravenously hungry, and her panic was beginning to overwhelm her. She saw the victorious light in Lorenzo's eyes, and it only made her more frantic.

"Dad?" she called, but Stephen was still dueling with the other guard. Lorenzo was walking toward her. She looked at the river with longing, wishing she could run toward its dark depths and swim away, but she knew she couldn't leave her father. In a last ditch effort, she ran toward Lorenzo, diving down and curling into a ball at the last minute to knock his legs out from under him. The ground felt like nothing. The only pain she registered was the sharp slice in her arm, which had been healing, but broke open again.

"Oh," Lorenzo said, laughing in a heap on the ground. "Are we supposed to fight hand-to-hand now because you've lost your weapon? Precious thing, don't you know I don't fight fair?"

He popped up, grabbing his own saber where it had fallen. Beatrice was crouched on the other side of the clearing, clutching her arm and waiting for his approach. She could still see her father battling the last guard, but now, both were drawing from the water in the river, throwing waves toward each other as they tried to throw the other off balance.

"Giovanni and Baojia are coming," she panted.

"But they're not here *now*, are they?" Lorenzo kept walking toward her. He curled his lip and ripped at the front of his robe, tearing it from the collar and tossing the blood-soaked rag in her direction. Beatrice caught the sweet smell and turned toward it instinctively, snapping at the cloth as it covered her face. She was blind when he kicked her to the ground.

"Did you think to challenge me?" he yelled. She tried to gather her energy. The world swam around her. She was hurt. Hungry. Her head swam from smoke and blood.

It was too much.

Her father grunted at the edge of the clearing opposite her.

Her arm throbbed, itching and aching as it tried to knit together.

The edge of a blade hooked the blood-soaked rag and pulled it from her face. Lorenzo stood over her with a grin, laughing at the tears in her eyes.

Too much.

Beatrice felt the tip of his sword slowly pierce her stomach, thrusting into her gut as he ran it through her body and deep into the ground below. Blood spilled out beneath her. She coughed once, and it flooded her mouth.

"It's all quite overwhelming, isn't it?" he whispered, bending down to stroke a finger along her jaw. She felt his finger gather up the blood as it dripped from her mouth. He lifted it to his lips and tasted. Then he grinned and bent down, licking the drips that ran down her neck.

"Mmm," he growled as his cold tongue drank her in.

"Go—" She tried to turn away, but the blade dug in deeper and she choked on her own blood.

"So sweet, my precious girl. Just wait... just wait." She could feel his cold hands run over her struggling body, and she cried in agony as the blade tore at her stomach.

Lorenzo laid a single kiss at the corner of her mouth before he rose, snapped off the handle of the sword, and ran toward Stephen, grabbing a weapon from one of the dead guards.

No! her mind screamed. She tried to grab at the blade and realized why he had snapped off the handle. Her hands quickly became slick with blood, and she could not grip the metal with enough force to pull it from the rough ground beneath her. She was pinned and weak from blood loss. It seeped out around her, and every time she struggled, it only tore her wound more.

"Dad?" she choked out, looking for her father. "Dad!"

Stephen had been holding his own against the guard, but once Lorenzo joined in, he was battling on two fronts with only one weapon. Their eyes met for one panicked moment.

Too much.

Beatrice sobbed and struggled against the sword pinning her to the ground, only to hear the quick snap when it finally cut her spine. Her legs fell still. She could no longer feel them. She closed her eyes.

Stephen yelled, "Beatrice!"

Too much.

Lorenzo was going to win.

Giovanni and Tenzin picked up Lorenzo's scent just past the courtyard where Baojia had left them, tracking him deeper into the mountain. They struggled through the scent of human blood, meeting only a few survivors. A few monks had hidden in corners, but most had rushed out to the courtyards, only to be cut down as Lorenzo's men found them.

The two friends entered the dim library. Old energy filled the room, but Giovanni could sense that no vampire remained. Scrolls, books, and tablets lay tossed on the floor. Two monks lay near the door, their necks snapped. Giovanni immediately picked up a faint human heartbeat on the far side of the room.

"Fu-han," Tenzin whispered as she rushed across the room. She picked up the old man, cradling him as his eyes flickered open.

"Tenzin?" he croaked. "My dear, why... what has happened? Who were those immortals? Why..."

"Shhh," she soothed the old man, rocking him as she held his head in her lap. "Fu-han, the book? Did they get the book?"

"They wanted Stephen's book," the old monk whispered. "I don't know why. They won't understand it. I finally..." He stopped and coughed up a little blood. "I finally found..." The monk's eyes flickered closed.

"What?" Giovanni asked. "What did you find, old man?"

He ignored Tenzin's sharp eyes, realizing that this must be Zhang's old pupil, who had been interpreting Geber's manuscript for them.

"He won't be able to... it's simply not what it seems. And he does not have the humility to see." Fu-han was looking into the distance, his eyes open, but empty, as the life drained out of him. "He is too arrogant. Too arrogant..."

"Who is too arrogant?" Giovanni knelt next to him. He heard the old man's heart falter, and he put his hands on his chest, sending an electric jolt through his body, which started the heart again. "What are you talking about? What did you discover?" he practically yelled.

"Giovanni!" Tenzin pushed him away, but he only crawled back, bending toward the monk in supplication.

Fu-han's eyes opened and locked with Giovanni's, momentarily lucid in the flickering light of the library.

"Learn humility, immortal. Look for the space between. The secret of the elixir lies in what is not there."

"What—"

"Do not forget the fifth element," he whispered as his eye flickered closed and his heart stopped.

The fifth element?

His mind raced and his heart pounded. There was something… something that Lorenzo did not see. Even if his son had the book, the old monk said he could not understand it. If Lorenzo could not understand it, there was still hope they could keep the elixir from him.

He felt the blow as Tenzin threw him across the room.

"Who do you think you are?" she yelled. "Have you no respect for my father's pupil?"

She raged, and he knew it was as much in grief for the destruction of the monastery as it was in anger for his actions. Tenzin tossed him around the library, and he did not try to resist, letting her vent her ire as she battered him against the cold, stone walls. Papers whipped around the room, churned by the wind she summoned.

"Tenzin—"

"This is your fault, you arrogant boy! Did you think your suffering so much worse than others? Did you think you were unique? This is the monster that *you* created!"

The whirlwind swirled around her, an outward manifestation of her anger and frustration. It was rare for Tenzin to lose her temper like this; he had only seen it once.

"I'm sorry, Tenzin."

"You are sorry? You're *sorry*? Your sorrow does not make this right!"

He narrowed his eyes. She was emotional. Too emotional. He suddenly realized his own blood was churning, and a twisting fear filled his stomach. He felt a phantom pain in his back, and his blood ached as it rushed through his body.

His blood… Beatrice's blood. His eyes darted to Tenzin, baffled by her uncharacteristic show of emotion. Her blood. *Stephen.*

"Tenzin!" He rose to his feet and rushed toward her. She batted him back with an angry wall of wind, and he fell into the alcoves that held the books as more paper whipped around him. "We must go to Beatrice and Stephen," he roared. "We must make sure they are safe. Something is wrong!"

The wind stopped and she cocked her head toward him. "Stephen?"

"Stephen." Giovanni nodded, rising to his feet. "There is something—"

"Stephen," she said again, blinking her eyes as if waking from a daze. She frowned at Giovanni and started toward the door. He followed her, only to halt when she suddenly stopped right before the open door of the library. Giovanni almost ran into her when he heard her gasp and buckle forward, as if something had punched her in the gut.

"Tenzin?" He placed a hand on her shoulder and she slumped to the ground. "Tenzin!"

He caught her and turned her in his arms. Her eyes were glazed over, hollow as the grave. The flames burst over his back when he heard her plaintive whisper.

"*Stephen...*"

CHAPTER TWENTY-ONE

Wuyi Moutains
Fujian Province, China
November 2010

"How shall I kill you, my Stephen?" Lorenzo slapped at his child's face with the flat of his sword. Stephen was hanging, trapped in a wall of water from which he couldn't break free. Lorenzo paced nearby, as his guard watched the stairs.

"You're so stupid. You have all this power, but no idea what to do with it. You should have spent less time with your books and more time practicing, like your daughter."

"Let me out of here," Stephen grunted, "and fight me like a man."

"Oh," Lorenzo laughed, "but I am not a man, you silly child. You're such an American. Can you do a John Wayne impression, cowboy?" Lorenzo chuckled at his own joke, and the silent guard smirked.

Beatrice was still trapped on the ground. Her hands continued to struggle with the blade that Lorenzo had run through her, but her palms slipped on the bloody sword, cutting her fingers as she struggled.

Stephen looked resigned. "Lorenzo, you already have the book. What else do you want?"

"To kill you, of course. I just can't decide… quickly or slowly? I would normally take my time since you've been such a bother the last few years, but I have a feeling"—he looked toward the stone stairs leading up to the monastery— "that we'll be having company soon, which makes me sad."

Beatrice saw Stephen's arm break free from the water and her father flicked his hand toward the river, summoning a stream of water that knocked Lorenzo over as he stood near the riverbank. The distraction was enough to break Lorenzo's hold on the water that had trapped him.

"Oh, you are clever boy!" Lorenzo laughed. "I suppose you're right, a fight is much more fun."

Stephen fell to the earth, reaching out and grabbing his sword before he sprang to his feet and met the silent guard who rushed him.

"Dad!" She had to get free. She had to help him. Beatrice tried to grab at the sword again, but she did not have the strength to pull it from the ground beneath her. She continued to spit out the blood that poured into her mouth as she struggled.

"Beatrice, hold on!"

"Enough," Lorenzo growled, looking toward the stone steps. Just then, there was a flurry of movement on the edge of the river as Beatrice saw her father leap up, sweeping down and beheading the guard he battled. He landed on the ground and started in her direction, only to have Lorenzo dart behind and slash the back of his thighs, cutting his hamstrings and bringing him to his knees.

"No!" Stephen cried out as he fell to his knees. Beatrice fought back the urge to scream when Lorenzo kicked her father's sword away from him.

No, no, no! Beatrice struggled harder, bloody tears coursing down her cheeks as she tried to break free. She choked on the blood that continued to fill her mouth. If she could just break free... Even if her legs wouldn't work, she could drag herself—

"Enough of this." She heard Lorenzo say as he bent over her father. "Enough playing, Stephen."

Beatrice spat out the blood. "Dad?" she choked. She could feel her wounds close around the blade in her stomach, but even that pain no longer registered as she watched Lorenzo circle her father with one hand gripping his neck.

"Dad!"

"Look at her, Stephen, isn't she beautiful?" Lorenzo ran a sword through Stephen's stomach and forced his neck around so Beatrice met her father's eyes as he began coughing up blood. She saw his lips form her name.

Mariposa...

"No, no... Lorenzo! Get away from him!"

"She's so lovely," Lorenzo murmured. "I have plans for her, you know? Such wonderful plans." He pulled the blade from her father's stomach and the blood poured out.

Stephen muttered through bloody lips. "Leave... leave her, Lorenzo."

"Take me! Leave him alone and take me if you want me!" Beatrice cried into the night. "I'll go. I promise."

"You have the book. Leave my daughter."

Lorenzo was watching her as his blade slid around Stephen's neck, drawing a thin collar of blood. "So touching. And I won't kill her. I have plans for her. If I could only keep you around, you could see them."

"No! Daddy!" Beatrice screamed as Lorenzo drew back the sword. Her eyes locked with Stephen's, and she saw a strange euphoria fill her father's face. Her eyes raced to Lorenzo, who only cocked his head as he stared at her with a small smile.

"Sadly," Lorenzo said. "I have to travel light."

The blade descended, cutting off Stephen's head in one swift stroke. It rolled toward her, coming to rest a few feet away as his lifeless brown eyes stared into the dark heaven above.

Beatrice screamed as her father's lips moved in one last silent prayer.

She heard Lorenzo walking toward her, and she stopped struggling when the pain caused her head to swim. She thought she was strong, but what use was her strength in the face of this monster? Lorenzo's black dress shoes came to stop in front of her face.

She heard Giovanni's voice in the back of her mind. *"Survive... that is your victory..."*

Lorenzo knelt beside her. He held the manuscript in his hands; Beatrice stared at it. It wasn't as big as she thought it would be, no larger than a typical hardback, and not even as thick. The dull, leather cover was stained with her father's blood. A single drop trickled down the side. It smeared when Lorenzo placed the manuscript in a large plastic bag and stuffed it in his shirt, securing it to his body as he ran a bloody hand through his blond curls.

"Oh"—he curled his lip as he saw the smeared blood on his fingers—"that's disgusting. Good thing I'm going for a swim. Tell *Papà* I said hello, and I'll see him later. I wish I could take you with me right now, but like I said, I am traveling light, so we'll have to catch up later."

"I hate you," she spit out through bloody lips. "I hate you, I hate you. I'm going to kill you if it's the last thing I do."

"Do you think so?"

She couldn't stop the sob that escaped her lips when she saw her father's lifeless eyes. "You will die, Lorenzo, and I will make it painful. You will scream in agony."

"So much anger," he murmured. "It's beautiful."

"It is my only purpose in this life, do you understand me?"

He leaned down and left a lingering kiss on her cheek before he whispered in her ear. "I know you think that you'll kill me, but I'm quite sure there will come a day when you will be putty in my hands. I'm quite looking forward to it."

"Never."

"Oh." He stood and wagged a finger at her. "Never is a long time in our world, precious girl." He winked before he ran and jumped into the river, sinking out of sight beneath its black currents.

"No!" she screamed in frustration before she caught sight of her father's head again. "No, no!" She sobbed bloody tears as she continued to struggle against the blade that pinned her to the ground. The night was silent, marked only by the soft sounds of night birds and her own cries. A few moments later, she heard a rushing sound and Baojia leaned over her.

"No," he groaned. "No, Beatrice. Not this." His voice as pained as she had ever heard it.

"He killed my dad." Beatrice couldn't tear her eyes from Stephen's head.

"Hold still, B. You're going to be all right, but hold still."

"My dad's dead, Baojia."

She heard him choke, but her eyes were still locked on her father's staring face.

"Damn it to hell!" he yelled as he stood. "Hold still, this is going to hurt you again. You're healing too fast."

"It won't hurt. I don't feel anything anymore." It wasn't strictly true; she was beginning to feel twitching in her toes as her nerves knit together around the blade in her spine.

"I'm going to pull the sword out and it's going to break your spine again, so just hold still."

She finally looked up at him. His eyes were red and there was a deep cut around his neck, as if someone had cut his throat from ear to ear.

"What happened to you?"

He shook his head. *Anguish.* He was anguished. "It's not important," he whispered. "Hold still." He gripped at the sword in her stomach, grasped it with both hands while his blood ran down, and pulled.

Beatrice screamed as her shoulders bucked up. She fell back to the earth with a thud, feeling the blood spill out beneath her again. Baojia tossed the sword away and came to cradle her head as she lay on the ground.

"Hold still, B. Please, hold still." There was a gaping wound in her stomach where the sword had torn her abdomen, and she couldn't feel her legs again. He stroked her hair back. "Shhh. Don't move. Give your body time to heal."

"Gio," she whispered, aching for her mate. "I need..."

"Giovanni Vecchio!" Baojia screamed into the night. "Where are you?"

No sooner had he called out than she heard quick footsteps on the stairs and felt his familiar energy rush toward her. She looked up and saw him, pale face and furious eyes, cradling Tenzin in front of him.

"Take her," Giovanni called to Baojia before he rushed over. Baojia gathered Tenzin in his arms, but she lifted a pale hand, reaching toward Stephen's body by the riverbank.

Beatrice began crying again as Giovanni knelt beside her.

"My dad, Gio. He killed my dad." She clutched at his shoulders as Giovanni cradled her in his arms and lifted her from the cold ground.

"Please, Tesoro, you need to go in the water."

"My dad."

"I know," he choked out. "Tenzin collapsed in the library. I came as quickly as I could. I had to carry her."

"He took the book and jumped in the river."

Beatrice heard the splash as Giovanni waded in. He dipped her down, submerging her in the river as the water swirled around her

211

body, embracing her in its cool, healing depths. She looked up at Giovanni through the rippling surface of the water. For the first time, she saw his own tears fall as he watched her pain. They dropped into the water over her face, meeting her drifting tears before the river washed them away.

"Take the water in, Beatrice. As much as you can. Let it heal you." He shook his head and blood scattered over the water.

"My dad," she mouthed, as the water filled and covered her.

"I know."

He lifted her head out and pressed their cheeks together, leaving her body in the water to heal. She felt tears on her cheeks, but she didn't know who was crying.

"Lorenzo killed him."

"I know."

"Where was everyone? I tried. I tried so hard, but there was so much blood and there were too many of them."

"Shh, don't talk." He held his wrist in front of her mouth and she bit into it, taking in his blood as her body floated in the stream. She could feel her bones knitting together. Her flesh stretched over her wounds. The prickling in her legs grew as her spine healed. Soon, her body was itching all over as her amnis joined the water to make her strong again. She continued sucking at Giovanni's wrist, and he watched every wound, examining them as they healed.

A few minutes later, she released his wrist and reached out, leaving the safety of the water as she threw herself into her mate's embrace. He lifted her up, and she wrapped her legs around his waist as they trudged to the edge of the riverbank. She dropped to the ground and looked for her father.

Stephen's body was laying on the edge of the river, and Tenzin was crouched beside him, stroking his lifeless cheek. She had laid Stephen's head next to his body and Baojia stood over them both, watching the night sky.

"Where are Zhang's people? They should be here by now."

"They had to travel fifteen hundred kilometers by air in one night," she heard Giovanni say as she sat by Tenzin and took her father's hand. Tenzin's eyes darted to her, and Beatrice saw her tense before her shoulders relaxed.

They all sat silent over Stephen's remains before a low keening began from Tenzin's small form. She rocked back and forth, one hand on Stephen's cheek and the other braced on his chest. Beatrice heard her murmur a low chant in the old language she shared with Zhang, and she felt her tears fall again.

Giovanni knelt down behind her and tried to pull her away from her father, but she shrugged him off and reached over to embrace Tenzin. The small vampire curled her shoulders, but Beatrice kept her hands out until finally, the small woman turned to her and Beatrice could see the desolate look in Tenzin's grey eyes.

"Tenzin?" Beatrice whispered. Tenzin reached over, pulling her into a fierce embrace. The two women rocked together until they heard a sound like a flock of birds flapping in the wind. Tenzin quickly dried her eyes.

Zhang's men landed in a crouch, eyeing the bloody clearing and the bodies of Stephen and the three guards that lay around them. The leader approached cautiously as Tenzin rose to her feet, stoic again in the face of her father's men.

"Mistress Tenzin." He nodded deeply to her. "Your mate… Elder Lu's monks?"

"The monks are dead. There is a small group of boys who escaped out the southern passageway. Follow the river down, and you should find them. Help them to find shelter in the nearest village until we hear from Lu. They should not go back to the monastery."

"Yes, Mistress." The leader motioned toward two of his men, who took to the air.

"Zhongli's guards are in the forest. His 'honored guest' slaughtered his men before he went up to the monastery." Beatrice watched as a flicker of confusion passed over the vampire's face at Tenzin's words. She could see Tenzin sag almost imperceptibly, and Giovanni's hand reached out for her arm.

"The monastery was ransacked," he said. "Most of the monks were killed. Master Fu-han among them."

"And Miss De Novo's property?" the guard asked.

"Stolen by Lorenzo," Beatrice said as she looked down at her father's body again. As if she cared about the book. Part of her knew it was important, but she was frozen in her grief.

"Mistress Tenzin." Zhang's guard bowed again and spoke softly, "may we help you with Stephen's body?"

"No!" Tenzin bent down, then looked at the body and shook her head. "I mean… yes. Take him up to the monastery." She turned and glanced at Beatrice before she took to the air.

Zhang's guard split up. Some of them followed Baojia to the edge of the forest where Zhongli's men lay; others gently lifted her father's remains before they followed Tenzin up the mountain.

She felt Giovanni grasp her shoulders. "Beatrice, we need to find you some blood. Most of the monks were killed and you need fresh—"

"I don't—" She broke off, overwhelmed again. "I'm not hungry. I don't want blood. I just want my dad. I want to be with Tenzin. Can we follow—"

"Beatrice," he broke in with a hoarse voice. "You need blood. You drank from me, but you had a terrible injury. I'll find an animal in the forest if you want, but you need to feed."

For some reason, the idea of killing a helpless animal seemed to break her. She slumped into Giovanni's chest as his arms wrapped around her, and she shook with tears.

He held her close. "You survived, Beatrice. You survived. That is a victory. You and your father faced four opponents, and you *survived*. Even Baojia was gravely wounded by those men."

"But my father didn't survive."

She heard him clear his throat and sniff. He pressed a kiss to her forehead and whispered, "I would take this pain from you if I could."

"I need to go to my father."

"Beatri—" Giovanni broke off and turned toward the forest. There was a rustling sound as a monk walked through the trees. Giovanni grasped Beatrice's shoulders, holding her still as the scent hit her nose. Though the smell wafted over her, and her fangs descended, she had no desire to pursue the human.

"You should be with Zhang's men," Giovanni said.

The boy answered in Mandarin, and the two had a quick, heated exchange she couldn't understand. She stared at the guard she had killed and the blood she vomited over his corpse. She imagined that it was Lorenzo's head the lay next to the body. The thought brought her some comfort and a hint of satisfaction.

Beatrice felt Giovanni's hands tighten on her shoulders.

"Tesoro, this monk has offered to feed you. He will hold out his wrist—"

214

"No!" Beatrice had no confidence that she could eat without harming the young man. He had come closer, and the churning in her stomach increased. Her fangs were sharp in her mouth.

"You will drink from his wrist, and I will make sure you do not take too much, but it is the best thing for you."

"I'll hurt him."

"No, you won't. I'm here. I won't let you hurt him."

"And I am, as well." She heard Baojia approach. The two grasped her shoulders as she turned and faced the young man. He was no more than sixteen or seventeen, and his head was shaved like the monks she remembered from Mount Penglai. He wore saffron robes and a resolute expression. She hissed instinctively, but shrank back when she saw the look of fear enter the young man's eyes. Still, he held up his wrist to her face, and Giovanni held her hair in his iron grasp as Beatrice leaned forward and latched on to the young man's wrist.

It was heaven. Thick, sweet blood flooded her mouth, slid down her throat, and filled her angry stomach. She could feel the boy's pulse, and she sucked in rhythm to it, watching him with hungry eyes as she struggled against Baojia and Giovanni's grasp. She eyed the pulsing vein in the neck, watching it like a predator as she drank. Soon, she could feel the aching in her throat lessen, but she did not release. She could see the boy pale in front of her, and a surge of satisfaction ran through her as the hint of fear permeated the air. If she could just get free of their hands...

"Enough!" Giovanni's fingers pinched her nose and pulled her away from the vein.

"No!" she snarled, lunging at him before Baojia pulled her back. Giovanni quickly healed the boy's wrist and spoke quietly to him in Mandarin before the young monk disappeared into the forest. Then he turned to Beatrice, and Baojia released her into his embrace.

"We must go up to the monastery. Dawn is coming and Tenzin needs you."

She blinked as her reason returned. She walked toward the stairs, holding his hand as they climbed the old staircase together. Baojia trailed behind them.

Beatrice turned and gave one last look at the clearing where her father had died. Though his body lingered, she knew Stephen's soul had fled. She clung to the vision of his peaceful face the moment before he was killed. Whatever her father's last vision had been, it had brought him joy, and she sent a silent prayer that his soul had found the home he had sought for so long in life.

She turned back to Giovanni. Her husband met her gaze, then bent down and picked her up, cradling her in his warm arms as they made their way to shelter.

CHAPTER TWENTY-TWO

Wuyi Moutains
Fujian Province, China
November 2010

They were ensconced in the library when dawn came. Giovanni carried Beatrice past the reek of blood by the door, guiding her to an alcove where low cushions lay scattered.

"Where are Tenzin and my father?"

"Here," he said as he laid her among the cushions. "At the back of the library. Tenzin is with him."

The monastery library was a long hall, dug deep into the mountain and carefully lined with shelves for the books and scrolls. Small alcoves branched off from the main hallway, most lined with low cushions and some with tables, the ideal location for quiet study and contemplation.

"I want to go to her." Beatrice couldn't explain it. It wasn't just that she wanted to see Tenzin; it was as if she needed to. She felt a pull of longing past understanding, even as she fought against exhaustion.

"You need to rest."

"Please, Gio."

He knelt down next to her, studying her face before he nodded silently. He stood and walked down the hall. A low murmur reached her ears before a rush of air and then Tenzin was beside her. She placed her arm around Beatrice and lay next to her; the comfort was instantaneous. Giovanni silently paced the hall while Beatrice blinked back tears.

Tenzin spoke in a low voice. "It is his blood, do you understand?"

"Yes."

"I will guard him today. You will help me prepare the body tomorrow night when you rise, as a daughter should."

"Yes."

"My father's guards are here. They are numerous, and I have sent for more."

Beatrice could only nod.

"Rest, my girl. Let your mate care for you."

"You'll be nearby?"

"Yes."

After a few more minutes, Beatrice could feel her eyes start to droop as the sun rose in the sky. Tenzin slipped away, and she felt Giovanni come to her, lying down and gathering her in his arms as the dawn took them both.

He was there when she woke, his arms wrapped tightly around her. Beatrice blinked for a moment in confusion.

"Where are we?"

He paused. "The library at the monastery."

In a harsh second, it all flooded back. Lorenzo and the four vicious guards. The current that radiated up her arms when she cut the head off one vampire. The sickening realization that Lorenzo had felt the same when he cut off her father's head.

Her father.

She began to shake, burying her face into Giovanni's chest; he stroked her hair until she was spent. Though her body was refreshed from sleep, her mind was still weary with grief.

"Wait here," Giovanni said. "Zhang's men brought blood."

"I'm not hungry."

His grip tightened on her shoulders.

"You must not stop eating."

Just then, Tenzin appeared in the hallway bearing two mugs of blood. Beatrice's fangs descended as she caught the sweet smell.

"Eat." She handed both to Beatrice.

Beatrice nodded and drank as Tenzin turned to Giovanni.

"Go get Baojia. I want to speak to him about yesterday."

Giovanni rose and walked down the hallway. Beatrice finished the first mug and started on the second as Tenzin sat across from her.

"You must not refuse to eat. He is worried because it is a common reaction of our kind to grief, but a dangerous one, especially for a new vampire."

"Okay."

They both fell silent as Beatrice drank. Though the burn in her throat lessened, she felt no satisfaction from her meal. After a few minutes, Giovanni returned with Baojia. She saw her mate inspect the cups she drank from. "I finished them both," she murmured. He sat next to her and took her hand as Baojia sat across from them. The deep cut across his neck had healed and the only evidence was an angry red line and his grim expression.

All four were silent until Tenzin spoke.

"Explain."

He nodded. "I was on my way back to the river when I caught the scent of vampires and human blood from another corridor. Thinking there were more humans being drained, I followed the passageway. It was similar to the one you had sent the boys down, but on the opposite side of the mountain.

"The northern route." Tenzin said. "Continue."

"The further I followed, the more scent I picked up. I smelled Lorenzo and the river, so I knew where he was going. I didn't want to turn back and waste time." His eyes narrowed. "I met six vampires at the exit."

"That must be the route Lorenzo took back to river," Giovanni said. "That's why we did not detect him." Tenzin only nodded as Baojia continued.

"I killed them... eventually. It took longer than I had hoped. These were not raw warriors. They had training and most of them, I would guess, were my age or older."

Beatrice whispered, "You killed six on your own?"

Baojia's eyes softened when he looked at her. "I have had many years fighting, Beatrice. You and your father did well against your opponents. Four against two. One of whom was your father's sire? Do not blame yourself for his death. Others bear that responsibility."

But Beatrice did. It was unavoidable. Her mind kept replaying

219

little things she could have done differently. If she hadn't panicked. If she had been faster. If she had better control of the bloodlust that had ambushed and distracted her.

"When I got to the river, Lorenzo was already gone. Stephen was dead. B was pinned—"

"Pinned?" Giovanni squeezed her hand.

"He pinned me to the ground with his sword. I tried to pull it out, but it was so deep. He broke off the handle so I couldn't... And then, I'm pretty sure it cut my spine and—"

She broke off when Giovanni grabbed her and pulled her into a fierce embrace. She heard Tenzin and Baojia quickly leave them as Giovanni rocked her back and forth.

"Tesoro," he whispered as he rocked her back and forth. "Beatrice, I should never have left you."

"You can't say that. You were trying to find Lorenzo. You were trying to protect the monks. I'm not the only person in the world, you know."

He said something low in Italian before he cleared his throat.

"Do you want to rest? Do you want to help Tenzin with your father? What would you do?"

"I'll help Tenzin. What... what will happen to his body?"

He paused. "It will linger for two more nights. On the third night, we return to our element. We will take him to the river."

She nodded. Beatrice was glad they were near a river. Some instinctual part of her recoiled at the idea of her father's remains dissolving into the earth. She peeled herself away from Giovanni, rose, and went to find Tenzin.

Giovanni and Baojia were silently sorting and replacing the scrolls on the shelves while Beatrice and Tenzin sat next to Stephen's lifeless body. Giovanni kept an eye on his wife even as he worked. He also watched in fascination as Tenzin performed the ancient mourning ritual over her mate.

She chanted a low, droning song, first washing, then covering his body in oils she had gathered from the monks' workrooms. She had closed his eyes and bound his mouth closed with a piece of saffron cloth, before covering his face with a white fragment torn from her own tunic. Tenzin rose to her feet, leaving the library on some errand, while Beatrice remained watching over her father.

Giovanni came to sit with her.

"I wish we had a priest."

"Rituals are for the living, not the dead." He knew Stephen had been Catholic, and he wished that Carwyn was there to comfort Beatrice.

As if reading his mind, she spoke. "Have you called Carwyn?"

"I sent a letter out to him and one to Kirby last night. Zhang's men will see that they are delivered."

"And Matt will tell my grandma."

"Yes."

"Because I can't."

He hesitated. "You can't see her right now, Beatrice. You're too volatile."

He heard her begin to cry again, and he put an arm around her, drawing her into his chest. He was grateful for the black robes that Zhang's guards had brought for them, as his shirt and her own were stained with bloody tears. Tenzin came back with a large white cloth and Beatrice pulled away from him, sniffing and wiping her eyes.

"What do we do now?" she asked.

Giovanni rose and let them continue. Beatrice tore the linen cloth into long strips, which Tenzin used to bind the body and head together. He watched in fascination as his friend took a dagger and cut her long hair at the shoulder, twisting it into a braid that she placed over Stephen's chest before she crossed his arms and began wrapping him in his shroud, tucking fragrant herbs among the linen. He had no idea where Tenzin had found the white cloth with which she wrapped her mate, but he watched carefully as Beatrice helped, following Tenzin's murmured instructions as they cared for Stephen's earthly remains.

Giovanni wondered what ancient rite they were following. He had never seen Tenzin grieve. Giovanni doubted anyone ever had, and he wondered if any human or vampire in the last five thousand years had sung the low song she chanted in her mother tongue.

No one entered the library or disturbed their quiet sorrow. Giovanni left briefly to check with Zhang's men, who were clearing the human remains and waiting for the company of humans and vampires that Lu Dongbin would send.

"The young monks?" he asked Zhang's lieutenant as he stood near the gates and watched them work.

"Have been taken to Penglai. They will go to another monastery. One only Lu has knowledge of."

"Please tell Elder Lu that we are sorting the library as best we can. It was left in shambles."

The wind vampire said, "The elder will be most grateful. After Mistress Tenzin has mourned her mate, his people will take care of the rest."

Giovanni nodded and slipped back into the dim hall.

Beatrice and Tenzin sat silently next to the wrapped body the rest of the night, while he and Baojia continued to put the library in as much order as was possible. Much had been destroyed in Lorenzo's frantic search for Geber's manuscript, but much still remained.

"I didn't love him, you know."

"What?" Giovanni looked up from sorting the next night.

Tenzin was still sitting by Stephen's body while Beatrice and Baojia swam. Like most of her kind, Beatrice was drawn to the water, taking comfort from its presence. She and Baojia had slipped away when the sun had set and they had fed. The water vampire had refused to leave Beatrice's presence since her attack, even sitting within eye distance while she rested for the day. Giovanni had allowed it, understanding the other vampire's burden.

"Stephen. When we started exchanging blood. I did not love him. We did not have what you and Beatrice... It was not the same."

Looking into her grief-stricken eyes, Giovanni knew that his friend had loved Stephen, no matter what she said. He only shook his head. "You do not have to explain yourself to me."

"I exchanged blood with him to protect him. And for Beatrice. I knew it was his fate to sire her, and he needed to be strong."

"He was as strong as you could make him, Tenzin."

"I was overconfident."

"We all were."

She fell silent before she left Stephen's body and came to sit next to him. He handed her a stack of loose paper, which she began paging through.

"What will you do now?" she asked.

"Try to get it back."

"I think you need to find out who his partner is. Someone

provided him with those guards. Someone other than Elder Zhongli."

"Yes, I know."

They worked steadily for another hour.

"You will take Beatrice to Cochamó?"

"Yes."

"I know you think it was a mistake to turn her. That it left her vulnerable to the bloodlust, but—"

"I don't want to talk about it."

She looked up. "Surely you must see that she would not have survived if she had not turned."

Giovanni clenched his jaw in frustration. "Did you see the council giving her the book? Did you see them forcing Lorenzo's hand? Causing this confrontation? Did your mystic eye see that, Tenzin?"

"Lan would have voted with you if there was no other option," Tenzin said in a firm voice. "They would not have allowed you to kill him on the island, you know how they are."

"And then Lorenzo would have done this anyway."

She made no response, only continued to quietly leaf through the old papers.

"Stephen told me he would not live long."

He frowned. "What?"

"He told me months ago that he felt he was 'living on borrowed time,' as he put it. That he would not escape this fate. He was peaceful about it. Stephen claimed that he should have died years ago when Lorenzo turned him. That all this time was only a gift."

"Because he saw Beatrice again."

She nodded.

"But you did not see this fate for him?"

"No, I did not see this."

"Or you did not choose to."

Tenzin looked at him with guarded eyes. "Perhaps, I did not choose to."

Giovanni cleared his throat. "Will she… will she join him?"

It had weighed on his mind more than he wanted. As much as Beatrice loved him, new immortals were impulsive and irrational, and he clearly remembered his own sense of despair hundreds of years before when he had murdered his own sire. Despite Giovanni's loathing for him, there was a gaping hollow where he felt Andros's loss.

"Gio, you know her better than that."

223

"Do I?"

Tenzin frowned. "How can you ask that?"

"She is the same to me, but more. Surely you can see it."

His friend placed her hand on his arm, squeezing slightly. "She is… exactly who she will need to be, my boy."

He took a deep breath. "Beatrice is as much your daughter as she was Stephen's, Tenzin. Please, don't disappear."

Giovanni saw her grey eyes shutter. She slipped away and went to sit by Stephen's body again, and in his heart, he knew she was already gone.

Two nights later, a solemn procession slipped down the steps from the monastery. Giovanni walked ahead and lit the stone lanterns on the path before four of Zhang's men, who carried Stephen's body. Tenzin and Beatrice followed them. Lu's water vampires had arrived the night before and stood near the edge of the river, watching the procession in silent respect.

The four wind vampires carried the body to the edge of the river where Tenzin and Beatrice, both dressed in white robes, held out their hands and cradled Stephen between them, waiting until the water claimed its own.

He felt a flutter of wind and looked to his right to see Zhang light on the stone steps and walk to him. They nodded toward each other.

"Giovanni."

"Zhang."

"How is your wife?"

"Beatrice will be fine. She is very strong."

He heard a slight hoarseness in Zhang's voice. "And how is my daughter?"

Giovanni paused. "She will be fine."

"The elder has been executed. Lu carried it out himself. The whole council was displeased by his actions."

"He broke their trust."

"And sacrificed a sacred place of learning for a human."

Giovanni couldn't help but think that he would have done the same if the human had been Beatrice, but he remained silent.

"Does your son have Beatrice's book?"

"Yes. She saw him take it."

"You will retrieve it. The book was given to Beatrice as a scribe of Penglai; it is rightfully hers. If the council of the Eight Immortals can help you, we will. We do not care to have our will averted."

"It is the Seven Immortals now, isn't it?"

Zhang was silent for a moment. "Surely you must know that the council is immortal. There will always be eight."

"But—"

"Elder Zhongli is more than the vampire who wore his name."

Giovanni nodded in understanding. So, another Elder Zhongli Quan would be chosen. Giovanni wondered how that would come about, but chose not to ask, knowing he would receive no answer. He wondered if Zhongli had been the original vampire of legend, or whether he had been a replacement himself.

"Of course, Elder Zhang. Continuity is important."

"As is balance."

"Yes." Giovanni looked to his mate. She stood proud and solemn across from his oldest friend. He thought of Beatrice and Tenzin. Of Carwyn and himself. Water, wind, earth and fire.

Balance.

Four elements.

Always four.

His eyes narrowed and he glanced at Zhang, who only looked at him with a slight smile.

"Balance," Zhang said again, "is the key, Giovanni Vecchio. The wisest of immortals have always understood this."

A thought began to bloom at the back of his mind. A path in the darkness began to grow lighter.

Balance.

He nodded at Zhang a little more deeply. "Of course. Thank you, Elder Zhang."

Giovanni turned back to the river; he could feel the change in the air. Beatrice's heart began to beat more rapidly, and he and Zhang stepped closer as the air became charged.

It was only a ripple at first. The solid shroud of Stephen's earthly form seemed to shudder in the current. Then, little by little, it grew thinner. The strips of cloth that had bound his feet came loose, curling in the water as the river teased them. Then, as if by silent command, the white cloth slipped away from the women's grasp, unfurling like a silken cocoon as the pure white linen was washed away in the stream.

He watched it spread, a silver web scattering in the curls and eddies of the Nine-Bend River, washing down the mountain and into the sea.

He watched Stephen's shroud until the turn of the river took it out of sight, then his eyes sought his mate. She was standing in the shallow water, watching with dark eyes. He could see the longing in them, and he knew that she felt the call to follow him, to lose herself within the soft embrace of her element. He sent a silent plea to her, willing her eyes to turn toward his.

She was poised on the riverbank. One foot on the muddy ground and the other sunk in the water. Finally, her head turned, she looked at him, and he felt her return. Beatrice climbed from the edge, and he caught her in a tight embrace.

"I want to go home," she whispered. "There is nothing here. Take me home."

"We will leave tonight."

Beatrice pressed her face into his chest as Giovanni watched Tenzin walk toward them. His friend stopped and spoke a few words to her father in the old language, then walked to them. Beatrice turned, and Tenzin put one hand on her cheek, wiping the tears that stained it as she pulled Beatrice toward her, laying a soft kiss on her forehead and whispering in her ear before she stepped back.

Tenzin met Giovanni's eye, nodded once, and took to the air, silently disappearing into the black shroud of night.

CHAPTER TWENTY-THREE

Los Angeles, California
November 2010

"Where is she?"

"A small airport outside of Chino. It smells more like cows than people there."

"And she's alone?"

Giovanni paused, looking at Beatrice's grandfather. Ernesto's measuring gaze bored into him. "She prefers the solitude. She asked that I lock her in while we had our visit."

Ernesto waved a dismissive hand at him. "I will be by to visit later tonight. She will see me."

Giovanni cocked his head. "You are welcome to try. Kirby is guarding the hangar. Call him for directions."

"And the boy?"

"I've already sent him south. He's being looked after."

Ernesto nodded, quietly tapping the arm of the leather chair in his study where he met with Giovanni. They were sipping red wine in Ernesto's mansion in Newport Harbor. Quiet servants scuttled about in the background, but no one disturbed their quiet conversation.

Beatrice and Giovanni had arrived in Southern California the night before to return Baojia to his sire. Giovanni was meeting with family and associates for the next two nights; then he and Beatrice would leave for Chile.

"You'll be in South America for a year?"

"Yes."

"And where can I reach my granddaughter if I want to contact her? I need an address of some kind."

Giovanni smiled and avoided the question. "You may reach us through Kirby, of course. And we'll also be making sure that Isadora is kept informed of Beatrice's progress."

Ernesto may narrowed his eyes, but Giovanni suspected the old vampire knew he would not get more, no matter who he was related to.

"You may be sure that I'll be keeping a close eye on Isadora while you are away."

Threat or promise? Giovanni suspected that for Ernesto Alvarez, it was a promise. "I'm sure Beatrice will appreciate it. As do I."

"I'm not doing it for you, di Spada." It had not escaped Giovanni's notice that Beatrice's grandfather was using his more notorious name. "Beatrice may be under your aegis—"

"She is under no one's aegis but her own."

"—but she is still my granddaughter. It is my responsibility that Stephen was lost, and I will not risk her. I only let her go with you now because you are her mate, and I know your reputation."

Giovanni forced down the instinctive surge of fire that flowed under his skin and narrowed his eyes at the old man. "Let me be clear, Alvarez, no one will be allowed to interfere with my family. Particularly with my wife. She is no one's pawn, no matter how they may care for her. Be very careful in your presumptions."

The old man's eyes gleamed for a moment before a smile curved his mouth. "Excellent. She has chosen a good mate in you." Ernesto sighed and leaned back into his chair, showing his age more in the slump of his shoulders than the lines that marked his face. It was the least guarded Giovanni had ever seen him.

"How is she, really?"

Giovanni took a deep breath and tried to release the tension. "She is grieving. Her father and her sire."

"It would have been better if I had sired her." Ernesto waved a hand as Giovanni opened his mouth to protest. "I know you think I have my own designs on her future, and I will not deny it. She was an extraordinary human, and she will be an even more extraordinary immortal, even the Elders of Penglai recognized it."

"She already is."

"But now she grieves doubly for Stephen De Novo. It would have been better if I had been her father in this life."

Tenzin's words echoed in his mind. *"She is exactly who she will need to be."*

"I think," Giovanni began, "things had to happen exactly as they did, Alvarez. Some things happen for a reason. Even if we cannot see the purpose of it."

Ernesto looked amused. "You have been spending time with the holy men, di Spada. That is not the rational man that I have come to know."

Perhaps not. But Giovanni only shrugged.

"Or." Ernesto smirked. "Has marriage softened you?"

"If it has, I'd better toughen up. Your granddaughter is not a woman, or a vampire, to be underestimated."

The old man burst into laughter. Giovanni only smiled as the immortal took another sip of wine.

"My son"—Ernesto curled his lip briefly—"says that her fighting skills are quite advanced."

"They are. And she says Baojia is an excellent instructor."

Ernesto's shoulders straightened. "Baojia failed in his mission. He will be dealt with."

Giovanni frowned. "He was a fierce ally in our battle. I would gladly fight at his side again."

"My son had one job. To protect my granddaughter from harm. It was not to rescue some humans or retrieve a book. One task was required of him, and he failed. He will be dealt with."

Giovanni's instinctive reaction was to defend the water vampire, but he closed his mouth. Beatrice may have been under her own aegis, but Baojia was not. He still answered to his sire, and Giovanni knew he must respect that.

So he nodded and rose to his feet. "I hope you understand, but I must leave you. I have much to do to prepare for our journey."

Ernesto rose and shook his hand. "Of course. I'll call Kirby and go by the hanger to see my granddaughter tonight."

"Of course." Giovanni turned to go, but halted when he heard Ernesto's voice.

"You will take care of her, di Spada. You may be her husband, but I am her kinsman. If any harm should come to her—"

Ernesto halted when Giovanni turned. The waft of smoke that drifted across the room matched the low growl of his voice when he finally spoke. "It would be wise of you not to finish that sentence, Don Ernesto Alvarez."

The two vampires stood, measuring each other from a distance. Finally, it was Ernesto that let a smile touch his lips. "Welcome to the family."

Giovanni turned and left the room, shutting the door firmly behind him. He had only taken a few steps when Baojia appeared out of a dark hallway.

"Di Spada."

"Baojia."

They stood in silence. When Baojia finally met his eyes, Giovanni saw the flash of quick grief the water vampire carefully smothered. Then, as before, his dark gaze revealed nothing.

"You will give my regards to your wife."

"I'm sure she would return the sentiment."

The shorter man offered a rueful smile and looked over Giovanni's shoulder, down the dark hallway were he had emerged. "I'll be going to San Diego for some time. I may not see you when you return."

"San Diego?"

"As you may imagine, my father is displeased with me at the moment. I go where he chooses to send me."

Another silence filled the hall until Giovanni finally spoke. "She does not blame you."

Baojia only hummed a little and nodded. "She should." He walked past Giovanni, toward the study where Ernesto waited. "She *should* blame me."

Cochamó Valley, Chile
December 2010

"When will I be able to see her?"

"Probably not for some time. Around a year. But I put a radio at our house, so you'll be able to call from the lodge."

Ben sat silently for a few minutes, playing with a torn seam on Isabel and Gustavo's couch.

Giovanni cleared his throat and knit his hands together. "How is your room here?"

The boy shrugged. "Good, I guess."

"You realize that I'm only a few minutes away if you need me."

Ben rolled his eyes. "Gio, I'm not a little kid. Isabel and Gus are cool. And the Revertes are cool, too. I'll be fine."

"We'll continue to study as we used to, and we'll take a trip into Santiago after the New Year. I'll show you some of the city."

"Yeah," Ben nodded. "Sounds fun."

"And you can teach the Reverte boys how to play basketball."

Ben snorted. "Really, I'm fine."

Giovanni still felt guilty pulling the boy away from the friends he had made in his semester at school. Ben was a social child, and Dez said he had thrived at the private school he had been attending.

"It's only for a year; it will be a good experience. Your Spanish will get much better. You can learn how to ride a horse, go mountain climbing. I'll teach you to shoot, and we'll start training soon, as well."

"Gio," Ben squirmed. "I really don't think I have to learn all the sword stuff, you know? I mean, we're not living in the dark ages, I—"

"It's not an option, Benjamin." He crossed his arms. "I will not have you unable to protect yourself."

"It's just, swords are kind of old, you know? I mean, the martial arts stuff is cool, and I'm excited about jujitsu with Gus. But swords…"

"Are very practical in our world. You need to learn how to used one, and you are fourteen now. By the time I was fourteen, I could already handle a blade. You're more than capable. You're strong now, and you'll get stronger. It is important to train your muscles young."

"I just mean, I'm already pretty good with a rifle, and if you teach me how to shoot better—"

"Do you think that any gun will kill a vampire?"

Ben reddened at Giovanni's harsh tone. "No, I just—"

"It is not an option. We are taking this year to regroup, but that is all. You are old enough to know now. You are old enough to defend yourself and others." Giovanni tried to soften his voice. "Do you know what it would do to her… to both of us if anything were to happen to you, Benjamin?"

The boy blushed a deep red from either anger or embarrassment. "Okay."

"We will start after Christmas."

"I said okay."

Giovanni let the hint of defiance pass unmentioned.

"What does she do up there all by herself? Is she bored? She can't use her computer anymore, can she?"

He looked up at Ben, noting the look of concern on the boy's face. "She reads. And runs at night. Or swims. She likes both."

Benjamin smiled. "I bet she's super fast now, huh?"

"Very super fast," he said.

"Is Carwyn really coming for a visit?"

"Yes."

"That's good. She'll be happy to see him."

Giovanni nodded. His wife had been quiet, speaking more with Isabel than with anyone else. He hoped that Carwyn's visit would help to heal her wounds. He knew from his own experience that most healing only came with time.

"Hey, G?"

He looked up at Benjamin's plaintive tone. "Yes, Benjamin?"

"She's going to be all right, though. Right?"

He stared at the boy for a long moment, wishing he could will the months away.

"She'll be fine."

He entered the house quietly, careful not to disturb her as she sat near the fire, reading.

"How is he?"

Giovanni slid behind Beatrice on the couch, picking her up so she sat on his lap. "He's fine. He likes Isabel and Gustavo. He'll get to know the Revertes soon enough."

"Does he know they have a very cute daughter his age?"

"I have a feeling that information will brighten his outlook considerably."

She nestled back into his chest, and his skin hummed happily wherever she touched.

"You're going to start training him soon, right? You and Gus?"

It had been Beatrice, even more than Giovanni, who had been adamant about Ben receiving self-defense, shooting, and weapons training. He had been reluctant to force the discipline on the boy, but she had insisted to the point of tears. Giovanni knew it was a good precaution, so he had pushed the memories of his own forced training from his mind and focused on what was best for Ben.

"We will start after the holidays, Tesoro. Don't be anxious. Give him some time to get adjusted."

"Okay." She fell silent again, and he looked down to what she was reading. It was a collection of C.S. Lewis essays he had seen her paging through more than once. He pulled the book from her fingers, making sure to mark the page she had been reading.

"Carwyn is coming in a few weeks."

"That's good. It'll be nice to see him."

"I thought so."

She was silent for a few minutes more, staring into the fire as he stroked her hair.

"You should see whether Gus and Isabel can get a wrestling match on their satellite dish."

He chuckled, pleased to hear the spark of humor that lit her voice. "I should."

There was another silence, and the only sound was the pop of the logs crackling in the fireplace. Even in the middle of summer, Beatrice asked for a fire if he was leaving the house. She seemed to be almost constantly chilled.

"I'm fine, you know. I'm going to be fine."

He nodded and tucked her head into his shoulder. "I know."

"So don't hover."

Giovanni grinned and picked her up, carrying her to the bedroom. "Wanting my wife's attention is hovering?"

"Oh… I just realized." Her head fell against his shoulder. "We're going to hear it from Carwyn about the wedding thing, aren't we?"

"I'm sure needling us about that is on the agenda right after wrestling."

She kissed his jaw and leaned up to whisper, "Can we un-invite him at this point?"

"No." He kicked the bedroom door closed. "But you can feign irrationally losing your temper as much as you like. He'll be expecting that from a young vampire."

She put her hand on his cheek, turning it so she could look into his eyes. For the first time in weeks, Giovanni saw a glimpse of the warm joy that usually marked her gaze.

She smiled. "Excellent. It's good to have a plan."

He tossed her in the middle of the bed with a mischievous smile. "Yes, it is."

London, England
March 2011

The Swan with Two Necks had lost none of its grimy Docklands charm in the year since Giovanni's last visit. As he sat in the booth, waiting for Tywyll, he looked at the printout of the e-mail Carwyn had sent through Benjamin.

Giovanni,
We're having far more fun without you here. No lessons are being completed. Ben and I drinking, smoking, and chasing women in Santiago next weekend. Please stay in the cold weather as long as you like, it's nice and warm here. Also, I've bought my nephew an off-road motorbike. I am now his favorite uncle.
Your wife is fine. I'm only calling her your wife now because I was able to properly marry you two. Thank the heavens you're no longer living in sin. Sadly for you, she has finally decided that I am more fun to be with, so we will promptly be tempting God's wrath to run away together to Hawaii. Also, we went hunting last week. She likes pigs as much as you do.
Carwyn
P.S. She's well. But take care of things and come home. You are missed.

He felt Tywyll enter the pub and looked up. The old water vampire motioned to the man behind the bar before he sat across from Giovanni, taking out a brown-wrapped parcel from under his arm and setting it on the table.

"This is for yer wife. Some journals that Stephen left with me."

"What kind of journals?"

"Did ye ever buy that boat you were talkin' about?"

"Why did I need to come all the way to London for these?"

"Did ye go with a powered vessel, or a sailing one? I always recommend sails, less mechanics to go wrong fer our sort. Of course, with the *Mariposa* being as she is, any further form of propulsion is somewhat redundant, isn't it?"

He placed his hand on the package, sliding it across the scarred table and looking into Tywyll's eyes.

"Why," he asked again, "did I need to come here for these? You could have sent them with Gemma's father. Why did I need to leave my wife to come fetch these like an errand boy?"

Tywyll paused, a look of sadness flickering over his rough face. "How is she?"

He paused for a moment. "She's coping. She's adapting very well to this life. She is extremely strong."

"Did I hear correctly that your old partner had a hand in that?"

He paused before deciding to confide in Tywyll. In reality, the old vampire seemed genuine. And if Stephen had trusted him...

Giovanni had received a letter from him the previous month, volunteering the information that Beatrice's father had left things with Tywyll in the event of his death that Stephen intended for Beatrice. Tywyll, much to Giovanni's annoyance, had insisted he collect the items in person.

"She did. Tenzin and Stephen were mated, so yes, Beatrice is partly of her blood, which is... very strong."

"Oh," Tywyll grinned. "Clever Stephen. Well done, lad. And well done, Tenzin."

As always, Giovanni wondered how extensive the immortal's connections were. He seemed to know a little bit about everyone and everything, though Giovanni had never heard of the old man traveling farther than up and down the river.

"She'll be a day-walker, as well. As Stephen became."

A smile lifted the corner of Tywyll's mouth. "Excellent. You'll give her my regards and my condolences."

Giovanni nodded. "My condolences to you, as well. I know you considered him a friend."

Tywyll paused as the barman set down two pints on the old table. "I did. I *do*. I don't happen to believe that significant things like souls just disappear. That's energy, isn't it? That's our element. And if there's one thing we know, the elements always remain."

"Nothing remains, save us and the elements."

The old memory from his father startled him. Giovanni blinked and took a sip of his beer, enjoying the sharp bite of the hops on his tongue.

"Tywyll?"

"Aye, lad?"

He paused before he took a chance. "Do you consider me a friend?"

The old man cocked an eyebrow at him. "Not yet."

"Do you consider my wife a friend?"

"I consider her a responsibility. But a pleasant one."

"I know you told Stephen you would care for her if he died."

"Ye've known that for over a year." He took another drink. "What do ye want, fire-starter?"

Giovanni paused, weighing the odds before he spoke. Someone had found Stephen. In the years he had hidden from the immortal world, one vampire had always found him. Whatever Tywyll may have said, if the old vampire had taught Stephen how to hide, then he could teach someone else how to find him.

"Who was Stephen's contact in Rome?"

A minute flicker in Tywyll's eye let Giovanni know that he'd hit his mark.

"Who says I know what yer talking about?"

"I do. There was a contact. An information source. One who knew exactly what Stephen had and whom he was hiding from. One who knew how to find him and get in contact with him when he wanted to."

Tywyll didn't look at him; he quietly sipped his pint as his eyes scanned the pub.

"And what if he did? What business is that of yers? You don't have Stephen's book now, do you?"

"No." He leaned forward. "I don't, but my son does. And I don't know exactly what was in it. I don't know the formula that Geber wrote, but I know what Stephen claimed it contained. And I know that Zhang Guo's most brilliant student told me that there was something that my son wouldn't understand, even if he got his hands on the formula."

Tywyll narrowed his eyes. "I'm not interested in formulas or elixirs, fire-starter. I have no use for them. What is it that you want? Speak plain or leave me to my beer."

"I want the name of Stephen's contact. And I think you know who it is, because I think you told him how to find Stephen."

Giovanni sat back in his seat, watching Tywyll deliberate in silence. Stephen's contact had pointed him in the right direction too many times for his involvement to be coincidental.

"And if I do know of this contact's name, why would I give it to you? You've no need to stay one step ahead of Lorenzo."

"On the contrary, I have even more reason to stay one step ahead of him. My son has this book. If it does what Stephen thought it did, he has a purpose for it, and it won't be a good one. Anyone who has truly studied it is dead or missing. Anyone who had any sort of understanding of it is gone... except for four vampires that I can think of."

A strange gleam came to Tywyll's eyes. "Four, eh?"

Giovanni nodded slowly. "Four immortals, who are hopefully still living. Balanced. One water, one wind, one earth, and one fire. Whomever Geber used in his research knew about the formula, possibly better than Geber himself. If Geber's manuscript is out of reach, then I will make it my mission to find the immortals who helped author it, and I think Stephen's contact was one of them."

Tywyll took another drink. Then he smiled. The old vampire chuckled and slid the brown-wrapped parcel across the table.

"Well then, Giovanni Vecchio, I suppose ye have some reading to do."

EPILOGUE

Plovdiv, Bulgaria
March 2011

Dr. Paskal Todorov shut off the light in the empty lab and shrugged on his brown overcoat to face the brisk wind outside. He sighed as he looked around the empty laboratory that had once employed so many men and women making high-end cosmetics for the European market.

Though their corporate office in Rome had given them enough funding to keep the building in good repair and to employ a few of the highest-grade chemists, they had not worked on a new project in months, and the majority of the employees had sought work elsewhere in the city's growing economy.

He was walking out of the lab and to his warm office late on Friday night to shut down the computers when the lights in the hallway flickered. He frowned and made a mental note to ask the janitor about the wiring. It had been replaced only the year before, right before they had ceased regular operations.

Todorov turned into his office and started when he saw the corporate representative who had visited them right before the shutdown sitting in the chairs and playing with one of the perfume samples that sat in a small beaker on his desk.

"Signore Andros! What a surprise. I was just closing the lab and getting ready to return home for the weekend. I hope you have not been waiting for me long. Did you call the office to tell them you would be arriving tonight? If you did, I am sorry. I was not informed."

The blond head covered in curls turned. A smirk twisted his mouth. "This is rose oil?"

Todorov frowned. "Yes, it is. The finest Bulgarian rose oil. My country is known for it."

Andros nodded and set the beaker back in its wooden cradle. The young man had always set him on edge, though Todorov could never say exactly why. Andros smiled, then held a hand toward the doctor's chair, but no warmth reached his vivid blue eyes.

"I came quite at the last minute, Dr. Todorov. I hope you don't mind. I am only glad I was able to catch you before the weekend."

"Well." The chemist took off his overcoat and sat behind his desk, picking up the silver letter opener his wife had given him for his birthday and fidgeting with the handle. "How can I help you, Signore? I hope that our reports have been favorable. I confess, we are eager for a new project to keep our employees busy. I hope that there has been no irregularity that has caused—"

"No irregularity, Doctor. None. Your records indicate a very well-run lab with seven chemists on staff. Your specialty was in botanical cosmetics, was it not?"

Todorov nodded. "Indeed it was. We had excellent results using the traditional botanicals produced locally and incorporating them into high-end cosmetics. Our products were very well received."

"And were all the botanical ingredients produced organically?"

Todorov nodded again. "Yes, it is what the corporate office requested. It costs more, of course, but the results and marketing made it—"

"Cost is not an issue on this proposed project."

The scientist brightened. "So there is a project from Rome? How excellent. The chemists will be—"

"There will be a project." Andros reached into his coat. "Providing you have ready access to these ingredients produced organically. And you have the quantities indicated."

Todorov took the paper from Andros's pale hand and looked it over. Some of the ingredients were unusual. A few, almost medieval. He frowned. "I'm afraid, Signore, that some of these are not produced commercially in Bulgaria." He glanced up to see the pale Italian's eyes frost over. "However," he continued quickly, "most of them are, and the others can be quite easily obtained. In fact, I know of a farmer we have used for specialty products who works primarily for the perfume industry. He can grow almost anything if it is ordered. Indeed, that would be ideal because we could ensure all the ingredients meet your particular requirements for quality. He even has extensive greenhouses."

Andros's smile immediately warmed. "Excellent. And when can we expect those ingredients to be ready?"

"It is March now." Todorov shrugged. "If money is no object, we could, perhaps, have some within a few months. I will have to talk to the grower."

"Of course, Todorov. I'm so happy I chose you; I was told you had a... flexible mind."

The scientist cocked his head. "Oh?"

"Indeed." Andros rose and turned to leave the office. "We will start production on the formula next winter, if all goes according to projections."

"May I ask, Signore?" He examined the odd formula at the bottom of the page. "What is it that we are producing? I confess, I have never seen anything like this. It is most..."

Andros cocked his blond head innocently. "Yes?"

"Unusual, Signore Andros. It is quite unlike any other formula I have worked on."

"Oh," Andros chuckled. "I'm quite sure of that."

A niggling fear began to work its way into Todorov's mind. "Signore, while none of this appears dangerous, I feel I have a responsibility to my employees and your customers to make sure that nothing we produce could ever be considered—"

Andros's laugh cut him off. "Oh, it's quite harmless, Todorov. It's an old beauty formula. A 'lost secret' so to speak. It was recently discovered and our marketing team thought it worthy of investigation. The sales pitch alone was enough to tempt them. 'An ancient formula for health and rejuvenation.' Buy the wisdom of the ancients for a reasonable price!"

"Oh." Todorov almost chuckled at his own paranoia. "So it is a beauty product?"

"Oh yes." Signore Andros smiled again and an inadvertent shiver ran down Paskal Todorov's spine, despite the warmth of his cozy office.

"One could almost call it… the elixir of life."

THE END

A first look at the finale of the
Elemental Mysteries series:

A FALL OF WATER

Coming in JUNE 2012

And please visit
ElementalMysteries.wordpress.com
for more information about the series and future projects.

CHAPTER ONE

Fifteen months later…
Los Angeles, California
March 2012

Giovanni woke with a start, and Beatrice looked up from across the room. He sat up, swung his legs over the side of their large bed and stared at the photograph of the Ponte Vecchio, which hung on the wall of their bedroom.

"Hey."

He blinked before he looked over at her, and she smiled. Her husband looked as if he was still halfway dreaming.

"Good evening, did you rest at all today?" He rose and walked to her, bending down to kiss her bare shoulder. He still refused to wear any sort of clothing to bed. Since their room was blocked by a sturdy, reinforced door, multiple locks, and an electronic monitoring system that she'd had custom made for them, Beatrice just decided to enjoy the view. No one would be breaking in.

"I rested a couple of hours. You looked like you were dreaming. What was it about?"

He shrugged and walked to the small kitchen area, heating a bag of blood and leaning over to sniff the coffee pot she'd added.

"Was it about your father again?"

He was silent for a few minutes, but she didn't try to fill the space.

It was one of the things that allowed them to be as close as they were. They both appreciated quiet.

Giovanni finally turned with a frown on his face. "I don't know why I'm having so many dreams about him."

She cocked her head. "Because of me? Because of my dad? Because we've been talking about that?"

"Perhaps."

She had finally taken Tenzin's advice and confided in Giovanni about the gaping wound that Stephen's loss had left. As predicted, he understood completely. Just sharing the hurt had done more to lessen the grief than any of her own efforts.

"Gio… there's no chance that Andros could be alive, is there? I mean, you didn't actually see him die, right? He was just ash when you woke up. Lorenzo was the one who saw—"

"Beatrice, how did you feel when your father was killed?"

Tears sprang immediately to her eyes. "Like… something was ripped from my chest. Empty. Physical pain would have been a relief."

He only looked at her and nodded. "I felt the same. Despite how much I hated him, I loved him, too. And the pain of my father's death woke me from my day rest, even though it was practically impossible to wake me when I was that young. I know he is dead."

"Okay," she whispered. "I'm sorry. I just—"

"It's a valid question. Don't apologize."

He turned and picked up the bag of blood he had heated in warm water, drinking it quickly before he walked across the room, picked her up, and brought her back to the bed. Though she didn't need to sleep, his presence, the silent meditation of his touch, allowed Beatrice to rest her mind.

The sun still peeked through the edges of the windows, so they lay silently, curled together as her amnis wrapped around its mate. Though he didn't move, she could feel Giovanni's invisible energy stroking along her back and neck, fluttering over her skin and soothing her busy mind.

"What are you doing tonight?" she asked in a drowsy whisper.

"I'm introducing one of Gustavo's sons to Ernesto. Diego has some business in Los Angeles, and he asked for an introduction."

"Oh, you get to play politics. Lucky you."

He pinched her side when she snickered.

"Your grandfather asked for you to come, as well, but I made an excuse for you. I'm not going to next time."

She leaned over and kissed him. "Thank you. You're the best husband in the whole room."

Beatrice squealed when he dug his fingers into her sides. Immortality had not lessened how ticklish she was. If anything, it had made it worse.

"Why? Why did I sign up for this abuse for eternity? What have I done to deserve this woman?" He chuckled as he continued to tickle her. Soon, she was gasping under him.

"Stop!" she panted. "Stop. I'll…"

An evil grin spread across his face. "You'll what?"

She brought an arm around and trailed her fingers down his back, teasing his spine as he shivered. Giovanni may not have been ticklish, but she knew exactly how to torment him.

"I'll… save some hot water for you!"

She darted out from under him and into the luxurious bathroom, locking the door behind her. She laughed and started the shower, only to hear the door splinter. Giovanni tossed the broken wood to the side and strode into the room.

"We didn't need that door."

Beatrice drove the grey Mustang through the busy streets, pulling up to the old warehouse where Tenzin had set up a practice studio. The ancient wind vampire was already there, and Beatrice could hear her pounding on one of training dummies.

"You're coming later, right?" Ben grabbed his gym bag and opened the door.

"Yeah, I'm just meeting Dez for dinner, and then I'll come back and practice with you guys for a while."

"No rush. I think she's meaner to me when you're there."

Beatrice laughed and reached across to ruffle his hair as he tried to squirm away.

At fifteen, Ben Vecchio had all the marks of a boy on the verge of manhood. He had shot up the year they had been in Chile and was far taller than she was. Beatrice guessed he would be almost as tall as Giovanni when he was full-grown. His chest was starting to fill out and lose its scrawny appearance, helped along by the intense physical training that Beatrice and Giovanni insisted on for his safety. His curling hair, deep brown eyes, and mischievous smile already attracted enough female attention to keep a grown man happy, much less a teenage boy.

Ben Vecchio was well on the way to breaking a few hearts, and Beatrice absolutely adored him.

"Tell Dez I said 'Hi' and let her know I'm here when she gets tired of the old fart."

"She told the old fart she'd marry him, so I have a feeling you're out of luck."

He leaned down and winked. "Engaged is not married, B. There's hope until there's a ring on her finger."

She shook her head. "You're shameless."

"Yep. But I'm cute, too. See ya!" He slapped the top of the car and walked into the warehouse, whistling.

"Shameless," she said as she pulled away.

She turned on to El Molina Avenue and parked on the street, glad to have found a parking spot so near the café where she and Dez met on Thursday nights. She could already hear a new band warming up inside, so she grabbed a table outdoors, glad for the clear night sky. Dez arrived a few minutes later, and Beatrice shoved down the instinctive hunger that tickled the back of her throat.

Though she was used to the scents of her family, close contact with other humans still awakened her instincts at times. Her best friend, for whatever reason, smelled particularly appealing that night.

"How are you, hon?" Dez chattered as they both settled into their seats. A waiter came out and they both ordered a coffee and dessert. "How was your week? Matt and Gio are both at that thing at your grandfather's tonight, right? What's Ben up to?"

"Other than still plotting how to steal you from Matt?"

She giggled. "Of course."

"He and Tenzin are practicing."

"How's school going?"

Beatrice nodded. "Good. He seems to have swung right back into his classes since we've been back. Of course, Gio's way more demanding than his high school teachers, so that's not really a surprise."

"Of course."

"The boy could probably pass most college-level classes at this point."

"Has he thought about early admission anywhere?"

Beatrice shrugged. "It's not a priority for him. He still does most of his learning at home with Gio. He only goes to school for girls, basketball, and to have something to do during the day."

They paused to let a group enter the cafe. The lively music spilled out as the door opened, quiet to Dez, but distractingly loud to Beatrice's immortal ears.

They chatted as they sipped their coffee, Dez happily filling Beatrice in on her wedding plans. She and Matt had been engaged the previous summer, but had waited until Giovanni and Beatrice had returned from Chile to get married. The wedding was only a few weeks away.

"—so the guests will have the option to eat either chicken or beef. I liked the idea. Of course, the cake looks amazing, but then, it's chocolate, so how it looks isn't all that important. B?"

"Huh?"

"You've been staring at my neck for the past couple minutes, hon."

She blinked. "Oh, sorry."

"No problem. Did you forget to eat before you came? You haven't touched your coffee."

Beatrice wrinkled her nose. "It's really strong. And are you wearing a new perfume or something?"

Dez frowned. "No, nothing different."

"Are you..." Beatrice struggled, trying to determine what it was that was triggering her awareness. Scent had taken on an entirely new dimension for her since becoming a vampire. Everything smelled. She had quickly learned to block out as much as possible, so as not to become overwhelmed, but there was something about Dez that night...

"You're pregnant!"

Her best friend blinked. "Uh, what?"

"I think that's it. You smell... more. I don't know what else it could be. You don't smell sick, and I know you went off birth control a while back, so—"

"How did you know that?" Dez almost looked offended.

Beatrice just shrugged. "Your scent changed. Matt liked it; I could tell."

Dez rolled her eyes. "And I thought being your friend was weird before... and I'm not pregnant. It's only been a couple months, and I haven't even missed my period."

"Well, you will. I'm pretty sure that's it."

Dez just gaped at her. "How… I mean, what—"

"I told you; you smell different." Beatrice shrugged again and sipped her coffee. It really did smell better than it tasted now. Unless she was at home and she could make it watered down, it was overwhelming. "You don't smell *bad*. You smell more… female, if that makes sense. I'm sure it's the hormones. Matt's probably been going nuts around you lately, huh? Humans react to that stuff even if they don't know what it is."

Dez cocked an eyebrow. "Humans, huh?"

"Yup." Beatrice smiled. "So you believe me?"

She shrugged. "Well, since you're a big, bad vampire with a super-strong nose, I guess I have to, though I think I'll still wait for the pathetic human doctor to confirm before I tell my fiancé."

Beatrice grinned. "Congratulations! So were you trying?"

Dez flushed. "We weren't *not* trying, if you know what I mean. Matt's older than me; he didn't want to wait. I was game for whatever. I knew I wanted kids and I'll be thirty next month. We're getting married in a couple weeks. No one will care we started a tiny bit backwards."

"I bet Matt's going to be really excited."

"I bet he'll be surprised. I don't think he thought it would happen this fast." She paused. "Hell, I didn't think it would happen this fast, but I suppose this is the logical result of all that sex."

Beatrice snorted. "You're so smart for a human."

Dez narrowed her eyes. "'For a human, huh? I'm smart for a human?" She tossed her hair, picking up a menu and waving her scent toward Beatrice. "Oh, look at the poor pathetic human tempting the big, bad vampire. Poor vampire. Hungry are we?"

Beatrice growled low in her throat, feeling her fangs descend, even though she knew she wasn't hungry. "Thtop it."

"Oh," Dez gasped in mock surprise, "are those your fangs? How embarrassing. Is there anything you can do about that little situation?"

"You think you're tho funny."

"I *am* funny." Dez grinned. "Know what else is funny? Your lisp when you have to say the letter 's.'"

Beatrice swallowed the burn in her throat and willed her teeth to retract. "One of these days, I'm going to bite you. Then you won't think it's so funny."

"You better not. According to your accounts, I might like it a little *too* much."

"Haha."

Dez cackled. "It's hilarious, you look like you *should* be blushing, but you can't."

"Why am I still friends with you?"

"Because I'm awesome. And you're going to be an auntie."

Beatrice couldn't stop the smile that spread across her face and the tug at her heart. Though she had no desire for children, she was thrilled for her friend. "You're going to be an amazing mom, Dez."

"Oh." Her face fell. "I'm going to get totally fat now. And you'll never get fat. I kind of hate you for that. I wonder if Matt's going to get grossed out by that."

Beatrice shook her head. "Please. Matt adores you. He's going to be—"

"B?"

She halted at the familiar voice of her ex-boyfriend.

"Beatrice?" She didn't turn around. Beatrice looked across at Dez, who just looked panicked. "Dez?" She could hear Mano approaching the table. With lightning speed, she turned and grabbed his hand, clasping his bare skin in her cool palm and letting her amnis crawl up his arm. She stood and turned, never letting his hand go.

"Hi, Mano." She looked over his shoulder, but he appeared to be alone. She looked back into the eyes of the man who had loved her. He blinked at her, his eyes already swimming with her influence.

"You look different, baby."

"I know."

"You need some sun. Let's go out on the boat tomorrow."

She shook her head. "No, Mano. I'm fine."

"Where have you been? I missed you."

She swallowed the lump in her throat, searching his mind, pained at the loneliness she found. The longing. "I'm fine. And so are you."

"I am?"

"Yes. You saw me and you realized that you had moved on."

"I did?"

Beatrice gripped his hand, stroking her thumb along the calluses on his palm "Mmhmm. And you're ready to meet someone new. Someone great."

"I am?" He blinked at her.

"Yep. You saw me, and we caught up. And you heard that Gio and

I are married and really happy now, and you were happy, too. Because you realized that you don't love me anymore."

He shook his head, and she forced herself farther into his mind, forcing back the tears at his familiar scent. Mano still smelled like sunshine and the sea.

"Right," he finally said with a small smile. "You look great. I don't love you anymore."

"Nope," she choked out. "And you're going to meet someone great. And you're going to fall in love."

"I am?"

"You are."

"I missed you, B." He smiled at her again, the soft smile he wore when he was sleepy.

"I missed you, too." It wasn't a lie. She *had* missed Mano, even though she loved Giovanni. She forced out a smile. "Good-bye, time to go home now."

He leaned down as if to kiss her, but she backed away. He only smiled.

"Bye, baby."

She finally let go of his warm hand, and he turned and walked away down the dark street. Beatrice turned back to Dez, pulled her wallet out of her pocket, and threw down some cash. Dez reached over and squeezed her hand.

"I need to go."

"That the first time you've seen him?"

She nodded, forcing back the tears that threatened her eyes. "Yeah."

"You okay?"

"Yeah." She took a calming breath and smiled. "It was just a surprise, you know? I was surprised."

"Well, you did great. And you were really kind to do that. He, um, he called Matt for months, you know? He was worried about you. Will he remember anything?"

Beatrice waved her hand as Dez stood. "Just… vague stuff. He should remember he saw me, but the exact memories will be vague. Hopefully, I did it right."

"Are you going to tell Gio you saw him?"

"Yeah, he'll smell him, anyway."

Dez just blinked at her before she walked down the street,

Beatrice following after. "Vampires are weird."

"I'll remind you of that when you have a giant human parasite sucking the life out of you and making you ill."

"Shut up, bloodsucker."

Beatrice walked into the kitchen behind Ben who immediately ran upstairs to shower and call one of the girls who had been texting him during his practice.

"Ben," she called. "It's eleven o'clock, and you practiced hard. You better get some sleep."

"Sure thing, B!"

"Goodnight."

"Night! Night, Isadora!"

She glanced at her grandmother, who was sitting at the kitchen table, reading a book. "Good night, Benjamin."

Beatrice leaned down and placed a soft kiss on her grandmother's delicate cheek. At age seventy-eight, Isadora Alvarez De Novo Davidson had lost none of the liveliness from her vivid green eyes; though her step was slower, her mind was not.

"And how is Dez?"

"Pregnant, but don't tell anyone. It's early."

"Oh!" Isadora smiled. "How wonderful. And the Kirbys will be thrilled."

"It's really early, so Matt doesn't even know. That's why you can't tell anyone."

Isadora frowned. "How early? Matt doesn't know?"

"Nope. I just told her tonight." Beatrice munched on an almond from the bowl her grandmother had out. "She smelled different. I got all fang-y."

Isadora was quiet for a minute. "You know, sometimes it's easy to forget you are a vampire, and sometimes, it's not."

Beatrice grinned and let her fangs run down. Isadora slapped at her shoulder. "Stop it, Beatrice!"

She giggled and took two almonds, sticking them on her fangs and muttering around them. "Yep, thcary, thcary vampire here."

They both broke into giggles, until Beatrice finally calmed down. "Where's Caspar?"

"He drove Matt and Gio to the meeting at Ernesto's."

"Ah."

"I'm going to go to sleep soon. I just thought I'd stay up to say hello. I missed you this afternoon."

"I was in the library."

"Looking at Geber's journals?"

"Yup." The journals, which her father had left in Tywyll's care, were all written in the alchemist's own strange code. In addition to learning old Persian, Beatrice was also trying to decipher the peculiar phrases and code words the alchemist had used to disguise his research. If she could decode them, they might learn the identity of Geber's original test subjects and be that much closer to solving the mystery of the elixir. Though they hadn't heard a peep from Lorenzo, his presence lurked in her mind, teasing her that the book Stephen had taken was in his possession again.

"Mariposa?"

"Hmm?" She looked up at her grandmother.

"I said I'm going to bed now."

"Oh." She rose and kissed Isadora's cheek. "Night, Grandma."

"I'll see you in the morning."

"I'll probably be in the library around ten or so."

"Have a good night."

Isadora shuffled through the door and down the hall toward the ground floor rooms that Giovanni had converted into a suite for Caspar and Isadora. She could hear Ben walking around upstairs and feel the quiet hum of the electrical currents and waves of Wi-Fi that Matt had installed throughout the house. It may have been quiet, but it was never really *still* the way their house in Cochamó was, and Beatrice realized why Giovanni would get frustrated if he was surrounded by technology for too long. The modern world, to the senses of an immortal, was relentlessly noisy.

She was happily lost in a novel and curled up in the living room when the sound of the Mercedes broke through. She smiled at Caspar when he walked through the door. The clock on the wall pointed toward one, and the old man bent down to kiss her cheek.

"Good night, darling girl. I'll see you in the morning. This old man is exhausted."

"Night, Cas."

"What time did she turn in?"

"A few hours ago."

CPSIA information can be obtained
at www.ICGtesting.com
Printed in the USA
LVOW11s1630110417
530416LV00001B/54/P